MASTER OF PLEASURE

A SCHOOL OF GALLANTRY NOVEL

DELILAH MARVELLE

DELILAH MARVELLE PRODUCTIONS

Portland, Oregon

Delilah Marvelle Productions, LLC
Delilah@DelilahMarvelle.com
Portland, Oregon
www.DelilahMarvelle.com

Publisher's Note: This is a work of fiction. Names, characters, places, and incidents are a
product of the author's crazy imagination. Locales and public names are sometimes used
for atmospheric purposes. Any resemblance to actual people, living or dead, or to busi-
nesses, companies, events, institutions, or locales is completely coincidental.

Book Layout ©2014 BookDesignTemplates.com

Master of Pleasure/Delilah Marvelle -- 1st ed.
ISBN-10: 1505206367
ISBN-13: 978-1505206364

*To the Kinksters who kindly took aside this
Vanilla Girl and entrusted me with a
glimpse into their private world. Your
intelligence, humor, and laughter, along
with the need to redefine my flavor of 'normal',
made this book possible. Thank you.*

This book wouldn't be in anyone's hands if not for a team of amazing people I adore and trust. A special smooch and big thank you to the ever fabulous Jessa Slade, Maire Claremont, Kim and Debbie Burke, Ronnie Buck, Kim Wollenburg, Jessie Smith, Cynthia Young, and Carol Ann MacKay.

PROLOGUE

We all wear proverbial masks to create an illusion.

These illusions, however, can be fatal, because we

soon begin to believe they are real.

-The School of Gallantry

The Abbey of Lagrasse, France
Spring of 1819

After the National Assembly methodically beheaded every last Maurist monk residing within the vast stone walls of the monastery, thereby confiscating their sizable property during the French Revolution so the government could pay its debts, a new order of men overtook the abbey and re-arranged the altars. These stern, overly-educated French luminaries weren't ordained by any one church, but rather by a private Christian organization which believed sex, and its endless array of sins, needed to be eradicated from the beating heart of humanity.

Despite being a Christian *and* a bonafide virgin, there was no doubt Malcolm Gregory Thayer had over-indulged in his fair share of sin by going against the word of the Lord. He had *never* been one to turn his cheek. In fact, he liked defending himself and others to the point of making cheeks, noses *and* mouths bleed. It was the only way to guarantee real justice, given hell was reserved solely for those who were dead.

Malcolm also worshipped and idolized false gods: women. He attended charity events for the sole purpose of watching them dance and would always wait for their skirts to lift just enough to reveal the silk stocking of an ankle that made his breath catch and his face flush. Sometimes, when he was feeling particularly roguish, he'd wake up early and sneak glances at the scullery maid whenever she scrubbed the floors because she had sizable breasts that jiggled. He had even cornered, grabbed and forcibly kissed the bishop's daughter during a garden party because he thought she was beyond delectable.

It was the worst idea he'd ever had.

These were his sins. And while they were incredibly viable sins worthy of a full confession, after living at Lagrasse for close to a year, he came to realize how exceedingly holy he was in comparison to the young men around him. Not even three tables to his left in the vast dining hall of the monastery sat seventeen-year-old Rafael Antonio Alfaro.

Rafael was the son of a wealthy Spanish merchant who made a vast fortune importing silks out of India. He was handsome, witty and could quote the poetry of Cadalso in three different languages.

Unfortunately, that was the extent of his good breeding. Rafael was nothing more than a maggot who brutally sodomized an eight-year-old boy he lured into his carriage back in Madrid. Because Rafael was far too rich to be sentenced for any crime, and far too sane to be confined to bedlam, his father opted to seek out 'religious' intervention by the internationally renowned Monsieur Bissette in southern France. Once a month, when it was allowed, Rafael wrote lengthy, apologetic letters to his parents, insisting he was a changed soul who found God and would never touch another boy again. It was laughable. Because everyone knew he still breathed out the name of his eight-year-old victim when masturbating in the privy late at night.

Malcolm was proud to say he had beaten the piss out of Rafael twice. Once for ripping out a page of his prayer book and the other time just because Malcolm felt like it.

The display of loathsome characters did not end there. Rafael was only one of sixty-nine sexual deviants, ranging in age from ten to twenty, who had been sent to Lagrasse by their wealthy families in an effort to unveil a truer connection to God.

And yes, Malcolm was one of them.

As part of their spiritual journey, it was imperative to understand the physical one. From the moment of their arrival, they were each assigned to labor on fourteen hundred acres of land where they toiled every morning and every afternoon, whether it was snowing, raining or the sun was hot enough to peel off one's skin.

After a long day of tanning leather, gardening and digging out boulders from the clay, they would gather in the library for lectures and spend their evenings silently reading from their prayer books. For those who didn't follow orders (and there were quite a few), a strap made of two pieces of leather with metal sewn between the halves, danced across their bare backs until blood filled their boots.

In Malcolm's opinion, grouping together so many depraved young men under one slate roof on the quiet hillside of the country was not a very good idea. It allowed too many souls to fester into something worse. He himself was barely hanging by a short twine. He'd never really considered himself normal. While he enjoyed the fact that he was far, far away from his brother, who only magnified the problem, it was coming at a very high price.

The din of male voices and the clattering of spoons against bowls reminded Malcolm he only had forty minutes to eat. Using the sleeve of his linen shirt to wipe the table clean, he settled into a chair set in the far corner of the dining hall. He always sat alone. Unlike the rest of the boys who congregated together during meals, he'd never cultivated any friends. Why would he? Most of these degenerates were looking for more than friendship. They wanted coitus.

No, thank you. Not now. Not ever. Not with them. Not with women. Not with *anyone*. Sex only turned people into mouth-foaming lunatics. Which he wasn't.

Bringing his hands together in formal prayer, Malcolm closed his eyes and whispered, "I thank thee, Lord, for this simple bounty and eat it knowing there are others who have far less. Please grant me the strength to survive these upcoming weeks so I may finally rejoin humanity in the manner I deserve and not kill my only brother whom I love so very much. Amen."

He opened his eyes and picked up his wooden spoon, mixing the oily, overcooked vegetables in his bowl. Scooping up the discolored sludge, he carefully pushed it into his mouth and paused. It sat like mud that had been urinated into. He grimaced and chewed the slimy vegetables, using his tongue to push away pieces that kept sticking to his teeth.

While everyone around him dined on mutton and burnt potatoes slathered in curdling gravy, his meals consisted of something far worse: old stew scraped out of the bottom of a cauldron. He had pummeled one of the boys for trying to suffocate a cat from the village. The cat couldn't very well serve as a witness and none of the other boys claimed to have seen it (even though they had). It resulted in Malcolm having his meals reduced and getting whipped.

He hated Lagrasse. He couldn't even rescue a cat without getting punished for it.

A piece of bread bounced onto his secluded table, falling into the sizable crack snaking through the wood. Malcolm's gaze darted to the left to see who had thrown it.

Rafael grinned and swept back curling, dark hair from his eyes. "It is for you," he called out in French, his Spanish accent marring his words. "The cat told me to thank you for your heroics. He said, '*Meow*.'"

Malcolm flicked the bread off the table and jabbed the spoon at that head. "Keep at it, Spaniard, and I will take your head and paint every last stone in this monastery red. I still have three weeks to do it."

"Then do it." Shoving more bread into his mouth, Rafael smirked and said in between hearty chews, "Whatever happened to your face, dearest? You never told me. It makes me want to lick you from chin to forehead. Let me."

Malcolm shifted his scarred jaw, *loathing* the way Rafael always tried to rile him. Monsieur Bissette had warned Malcolm that if he started another fight, more than the leather strap would descend. It wasn't worth it. In twenty-one days, he was set to go home. Which was going to be a whole other mess. "Unless you want to swallow every last one of your crooked teeth and shite them out for weeks, turn around and find *another* face to lick."

"You are a prude and you bore me." Rafael gave him a withering look, no longer conveying an interest. "I prefer younger boys anyway. Younger boys who…" He paused, his eyes veering to a youth who sat quietly reading the Bible at the only table whose wooden surface was covered with a white linen cloth. Delicately tracing a stubby finger along the seam of his shirt, Rafael lowered his chin and keenly observed the boy.

That was quick. Malcolm shook his head and glanced at the dark-skinned youth who had arrived days earlier. He knew very little about the newcomer, except that he was Persian, spoke various languages and was so intent on learning the Christian way he was always reading the Bible.

This Persian was not the typical resident.

Aside from the unprecedented fact that Bissette's strap still hadn't touched his brown skin, the youth wasn't mandated to labor and could wear whatever clothing he pleased. The Persian therefore did nothing but read the Bible while roaming the monastery in flowing silk garments that resembled Turkish robes. The rest of them were forced to not only dig out boulders from the clay ground at every hour, but wear rough wool trousers and a barely passable linen shirt.

It created a few disgruntled boys. Not that anyone bothered the Persian. He was usually surrounded by massive, dark-skinned servants in turbans who kept everyone away by merely crossing their arms over their chests.

For some reason, the young Persian sat alone today. There were no servants.

Rafael eyed the entrance hall where the luminaries were stationed, leaned over and whispered something to those at his table. The whispers intently escalated until one by one, the younger boys at the table sighed, got up and paged through their Bibles as they grudgingly went over to the luminaries with what appeared to be questions about a particular verse.

Apparently, Rafael was getting ready to lick.

Bastard. Now *he* felt responsible. Malcolm let out an exasperated breath. While he never looked for trouble, he never walked away from it, either. Grabbing his meal and spoon off the table, he trudged over to the newcomer.

Setting his wooden bowl onto the linen cloth, Malcolm pulled out the straight-backed chair and sat. The adolescent sitting across from him was actually pleasant-looking, with well-defined European and Arabic features that had yet to grow rugged and manly.

No wonder Rafael was interested.

Malcolm cleared his throat, trying to be social. "How are you?" He said it in French. It was the only common language everyone in the abbey shared. "What verse are you reading?"

The Persian glanced up from the Bible, his dark eyes fierce and penetrating. "I wish to be alone," he tossed out in French. "I am here to think and to pray. Nothing more. Leave."

Malcolm wanted to oblige. He really did. For all he knew the youth had been committed for molesting camels in the desert. But it wasn't in Malcolm's nature to abandon anyone in need. Especially when they didn't realize they were in need.

Digging his spoon into the stew, Malcolm started eating again. "Where are your servants? The ones who usually follow you around?" He chewed. "Why are they not with you today?"

The Persian hesitated. "I gave them a day of religious rest. Why?"

"Religious rest on a Friday? What calendar are you on?"

"It is *Joma'a*. Muslims pray on Fridays."

Oh. Malcolm swallowed what was in his mouth. "I don't mean to be a nuisance to you or your religion, but Rafael has taken a keen interest in you, which is never good. If there is any trouble, I will break his legs, then his arms and if there is time, you can do the rest. Agreed?"

The youth edged the Bible closer to himself, covering the large ruby ring on his finger. "I am trying to learn the Christian way."

Malcolm rolled his eyes. "Do you honestly think a good Christian would let people take advantage of other people? As I like to say, God is great and merciful but He still sent a flood. Otherwise, who would take Him seriously? No one." He shoved another spoonful of stew into his mouth and chewed more enthusiastically. It was nice talking to someone. "I hear you speak English. Do you?"

Those pinched features softened. "Yes. I do," the boy replied in clipped English to demonstrate. "I was raised in Persia, but my mother grew up in Wiltshire after her family fled France during the revolution. Mother and *Grand-pére* were the only ones in their family to survive. Although the title was revoked, *Grand-pére* still goes by the name of Vicomte de Chastain. He has grown incredibly popular in England given what he survived at the hands of the National Assembly and has become *very* involved in politics. Everyone in London knows him."

Startled at the irony of their meeting, Malcolm stared. "Even I know him. Your grandfather goes to our church. He ties red ribbons around eight candles every Sunday."

The boy sat up, eyes widening. "That is indeed *Grand-pére*. He had three brothers, one sister, two cousins, and two uncles who were all guillotined during the revolution. Red ribbons around candles is how he honors them. My mother, who was fifteen at the time it happened, remembers just as much and does the same."

Malcolm hesitated. "How did your mother end up marrying a Persian?"

"My father was always fascinated by Western culture. He was visiting London when he met my mother. Allah only knows what she saw in him, but she gave up her entire way of life to be with him. The two are disgustingly obsessed with each other." The boy eyed him. "Might I ask what happened to your face?"

The face, the face. Always the face. The only good that ever came of his ear-to-jaw scar was it prevented him from looking *exactly* like his brother. "My birth was a little rough." Malcolm kept eating.

Leaning into the table, the Persian quieted his voice. "How so? What happened?"

Sometimes, Malcolm wanted to make up stories about it. He was tired of repeating the same tale over and over to anyone who asked. Unfortunately, he wasn't much of a liar. "There were two of us in my mother's womb, and given her labor wasn't progressing, the doctor used more force than was necessary. Most of the damage you see was caused by an infection after the forceps sliced my face. For some reason, God was gracious enough to grant me the strength to live. It's been an unexpected blessing that distinguishes me from my brother. He and I are identical in every way. Even our voices are the same. It's annoying." Picking up his wooden spoon, Malcolm started eating again trying not to think about his brother. "So what do you think of our Bible? I see you reading it all the time."

The Persian sighed and drifted his fingers across the Latin text. "There is much here I do not understand. What is Christianity's view about sexual relations outside of matrimony? Is it permitted?"

Malcolm almost choked on the vegetables he was trying to swallow. He glanced toward the luminaries on the other side of the dining hall who were still occupied. "What in Satan's name is wrong with you? Are you trying to get us both whipped?"

The Persian flushed. "No. I..."

"If it were permitted, my friend, the church would have its own brothel and charge us all admission. No. It's *not* permitted. A true Christian awaits the blessing of a marriage by God."

"Are you certain? Because unlike our *Qur'an*, which is very specific about condemning such acts, this Bible of yours does not appear to condemn premarital relations at all. It merely speaks to sexual *immorality*, which is an incredibly broad term."

Malcolm gave him a withering look. "Oh, I see. Apparently, you're looking for an excuse to indulge. That is certainly your right, given you're a Muslim, but I was raised better."

"So you do not question your church or its beliefs? You simply accept what is written?"

Malcolm lowered his chin. "What I accept and what I believe are two different things. Let there be no doubt in that."

Those dark eyes brightened. "Ah. So you have doubts about your Christian faith?"

"All the time." Malcolm made sure there wasn't a luminary in sight. "This never leaves the table, but I firmly believe the church is part of a conspiracy to control world population. After all, the more people there are, the less they can control."

The Persian sat up. "Fascinating. Where is your proof?"

"In plain sight." Malcolm gestured to the open Bible. "In the Old Testament, for example, polygamy was the foundation of our culture. Exodus clearly states a man can marry an infinite amount of women without *any* limitation as long as he could provide for them, and yet in the New Testament it suddenly proclaims a man of the church can only have *one* wife. It's a conspiracy to control how we, as humans, reproduce. How do I know this? Because Jesus himself stated he upheld the Old Testament in its true form, which, obviously, *would* have included polygamy." Malcolm leaned into the table. "Pages are missing, my friend. *Missing.* But what do I know? I'm only a follower."

They stared at each other.

The awkward silence made Malcolm realize he'd spent *way* too much time in his own head thinking about religion. He was used to it. Even well before entering the monastery. After the unexpected illness and death of his mother, his father had become abnormally devoted to prayer, claiming her death had been a warning from God. In a desperate effort to reclaim God's favor, the earl did away with all extravagances, reducing their lifestyle to resemble the middle classes and tried to mold Malcolm and his twin brother at fourteen into the paragons of religious virtue neither of them were prepared to embrace.

Their tutors were dismissed and replaced with priests who taught them Latin and the history and beliefs of the doctrine and Bible. Their lavish clothes were donated and replaced with simple tweeds and wool. The ancestral lands and home were sold, after being stripped of all furnishings, and donated to local charities, so that instead of occupying thirty-two rooms, they only occupied four in a humble cottage on the outskirts of Wiltshire.

Malcolm's twin brother, James, who had been born three and a half minutes too late, was being prepped to attend a seminary to become a vicar as opposed to going to a university to be a surgeon. James didn't plan to cooperate. The idea of slicing people open and sewing them back up fascinated him too much.

By good fortune, Malcolm was spared that path. As heir, he was granted permission to go into the military until it was time to inherit whatever remained of the estate. Which was nothing given how often they donated to charities.

Despite their father having obsessive tendencies that included washing his hands as many as forty-five times a day, and refusing to let them near him if they weren't wearing gloves, the man did his best to love them. He simply didn't know how.

Setting aside that their father made them wear unfashionable clothing the upper crust snickered at, what was even *more* annoying was that all of the games the other adolescent boys played, such as cards, dice, pall mall, and cricket were no longer permitted. According to their father, it was a rake's sport that did not progress the soul. Charades were permissible (huzzah!) but only under the proviso that it involved Bible characters, parables and religious landmarks. Charades became an inside joke between Malcolm and James. It was how they communicated when they didn't want their father knowing what they were talking about: *women.*

Christmas did become more interesting. They began hand-delivering bibles to countless places in dire need of the Lord's word. Places he and his brother had *always* been curious about. One particular year, their father trooped them into a brothel where they set bibles on all of the beds before getting thrown out by the clients who didn't want them there. In vast appreciation, one of the prostitutes flashed her charms (both breasts) and yelled, "Happy Christmas to you and Jesus!" He and his brother laughed so hard, his father decided converting prostitutes was no longer a respectable option.

The Persian tapped the table. "So what is your name? You never introduced yourself."

A breath escaped Malcolm. "Forgive me. I was too busy preaching conspiracy theories. The name is Thayer. I'm set to inherit an earldom one of these days but there really isn't much to inherit outside the name itself, so I ask you call me Malcolm."

"A pleasure to meet you, Malcolm. 'Tis unexpected to meet someone so civilized among these walls. I am Nasser." The Persian set his chin. "I am sixteen and commenced fully shaving four months ago." He smoothed a hand over his jaw and angled closer. "Can you see the stubble on my face? Is it not magnificent?"

How adorable. This one took pride in being male. "Oh, yes. Very. You must be proud."

"I am. I have been waiting to shave since I was eight."

Malcolm eyed him with renewed interest. "You seem...*normal* to me. And I have been here long enough to notice what normal is. Why are you here? And how long is your penance?"

The olive tone of Nasser's face heightened. "I have no set penance. I have the freedom to leave anytime. My mother is actually waiting for me in Paris. She is being very supportive of my decision to be here. It could be a month or a year. It depends."

He made it sound like a holiday. "If you have the support of your mother and can leave anytime, why don't you?"

"Because I am ravaged by a sin I cannot control." Nasser lowered his gaze and smoothed his garb. "I did not want you sitting with me earlier, because I am physically drawn to men. I heard about the abbey's ability to cure depravity and decided to see if converting to Christianity might be an option."

Malcolm quirked a brow. "So you think surrounding yourself with sexually deviant Christian boys is a good option? Really? Whatever gave you *that* brilliant idea?"

Nasser glanced up, fighting tears. "What are you accusing me of?"

"I'm not accusing you of anything," Malcolm countered. "I have a cousin who is drawn to men. Not that anyone in the family knows about it. His father and my father are so incredibly religious, they would have carved a crucifix into his bollocks. So my brother and I decided it was best to say nothing. Trent owes us for life."

Nasser hesitated. "Why are you here? What did you do?"

"I'm an idiot who loves my brother too much." Malcolm puffed out a ragged breath. "If we are to lay out the gossip *and* the crime, I was accused of impregnating the bishop's daughter, Miss Silverthorn."

Nasser's lips parted. "Did you?"

Malcolm glared. "No. Absolutely not. I only cornered, grabbed and kissed her."

Those brows came together. "I do not understand. If you only kissed her, how did she end up pregnant?"

Swallowing hard, Malcolm averted his gaze. "She wasn't pregnant. The poor girl had never been intimate with anyone. Not even my brother, who, as it turns out, was *very* attached to her. Not that I knew. No one did. Those two kept their strange little bond a secret since they were children. Imagine my surprise when, after I grabbed and kissed her, she went and told my brother she was pregnant with my child. Needless to say, James tried to knock my brain out of my skull for it. And not in an angry, it-will-pass sort of way, but rather in a *'I will murder you and be branded Cain forever'* sort of way. The lunatic came at me with a blade and tried to stab me through the heart. My father had to tie him to a chair and whip holy water at him to calm him down."

Nasser's eyes widened. "Holy water?"

Malcolm sighed. "My father thought a demon had entered into his body. Little did the man know, that's who James really is. I'm no different. Had I been in his position, and she had been my woman, I most certainly would have done the same. But given I didn't touch her in that way, I got angry and confronted Miss Silverthorn demanding she tell my brother the truth. Imagine my surprise when she starts wailing about how *vile* their association was and how she was *trying* to be sent away to a nunnery to escape him. She kept saying she was afraid one of them would end up dead. She wouldn't go into detail but when I saw the same marks on her arms my brother branded into his, I knew they were a danger to each other. So I told her not to worry, and made everyone, including the bishop and my brother, think she and I had been intimate.

Which, of course, resulted in her being sent to a nunnery in Scotland, and me getting into trouble with my father. So here I am learning how to be 'celibate'. Even though I'm still a damn virgin."

Nasser's eyes widened. "Whilst noble of you, what if she had been lying?"

A raw grief overwhelmed Malcolm. "No. I know my brother. Much like myself, he isn't...*normal.* Whatever book I was reading, he had to read it, too. At the same time, mind you. He'd punch my arm to bruises until I held the book open wide enough for him to read because he never wanted me to get a word ahead. When I climbed a tree, he had to be on the same damn branch. Which, of course, caused said branch to snap and break not only my arm but his. He thought it was incredibly funny when we broke our arms. Pain was a game. And it was for me, too, but not to that extent. Things like broken bones take *forever* to heal."

Rolling his eyes, Malcolm shook his head. "Whenever I got tired of him and latched the door to keep him out, he'd leave the house, scale the wall and climb through the window after he knocked out the glass and bled everywhere. He was damn crazy like that. He once shaved his entire head and insisted I do it, too. When I refused, what did he do? He bloody sheared my hair while I was sleeping. My mother, bless her poor heart, was horrified. We looked like prisoners heading to the scaffold. I often wonder if we sent her to the grave early."

Malcolm was quiet for a moment. "All I can say is James and this girl got entangled in something dark. It was like she lit a wick to a morbid side of his mind even I didn't know existed. It scared me. So I did what I thought was best for him and got him out of it."

Nasser pinched his lips and carefully shut the Bible, pushing it aside. "So you lied."

"I had to. My brother wouldn't let her go any other way. We Thayers are crazy like that. Once we get attached to a person, it takes a knife." Malcolm let out an exasperated breath. "You have no idea what it's like having a twin. My brother touched a finger to my heart long before I even had one. Despite hating this monastery, it's been a blessing. It's allowed me to become my own person. Life away from my brother is certainly quieter. And tame. Very, very tame." Trying to shove aside all thoughts of it, he pointed to the boy's untouched plate of mutton, potatoes and bread. "Are you going to eat that?"

"No. I tried." Nasser pushed his plate across the table, causing the white cloth to crinkle.

Malcolm dragged the plate over to himself and smoothed out the cloth. Using his fingers, he grabbed up the dry mutton and frantically ate whatever meat he could off the bone, its rubbery texture squeaking between his teeth.

Nasser was quiet for a moment. "Do they not feed you?"

"They usually do." Malcolm bit off another mouthful of mutton and chewed. He gathered the burnt potatoes and slapped them into his bowl of stew before pushing the plate back across the table. "Simply not this week." He swiped his fingers against his wool trousers, scooted his chair closer and picked up his spoon again to finish the remaining stew. "I'm being punished."

"For what?"

"One of these morons tried strangling a cat." Malcolm tapped his wooden spoon against his scabbed knuckles. "I used more force than I should have. But I enjoyed every minute of it."

Nasser hesitated and lifted a section of his silk garment to reveal a leather satchel around his waist. He dug out a small glass jar and uncorked the lid, setting it onto the table. Scooping out the glistening yellow substance with two fingers, he edged it toward Malcolm. "Hold out your hands."

He eyed the substance. "What for?"

"This will heal them." Nasser stood, reached over the table and smeared the thick substance onto Malcolm's outer hand. "It is made of nightly cereus and is mixed with water pulled from the blessed well of Zamzam. Legend has it, if rubbed onto the skin of a man who is deemed worthy by Allah, he becomes invincible. Even a blade will bend to his touch."

"Sounds like witchcraft to me."

Nasser glared. "It is not witchcraft. *Davana ittar* is meant to scent and to heal and is reserved for a select few. How dare you insult my offering? Are you to be a friend or not?"

Puffing out a breath, Malcolm let his spoon drop into the bowl. "I accept your kind offering.
Forgive me for being so ungrateful." Turning over his hands, he rubbed the thick substance over scab-roughened knuckles and palms. It dissolved into oil against the warmth of his skin, softening the chafing. "Not bad." A fruit-like fragrance drifted toward his nostrils. "For something that is supposed to give strength, it smells overwhelmingly feminine. Should I be wearing this?"

"Cease. There is more strength in females than you think." Nasser corked the glass, tucking it into his leather satchel. "Have you ever seen a woman give birth? No man would survive it."

Malcolm hesitated. "You've seen a woman give birth?"

"Of course. My father has a concubine."

Malcolm gaped. "Your father has his own prostitute?"

"She is *not* a prostitute. Concubines are well-educated and devoted to serving one man. 'Tis very respectable."

Like hell it was. These Persians still lived in the Old Testament. "Surely your mother objects."

"Of course. But my father insists after eight children, she needs the rest. He won't touch her. She almost *died* giving birth to my sister three years ago. So he bought a concubine."

One would think they were discussing cattle.

A figure approached, making them pause.

Rafael's stubby fingers grazed the edge of the tablecloth. "I have been waiting and waiting for a moment alone with your new friend, Thayer. Do you mind?"

Malcolm slammed his wooden spoon against the table, spraying cold stew, and rose to his full height of six feet and four inches. "I would rather you sodomize someone else."

Rafael stared. "I pity your lack of trust." Angling away, his features softened. He grazed a finger along Nasser's silk garment. "I like this. The color suits you."

Nasser shoved Rafael's hand away. "You have no right to be touching me."

Rafael leaned in. "While the luminaries are still occupied, you and I are going to visit the privy, sweetling." Digging into his trouser pocket, he flicked out a shaving razor from its ivory handle. "Get up."

Nasser's eyes widened.

Malcolm lunged at Rafael from across the table to knock away that hand, but only managed to tumble over his bowl and jar the table.

Rafael swung the edge of the razor toward Malcolm. "I suggest you not get involved, English boy. This is between me and the Muslim."

Other boys at the surrounding tables scooted their chairs out of the way and kept eating in between glances.

Satan's blood. He had to do something. "Put the razor down." Malcolm slowly rounded the table, his heart pounding. "Put it down."

Rafael matched his motion and moved the razor closer to Malcolm. "Why are you *always* trying to be a hero?"

To make up for the fact that he would never be one. "Put it down. *Now.*"

"I am the one holding the blade," Rafael challenged. "Are you *wanting* to lick this? *Are you?*"

There were very few things that intimidated Malcolm. A blade was not one of them. Growing up with a brother who was as equally crazy as he was, he had survived well over thirteen dozen things, including a gunshot wound from a hunting accident when his brother swung the wrong way, a stab wound from trying to see how far a knife could go into him, broken fingers from slamming them in between too many doors and a fire he himself had caused when he was curious about what would happen if he knocked over an oil lamp.

This was nothing.

Edging closer, Malcolm kept his eye on the razor. "Maybe we can negotiate. What do you want?"

"You know what I want, dearest." Rafael squinted. "Are you willing to go in his place?"

Ha. No. Malcolm evened his tone in an effort to bide time. "If you put it away, I will lay on the floor with my trousers around both ankles and let you do whatever you want. All you have to say is *'Je vous en prie.'*"

Rafael paused.

Finally close enough, Malcolm jumped and snatched that wrist hard, startling Rafael. He snapped the razor up toward Rafael's own face and held it rigidly in place.

Rafael's hand trembled as the edge of the razor teetered closer and closer toward his own throat. "What are you— Cease—"

Snapping up his other fist, Malcolm gritted his teeth and punched Rafael twice, cracks resounding within that nose each time. Malcolm released the bastard with a violent shove, trying not to take *too* much pleasure in what he just did. "Don't *ever* call me dearest, you demented son of a tavern hag. I am damn tired of dealing with all you crazy people! *Learn how to be normal!*"

Blood gushed out of Rafael's nostrils and streamed from his chin. Rafael staggered as the razor clattered to the stone floor, echoing.

Nasser scrambled up from the table. "*Tawhîd.*" Grabbing the white cloth off the table that sent the porcelain plate shattering to the floor, he jogged toward Rafael and pressed the cloth against Rafael's nose with trembling hands. His dark eyes intently searched Malcolm's. "Was it necessary to make him bleed?"

Malcolm glared. "He almost had his way with you. *In the privy!* And you dare defend him?"

"No. But you are twice his size. You are also a Christian, are you not?"

"Oh, come off it. The Lord knows I mean well. I'm doing His work."

"*All of you!*" Monsieur Bissette boomed in French. "Stay where you are."

Everyone, including Malcolm froze.

Wiping his hands against his shirt, Rafael shoved Nasser away and pointed at Malcolm. "He tried to use the blade against me, *Monsieur!*" Smearing his fingers across his bloody nose, he stared at his hand and yelled, "This-this...*leviathan* tried to kill me!"

Malcolm narrowed his gaze. "If I had tried, believe me, you would have died."

"*Enough.*" Bissette strode over, his stocky frame garbed in all black, except for the high white collar and a tightly knotted linen cravat that was spattered with an unknown substance. If cleanliness were godliness, the man would find himself wanting. It was a known fact that every morning, Bissette soaked a filthy hair-brush in holy water and drew it through his hair. That was how he washed it.

Sharp, hazel eyes darted over to Malcolm before resting on the blade lying on the floor between their booted feet. "Where did the razor come from, Thayer?" Bissette coolly asked.

Widening his stance, Malcolm thumbed at Rafael. "Ask him."

Bissette swung to Rafael. "Where did you get it?"

Rafael stared but said nothing.

"I asked you a question, Alfaro."

Rafael still said nothing.

Bissette grabbed Rafael's face hard, digging his fingers into his flesh, causing more blood to gush out of that nose. "You clearly have not been here long enough to know what I am capable of. Answer or I will shackle you to the ceiling of the altar and leave you to hang there until your very bones slip through the iron. Do you think I care if you live or die?

No. I get paid by your parents either way. The real question here is…do *you* care if you live or die? *Do you?*"

Rafael trembled. "I stole it out of your shaving cabinet, *Monsieur*. I was trying to defend myself against Thayer. He has done nothing but assault me and lives to give pain!"

Wah, wah, wah.

Bissette shoved his face away. "Go to my office, Alfaro. When you get there, face the wall and recite *Te Deum Laudamus*. Your punishment will be determined when I see you. Go."

"*Oui, Monsieur*." Holding a hand against his still bleeding nose, Rafael darted out of sight.

Pulling out a stained handkerchief, Bissette swiped Rafael's blood off his hand. He folded the handkerchief so the blood wasn't visible and tucked it away. "As always, Thayer, you do nothing but disappoint me." Picking up the razor from the floor, Bissette snapped the blade back into the ivory handle. "I was supposed to approve your upcoming release, but due to your continued penchant for violence, your stay has officially been extended by another year."

Malcolm almost choked. "*A full year*?! But I wasn't even the one who pulled out the razor!"

"And yet somehow *he* ended up bleeding." Bissette glared. "You know full well why you were sent here. You are no different from any of these boys. So cease pretending that you are."

A suffocating sensation tightened Malcolm's throat. "My only sin is enjoying pain."

"And I assure you, Thayer, you will." Seeing Nasser, Bissette paused. "Forgive this chaotic display of inhumanity, Your Royal Highness. I wish to assure you, neither will be allowed near you or your studies again."

Malcolm froze. Nasser was…royalty?

Tossing aside the blood-spattered cloth, Nasser angled closer to Bissette and announced in French, "In the name of my father's crown, you cannot punish my new friend, *Monsieur*. He was only protecting me.

That razor should have been locked away. I am holding you responsible."

It was rather endearing having a Persian prince come to his rescue. Malcolm eyed Bissette. "I concur. Why wasn't the razor locked away? I find that incredibly irresponsible. I could have been hurt."

Bissette narrowed his gaze. "Go into the corridor for further instruction, Thayer, or your extended year will turn into two."

"But I already served a full year. You cannot—"

"Your father entrusted me to cleanse your soul and permitted me to decide on the length of your penance. It is done. You are staying. Unfortunately, the additional year will cost your father another thousand francs. Which I will remind him of."

Malcolm's chest burned in disbelief. The man only wanted money. Which his father barely had. The son of a— "How dare you take money for what is supposed to be God's work?" he breathed. "My father already paid you well beyond what this pit of hell is worth."

"You wound me, Thayer." Turning toward the gathering luminaries, Bissette boomed, "Take him out! Lest I bloody the very halls of this sacred space!"

****

Dried blood crusted sections of the tall grass and some of the surrounding stones, whispering of the penance that had been issued to other boys earlier in the day.

It left nothing to the imagination as to what was about to happen.

Several young faces peered down at Malcolm through the latticed windows of the old library. Their noses and cheeks touched the glass in an effort to better see. Shadows loomed behind the boys as they were ushered away from the windows by several luminaries in black coats. One of the luminaries, whose face was stern and pale with severe lines around his sunken eyes and mouth, lingered before paging through his bible and turning away.

The courtyard became eerily quiet.

Malcolm's throat tightened. He veered his gaze to Bissette. "Rafael almost raped him."

"I know. And that is being addressed. His father and I will be discussing the possibility of castration. But as I have repeatedly told you, you are not in the position administer justice. You are here for the same reason he is: to be molded into something more." Bissette watched him with a hard, stoic expression reserved for those who disappointed him. "You will write a detailed letter to your own father explaining why I extended your penance by another year. Be certain to include the costs involved. Am I understood in this? Or would you rather I write the letter?"

It was pointless to even argue. His father would only take the side of the luminary. God before son. "I will write to him, *Monsieur*."

"Good." Bissette pointed to the slab of stone set before him on the ground. "Let us now focus on your soul's perpetual need for restraint. Pray for the forgiveness only God can give."

Malcolm grudgingly knelt on the stone, his knees long accustomed to the ache of a hard surface penetrating his bones. Bringing his hands together and folding them in prayer, he lifted his gaze beyond the man, beyond the old tree and beyond the stoned walls of the garden that were too high to climb. "O Lord, prepare my soul for the punishment I deserve. Amen." It was the only prayer he could muster.

"Stand." Bissette wagged his fingers, demanding it.

Malcolm rose to his feet.

"Remove everything, including your boots."

Sometimes, he wondered if the bastard enjoyed whipping naked boys. Stripping his linen shirt with the shrug of both muscled arms, Malcolm tossed it aside onto the grass. Kicking off his boots and wool stockings, he unbuttoned the flap of his trousers and shoved them down along with his undergarments. The cool air tightened his bare skin.

"Gather them and set them aside."

Malcolm neatly folded his clothes and set them aside.

"Face me."

Squaring his bare shoulders, he faced the luminary and placed his hands against his cock for the sake of protecting it against blows. *Help me, Lord. I have stupidly gotten myself into a situation I cannot get out of. I thought my time here would be spent in Your presence and in prayer. Not this. This is not what I want to be.*

Bissette snapped up the leather and metal strap laid out at his booted feet and approached, crushing the tall grass with solid movements. Wrapping its end around his hand, he whirled the length of the thick strap, forcing the air to whistle around it.

Malcolm closed his eyes. The first lash was always the worst.

The blow of the leather strap bounced off his back and made him gasp. The metal sewn between the leather spliced into his skin like a blade, but he defiantly remained standing.

Grunting to keep the blows steady, Bissette struck downward with a full arm swing from over his head and down, skidding and dashing the strap into flesh and bone. "Four...five...six..."

Blinded by tears he could no longer control, Malcolm staggered beneath each skull-penetrating impact of metal and leather, his legs growing unstable and weak. His heart responded by pounding so fast and so out of control, it made him lightheaded. Glimmers of euphoria found him only to remind him it was nothing but pain. He choked and gasped for breaths, unable to hear the count and eventually stopped fighting it. He let that dark, dark morbid part of himself, the one he'd always shoved away, enjoy the pain.

He was now his brother.

A loud crack shook his core as the metal snapped in half against the flesh of his upper thigh. Everything whirled white beneath his eyelids as the taste of blood filled his mouth. Malcolm staggered forward and back, no longer feeling a part of the world. It was beautiful. In a pulsing void, he watched his own blood slowly finger its way down his arms and legs.

"*Enough!*" someone boomed, sending an echo throughout the court-yard. "*How dare you go against what I commanded? You were not supposed to touch him!*"

The air seemed to thicken. It was Nasser.

A flurry of blurring words were feverishly exchanged between Bissette, Nasser and all of Nasser's servants who grabbed the blood-soaked strap from Bissette. Malcolm couldn't focus long enough to deci-pher what was said. He slumped onto his hands and knees, the grass cushioning his fall. His trembling fingers dug into the thick grass, blood smearing over its green as he savored its unexpected softness. He drew in shallow half-breaths, reveling in the lull from all the earlier pain.

A quick movement rustled through the grass. Sensing someone stood before him, Malcolm edged into a kneeling position. Everything swayed. He squeezed his eyes to steady himself. It was so nice to feel numb. It was so nice to feel nothing after feeling so much.

"Upon my life, you will *never* be beaten like that again," assured a fa-miliar voice.

Malcolm slowly shut out the darkness he had let in and returned to being who he wanted to be: himself. He opened his eyes, willing each breath. Standing before him against the vast blue valley sky was Nasser dressed in flowing silk garbs of blue and gold. They flapped freely against the wind.

He stared down at Malcolm with intense, dark eyes, his jet-black hair hanging around his young, vibrant face. "The luminaries refused to tell me where you had been taken."

Feeling his wounds oozing, Malcolm gasped between breaths. "I…I'm fine."

"You most certainly are not. Do not move." Yelling something in Persian to his servants, Nasser tossed the bible he held, causing it to thud open. "If this is the God who is supposed to save me, I return my faith to Allah. We leave within the hour and head to Paris. My offer is not negotiable."

Surprise flitted through Malcolm as he squinted through stabbing breaths. *"Paris?"*

Nasser removed his long flowing shawl, leaned in and gently draped it around Malcolm's nakedness. "I am buying your freedom, *Dalir,*" he said in a low voice. "Monsieur Bissette is willing to release you for fifty thousand."

Fifty thousand? Malcolm choked. "I wouldn't even be able to repay you. My father isn't worth that much. He isn't worth anything anymore. No. I cannot accept such grace. I cannot—"

"I am *not* leaving you here another year knowing I was the reason for it." Nasser hesitated. "I welcome you to travel with me to Persia and see a bit of the world at no expense to you. Allow me to show you what a brother should be."

Malcolm swallowed. "I happen to love my brother."

"'Tis obvious you do." Nasser leaned in closer his lean face sharpening. "But the world does not need a martyr who disappears for one brother and one cause. It needs a hero who appears for every cause. While I admire your devotion to your brother, it is crippling you. Allow yourself to be more. What you did for me today can be replicated on a far greater scale. I have *never* seen anyone take on a blade with no fear like that. Do you know what you can do with a gift like that? My country is on the brink of war with Russia and needs true fighters. We need someone willing to swing a sword at those who only seek to make the world suffer. You can be that someone and help worthy people. But not if you feel your brother needs you more."

God was speaking to him through this young man. After too many years of carrying the burden of being responsible for an unruly, tempestuous brother incapable of being responsible for anything, God was finally offering him a greater cause. One worthy of his mind and heart.

For although, yes, he stupidly gave into temptation and kissed Miss Silverthorn, thereby damning himself to a situation he wished he'd never been a part of, he did not deserve to continue to punish himself for the sins of his brother. If he returned to England, he would never be his own man. Even if his brother forgave him, he would be nothing more than what his twin had always wanted him to be: his shadow, but even darker and more twisted. "I'm tired of Wiltshire and London. I want to be my own man. I want my own life. Separate from my brother."

"I can give you that." Nasser's voice softened. "Do you enjoy being at sea, Malcolm?"

A breath escaped him. "Very much so. Yes."

"Good. Because we have a long journey ahead. I will ensure you are knighted into the Persian Court by my father. You will be granted the new name of *Dalir*. It means...brave." Nasser's features softened. "I am honored you chose to protect me in the same way you chose to protect your own brother." Nasser knelt beside him, pushing his garb away from the movement of his legs. "My servants went to fetch salve and cloths. They will tend to your wounds."

Malcolm tightened his hold on the shawl that barely covered him. He could feel it sticking to his wounds. They were a little too deep for his liking. "No. I will do it."

"There are too many. Let them help you." Nasser leaned in and touched Malcolm's face with trembling fingers. "Are you all right?"

He had almost forgotten what brotherly love was supposed to be like. "I am now."

LESSON ONE

**When your closest friends are strangers you meet
on the street, it is time to introduce your neglected,
silly heart to a more meaningful beat.**

-The School of Gallantry

London, England, Spring of 1830
Clipstone Street – late morning

Miss Leona Olivia Webster was used to being a pariah. Yes,
there were days it was difficult to accept that her only rela-
tive and all of society thought she was a whore unworthy of
pity, but she had learned that wallowing in one's misery left very little
room for much else. As a mother, it was imperative she set a good example by showing her son one could and should remain optimistic. Even
during the worst of times.

Which was why, without any visible regret, she lingered by the steps
of the tenement and watched an array of her son's expensive clothing

and toys as they were carried down the cobbled street by unshaven creditors who spat out chewing tobacco every few steps.

Well. At least she didn't owe anyone anymore money.

A small hand tugged at her skirts. "Mama?"

"Yes, Jacob?"

"They took Jesus."

She paused. "What?"

"My bear," he whined. "The one you bought for me last week. I
named him Jesus like Mrs. Henderson told me to. And those men took
him. *They took him.*"

Leona glanced down at her six-year-old son with a quirked brow.
"Unlikely. I paid one of those gentleman two shillings to leave him behind. I was going to surprise you with it later. Mrs. Henderson had just
enough to save him. He is waiting upstairs on the table."

Jacob shook his head, sending strands of dark hair into his eyes. "No.
He isn't. They took him."

She squinted. "Are you certain?"

"*Yes.* They stuffed him into a crate and carried him off like
some...some...*criminal!* Whatever will become of him? I might *die*
knowing I'll never see him again." He gaped up at her. "Speaking of
death, Mrs. Henderson says children who aren't baptized go to hell. Is
that true?"

Leona tsked. "Don't listen to what Mrs. Henderson says. Her husband
used to commit forgeries for the aristocracy and was hanged for it. It
scared the poor dear into going to church far more than any person
should." The elderly woman, who was a very, very distant cousin, went
every morning, every afternoon and sometimes, when the spirit moved
her, she would knock on the locked doors of the church at night, yelling
about her need for salvation.

Jacob's brows flickered. "Why haven't I been baptized? Don't I deserve to be?"

She softened her voice. "Of course you do. But the circumstance of your birth makes it difficult."

"So I'm going to hell?"

"No. Of course not."

"How do you know that?"

"I don't. But if hell does exist, I hardly believe God would send a child into the flames merely because a bit of water wasn't splashed on its head. You're a good boy, dearest, and that is all that matters. Hell has nothing to do with it."

Jacob chewed on his lower lip before tugging on her skirts again. "Mama?"

"Yes, dear?"

"Please don't let the creditors take my bear. *Please.*"

She leaned down, and smiling as brightly as she could, tweaked his freckled nose. "I promise he isn't going anywhere. They should have left him on the table, but obviously there could have been a mistake. Let me see if they accidentally took him. I'll be right back."

Jacob's green eyes brightened. "Can we buy Jesus a new cravat? He needs one."

She sighed. "Aside from the fact that we can't afford it, can you please name him something else? It's incredibly inappropriate."

"But Mrs. Henderson thinks it to be a brilliant name."

"And it is. Believe me, it is. But Mrs. Henderson *also* thinks we should crawl on our knees to Jerusalem."

"I take it Jerusalem is very far?"

"Yes. Very. So far our knees would disappear in an attempt to get there. The sad truth is, Jacob, I cannot and will not support a religion that won't baptize you. It's wrong." She brushed his hair away from his forehead. "Now please. Name the bear something else."

Jacob tapped his chin thoughtfully with two fingers. "What about Mister Moses?"

She supposed there were worse things a child could believe in other than God. He could be worshipping the devil. "I...fine. That name will do just fine. Now stay here. We don't want Mister Moses disappearing into the Red Sea, do we?" Hurrying down the stone stairs of the tenement, she gathered her calico skirts and bustled down the busy street, dodging women and men on the pavement. "Gentlemen!" she called out to those loading the cart. "Gentlemen, pardon the delay, but my son seems to think you've taken his bear. Do you know where it is?"

One of them shoved her belongings further into the cart. Adjusting his sweat-soaked shirt, he playfully clicked his tongue at her. "I'll be your bear."

It was humiliating. And even worse? They didn't care that it was humiliating. "I don't associate with hairy clackboxes," she tossed back in a much sharper tone. "Now where is the bear? Don't make me climb into that cart, gentlemen, because I'll throw everything out of it and ensure you're here all week. Is that what you want?"

Eyeing her, they busily tied items into place with tangled rope.

Men. They thought because she was barely five feet in height, they could take advantage of her. She trooped over to the bearded male who had earlier taken her money. "I paid two shillings for my son's toy to be left behind. I put it into your hand when you first came upstairs collecting items. Now where is it? It was supposed to have been left on the table."

He shrugged. "I don't recall touching it." He lifted several items and passed them off to the others. "But if you yank on my cock a few times, I might remember."

They all laughed.

She glared. "You bring nothing but shame to your poor mothers. My only hope is they're all dead so they don't have to suffer knowing their sons are morons." Letting out a disgusted breath, she shook her head and rounded the wooden cart. Standing up on the tips of her slippered toes, she lifted her chin to peer inside. Only she couldn't see.

Propping up a leather slipper onto the cart, she hoisted herself up over the side to better see over the wooden railing and into the box below. She scanned the gathered items of mantle clocks, books, and other countless items belonging to other unfortunate souls whom the creditors had earlier called upon in the name of debt. She paused. In the very corner of all the clutter, directly below where she was propped against the cart, a bear made out of fuzzy grey wool with a satin cravat neatly tied around its throat caught her attention.

The bastards. Not even a child's toy was safe from the world.

Leaning forward against the laced constraints of her corset, Leona reached over the side of the wooden cart. After a few huffing swipes, she grabbed it by the ear using the very tips of her fingers and brought its arm up to her mouth knowing she had to keep her hands free to get down. Clamping her teeth onto the woolen arm, she leaned back and lowered herself off the cart, hopping back down onto the cobbled street. Removing the bear from between her teeth, she grinned and dusted it off in triumph, feeling as if she had climbed a mountain in Tibet for it.

Not that she would *ever* leave the country or climb anything outside of a few flights of stairs.

A grubby, hairy-infested hand seized her wrist hard, making her jump. "Put it back," the bearded man rasped, his breath as rotten as his teeth. "Before I make you regret you have tits."

She gasped. "You, sir, are as rude as you are disgusting." She tried shaking the man's hand off, while still holding onto the bear. "Now let go! I paid for it!"

The creditor grabbed the bear with his other hand and narrowed his gaze. "This here be the property of the debts you owe. Two shillings isn't going to save this bear or anything else in the cart. Now unless you're willing to fuck every last one of us right here on the street, you'd best put it back."

If she wasn't already wrangling for the bear with both hands, she would have smacked him into the street and out of England for such language. "Let go or I swear I'll swing at far more than your pea-sized bollocks, you-you...rumpot!" Thankfully her son wasn't within hearing distance, because she wasn't being a very good role model. She tightened her hold on the bear and gritted her teeth in an effort to hold on, praying the thing wouldn't rip in half. "Now let go!"

"Not until you pay the debt!" The creditor kept tugging on the bear.

"One would think I owe you a hundred pounds. And I don't. Now let go of the damn bear!"

A male figure loomed beside them. "Is there a problem?" The tone was like velvet, yet it was equally edged with steel.

"*Yes,*" she piped, still frantically tugging on the toy. "I paid two shillings for this bear. *Two!*"

"But you owe me five pounds!" the creditor yelled, sending spittle toward Leona. "*Five!*"

"*Minus two shillings,*" she sternly corrected, swiping at her face with her free hand. "Which means...I keep the bear. Now stop spitting on me!"

"I'll do more than spit on you, you damn—"

She winced and held up the plush bear rigidly between them, half expecting to be struck.

It didn't happen.

The creditor was yanked back hard and shoved against a nearby lamppost by a massive figure dressed in a great coat.

Leona blinked, awkwardly lowering the bear to better see.

The stranger, who was well over six feet, held the creditor firmly by the throat with one hand while digging into his own coat pocket with the other. His large gloved hand retrieved a five pound bank note which he crushed and tucked into the man's left nostril. "There. Now she owes you nothing. Carry everything back in for the lady before I introduce you to the back of my fist."

Leona bit back a smile. She had never seen anyone shove money into someone's nostril before. Creative.

The creditor stilled, his gaze locked on the looming figure that still held him by the throat against the lamppost. "I'll...have my men put everything back," the man wheezed, the bank note in his nose twitching.

"You damn well better," the stranger ground out. "*Now get to it.*"

Releasing the creditor with a rough push toward the direction of the cart, the gentleman let out a long audible breath. He paused as if realizing she was watching and swung back to her, his dark hair falling into his eyes. He cleared his throat. Adjusting the smalt-colored waistcoat that shifted against his broad chest, he shoved his hair out of his eyes and set his massive shoulders. "People these days have no manners." His voice broke with huskiness as he intently searched her face. "Are you all right?"

Leona's stomach flipped as she pressed the bear against her chest in disbelief. Tally-ho. It appeared Hercules had a brother.

LESSON TWO

Embrace the unknown.

It leads to tantalizing possibilities.

-The School of Gallantry

"A you all right, madam?" the man repeated.

Leona gaped up at the face of the unexpected angel who looked more like the fallen sort out of hell. He was enormous in stature, forcing her to crane her neck. "Uh...yes. I...thank you, sir," she managed.

Ice blue eyes held her gaze from where he towered. A thick, jagged scar marred the entire left side of his shaven face. "Next time, ask others for assistance before taking on a group of men. What under heaven were you thinking? You're the size of an elf. You could have been hurt." He gave her a pointed stare, then with the shake of his head, turned and stalked away.

She blinked, holding the softness of the bear tighter against herself and watched that massive, muscled body make its way through the crowd like a lion prowling its way through a herd of gazelles. There was an unspoken air of isolation surrounding him as people scrambled to get out of his way.

Usually when a man paid a woman's debt in these parts, he expected something. A kiss, at the very least. Not that she would ever entertain a man who looked like he could snap chimneys under one arm. "Sir?"

He jerked to a halt and glanced back at her, his hair falling back into his eyes. "What is it? Are they not moving fast enough?"

In unison, the creditors scrambled to unload the cart, stumbling to carry everything back to the tenement with the scuff of boots.

She burst into laughter. The man had earned her respect for life. "They are moving *much* faster now, thank you." Turning to her son, who lingered on the steps, she called out brightly, "Go inside to Mrs. Henderson, dear. I'll be right there!"

"What about Jesus?" he called back, holding out both hands and rattling them. "I want Jesus!"

"It's Moses now, remember? Moses. Now give me a moment!" Gad. Half the street heard that. She turned to the gentleman who still silently waited and cringed. "He is going through a religious awakening. Very normal for children his age. I'm hoping he'll outgrow it."

His blue eyes continued to hold her gaze as if expecting her to say something worthy of his time. "Am I to understand you don't support your child's view of religion?"

Apparently, he was the religious sort. Most people were. Not that she was most people. Much like her aunt who had raised her after the death of her father, she was more of a freethinker. Neither a believer or a disbeliever.

When she was younger, her aunt had wisely taught her to hide their radical views which included being independent from not only the church but men. As for hiding her views now that she was older? Why bother? Everyone hated her anyway.

"It isn't that I don't support his view, sir, I simply want him to be well-informed before he makes a decision that will impact the delicate core of who he is. You cannot turn a boy into a leader if you insist he only follow. One would hope every mother would be as infinitely thoughtful as I."

He stared.

She said too much. "Uh…can you please wait whilst I take the bear to him? I shall only be a moment."

He shifted his scarred jaw. "Why do you want me to wait?"

My, was he ever serious. "I wish to speak to you."

"About what?" he rumbled out.

Oh for the love of butterflies. "About your generosity. What else? Now might you wait?"

He skimmed her appearance, lingering for a moment on her stained apron, and then widened his stance. "All right. Go. I'll wait."

Leona awkwardly adjusted the apron around her waist with one hand, wishing she had taken it off before leaving the kitchen. She probably had flour in her hair, too, after her morning of making scones had been interrupted by the creditors banging on the door. She swiped at the sides of her hair. "I was busy in the kitchen all morning."

He held her gaze. "I can see that."

His level of intensity made it impossible for a girl to breathe. She edged away. "Excuse me."

Turning, she bustled back to her son who still waited on the stairs. She wagged the bear at him, leaned down and kissed his head. "Here you are. As promised. Now please. Call him whatever you like, even Jesus, Mary and Joseph, but don't ever say it outside the confines of your room."

She lowered her voice. "Setting aside what I think, people are very sensitive about anything relating to God. It's very personal, and we have to be mindful of how we make others feel. Do you understand?"

"Yes, Mama." He hesitated, then quickly leaned in close and whispered urgently from behind a small hand, "*What does fuck mean?*"

She gasped. He'd heard everything. "Don't *ever* repeat that word! Do you want your poor bear to faint? The word shouldn't even exist in the English language. Only rakes and bullies use it."

He blinked, lowering his hand to protectively cover the ears of his bear. "But those men used it."

She was such a sad example of a mother exposing her son to such men. "They only used it because they're too stupid to know any better. Remember. How you conduct yourself in anger reflects the depth of your soul. Which is why we never use such words. Ever."

Having been raised by her aunt, who was an overprotective country woman out to slap the world, Leona heard more than a few vile words uttered in her presence. But living these past six years amongst the middle classes in the big city of London, a girl learned all sorts of things she didn't want to learn. "Now go inside and think of how fortunate we are. Someone actually cared enough to help us. That doesn't happen every day."

Grinning wide enough to show off all three missing teeth, Jacob took the bear and nuzzled it. "Did Papa send him to pay for everything?"

Leona stiffened. She hadn't even thought of that. What if— Oh, no. Ryder would try to use this as an open invitation into their lives. An invitation he would *never* get. "It's important I speak to this gentleman at once. Can you go upstairs?"

"Why?" Jacob used his chin to point beyond her. "Who is he?"

"I have no idea. But I plan to find out. Now please. Go upstairs."

"What happened to his face?" Jacob eyed the man. "Why does it look like that? Did someone hurt him?" He pointed. "Look! His scar runs from his ear to his—"

Leona grabbed his hand, squeezing it and gently nudged him away. "It isn't our business to know. Nor is it polite to delineate physical abnormalities. Now please. I made a whole batch of scones and ask that you go upstairs and eat. Mrs. Henderson will set a plate out for you."

Jacob peered up at her. "Your scones hurt my teeth. They're too hard." He pointed to one missing tooth. "See?"

Leona cringed. "I will agree that my cooking is horrendous, but you and I both know your tooth was loose for weeks and my scone had nothing to do with it. Now go and...dip said scone into some tea and count to five. That should soften it. Because food is food."

"Yes, Mama." Jacob turned and trudged up the stairs, disappearing inside.

Letting out an exasperated breath, she swiveled on her slippered heel and paused, realizing the man was standing behind her. He had heard everything. Including the comment about his face. She shriveled at seeing his strained expression. "Forgive him. Jacob is only six and still learning how to conduct himself."

"I hardly took offence." His sun-toughened face now held a lethal calmness.

For all she knew Ryder sent this man. Her throat tightened. "Did someone send you to pay my debts? A certain gentleman from King Street?"

He stared. "No. You appeared to be in need of assistance so I offered it."

Her lips parted. "Oh." She was so relieved. Pathetic though it was, she had gotten to the point of preferring to owe complete strangers over Ryder. "Thank you, sir." She offered a smile. "I must say, I was rather impressed with how you stuffed that banknote up his nose."

A satisfied light came into those eyes. He inclined his head. "I did it with pride."

She let out a calming breath. It had been so long since she bothered to interact with men. She had almost forgotten they were actually people. Not just walking penises. "Might I offer you some tea?" She was certain there were a few leaves in the cupboard. "I made scones this morning." Hard as rock though they were. "Won't you join us?"

He hesitated. Then shook his head. "No. I don't have time." Despite that, he lingered.

Sensing he wanted to accept, she smiled. "There is no need to be overly polite. We have plenty of scones. I made well over a dozen. Sixteen, to be exact. They came out a bit overcooked, so I really need to get rid of them." Wait. She wasn't really helping her cause, was she?

He adjusted his linen cravat with gloved fingers. "No. I already ate." He still lingered.

It was obvious he was a man of few words. Fortunately for him, she was a woman of plenty. "Oh, come now. I can't have food going to waste and I most certainly won't be able to repay you in any other way."

"I'm not looking to be repaid, madam." He shifted his scarred jaw. "Will you be all right? Can I go now? Or did you need something else?"

Was this man real? He wasn't even looking to exploit the generosity he had shown. It was so unbelievably...*nice*. "No. I...no. I uh...I don't require anything else, thank you." Strangely, she felt rather depressed letting him go. After all, this man was breathing proof that not all of humanity had been lost.

He lowered his chin. "Your tone leads me to believe you're still in distress."

His cool level of seriousness was charming, as if he were parenting the entire world. "I'm not. I was only— My aunt used to say real gentlemen are like fairies: they don't exist. And yet here you are proving her and me wrong."

He studied her. "And what makes you think I'm a gentleman?"

Was he flirting with her? She couldn't tell. "I could be wrong."

"Yes. You could be. Be wary of the men you compliment. This world is full of deviants."

She snorted. "Oh, come now. You speak as if I were attractive enough to lure in deviants. Maybe seven years ago that might have been true. *Maybe*." She angled both hands before herself. "I had a glorious waist worth whistling at. Sadly, I've gained a few stone after having my son. The corset strings don't pull half as tightly as they used to."

An inexplicable look of withdrawal came over his face. "Are you prone to insulting yourself?"

"Sometimes." She dropped her hands to her sides and puffed out an exasperated breath. "It's been a long day and it's not even noon. Have you *ever* had creditors call on you? They dig through everything. Poor Mrs. Henderson's flat is a mess. I'll be cleaning it for days."

He said nothing.

She quirked a brow. "Are you certain you don't want any scones?"

"Quite." He edged back. "You seem well-educated and appear to live in a fairly decent neighborhood. Why do you owe money?"

How had her life become this pathetic? Here she was standing on the street between the shuffle of peddlers, explaining her financial situation to a stranger. "I was putting everything on credit thinking I'd get a chance to pay for it, which, of course, *never* happened. It's been a few months and I still haven't been able to find work. No one will hire me."

"I see." He squinted, crinkling the scar on his face. "I'll only be in London for another eight weeks, but maybe I can help."

This man was putting all the local charity houses to shame. "Oh, no, no. Please. That won't be necessary. You've already done more than enough."

"I will decide when it's enough. And it isn't enough." He widened his stance. "What do you usually do in an effort to earn a wage?"

May she keep herself from rattling that face in appreciation for what appeared to be genuine concern. He would be the first. "Well, I...there isn't a thing I haven't done. I've serviced kitchens and drawing rooms alike these past few years. As long as the pay is worth more than two shillings a week, I'll take up whatever household drudgery there is."

He glared. "Two shillings a week? Why not sign up for slavery out of Africa? What the devil is wrong with you? I would never pay a wage *that* low." He adjusted his coat, his features softening. "Mr. Holbrook and I share quarters. Given his dire financial situation, he is down to only one servant, has no clean clothes and eats in pubs I won't even go near. If you're willing to take on the responsibility of cleaning, cooking and tending to the house we are leasing, I can start you out at five pounds a week for however long I'm in London. Are you interested?"

She blinked. Rose buds. He was offering her a position *merely* because she needed one. Who was this man? "Five pounds a week? For cooking, cleaning and laundry?"

"Yes. To be paid every Saturday. By me."

She refused to trust it. "Might I ask why the pay is so inflated? Not even a lady's maid in the highest of circles makes more than fifteen shillings a week."

"I know. There is a reason." He swiped his gloved knuckles across his chin. "I've been at the house for a little over two months now, and it's alarmingly obvious despite the servant Mr. Holbrook keeps, it's *never* been cleaned. There are still chamber pots in some of the rooms that haven't been washed out from the previous owners."

Ew. "I may struggle with that one. I don't even like cleaning my own porcelain."

He arched a brow. "I don't expect you to clean any of them. We're grown men and can take care of our own, thank you. All I ask is that you tend to cooking and the cleaning of the house. If you take the position, I promise to pay five pounds a week *and* a bonus of twenty."

"*Twenty?*" Her pulse skittered. That was a lot of money. Enough to get her and Jacob out of London and into Shrewsbury well before summer.

She eyed him. "When would I get the bonus?"

"The moment you impress me."

She wasn't sure she liked the suggestive tone in his voice. "We are still talking about my ability to clean chamber pots, right?" she asked, spacing her words evenly.

His mouth tightened. "Last I knew. Why? Are you talking about something else?"

"No. Of course not. Why would we be talking about something else?"

"You tell me." He stared. "Do you have any references?"

She cringed. "No. I was terminated without any."

"Why? What did you do?"

"Nothing. I was loyal and worked very hard for every person who ever hired me."

"So says the woman with no references."

She set her chin. "If you must know, sir, I was terminated from every position I've ever had because the moment these women discover I have a child and no husband, they panic and come to the vile conclusion that I must have no morals *whatsoever*. That I may very well take it into my head to steal their silver *and* fondle every last footman in the house. People are disgustingly judgmental. They know nothing and assume everything. Not that you would understand."

He paused. Something flickered in his blue eyes. Some sort of emotion that appeared and disappeared within a blink. "I understand more than you think." He set both hands behind his back, broadening his chest to an even more intimidating size. "If your work is as sharp as your tongue, I would like to hire you. You'll get the bonus of twenty in eight weeks, which is about when the position will most likely end."

Her eyes widened. "I'll receive sixty pounds for only eight weeks of work?"

"Yes. So whatever you do, don't disappoint me or I'll terminate you without pay *or* references. Like the rest of your employers."

She gave him a withered look. "Is that supposed to be funny?"

"If it were, you would have laughed." He dug into his coat pocket and withdrew a small silver case. He flipped it open and straightened the cards within the casing as if it was imperative for each ivory stock paper to be aligned. He withdrew a card. "Mr. Holbrook usually isn't around and barely has time to sleep in his own bed. As for me? I'm only in Lon-

don on business. Once that business has been resolved, I'll be departing."
He snapped the case shut, tucking it into his pocket and presented the
card between two gloved fingers. "Seeing it's Monday, call on me this
Thursday afternoon at three. I'll be around."

Son of a blundering ox. No more London. And more importantly...no more Ryder. "Thank you, sir. I'll be there at exactly three. And
not a minute later. I'm very punctual. I have to be. I'm a mother." Egad.
She was rambling. "Thank you again, sir. I'm so very grateful to you.
Very. This goes beyond anything anyone has ever done for me. This
is...*Thank you.*"

He wagged the card closer. "Cease thanking me and take it. I have to
go. I have an appointment on the other side of town."

"Oh. Of course. How rude of me." She took the card, her bare fingers
grazing his. She paused. The leather of his gloves was provocatively
smooth. "Thank you."

He lowered his chin. "You already thanked me. Four times. I counted."

She cringed. "I'll stop thanking you."

"Good." A muscle now flicked in his jaw. "Your hands ought to be
covered in public. Why aren't you wearing gloves? Do you not own
any?"

Apparently, she had just been reprimanded for not being a lady. She
fingered the card. "I do, but I only wear them on special occasions. I can't
afford to spoil them."

He lowered his hand, flexing the one she touched. "What is your
name?"

She felt her pulse beat in her throat, sensing the contact of her bare
skin against his glove had somehow bothered him. "Miss Webster, sir."

"I want your full name. What is it?"

He was such a gruff and curt soul. It was as if he didn't care if he offended anyone by being who he was. "Miss *Leona Olivia* Webster, sir."

His countenance remained immobile. "If you have trouble finding suitable care for your son, Miss Leona Olivia Webster, he is more than welcome to remain at your side during the course of your service. Mr. Holbrook and I are hardly around the house anyway."

Her lips parted. "I'm allowed to bring my son to work?"

"Yes. All I ask is that you keep him within your sight at all times. Mr. Holbrook has books and papers that cannot be damaged."

Holy badger. She had found the perfect position. "So I can have my son with me at all times?"

"Yes. I do believe I just said that."

She eyed him in disbelief. "You, sir, have restored my belief in humanity."

He edged back, his features tightening. "Then you obviously know nothing of humanity."

She blinked. "Are you always this serious?"

He leveled her with a stare. "Yes. Does that bother you, Miss Webster?"

"Yes. It does." She fingered the card he had given her. "When one is too serious about life, one misses out on it. My poor Aunt Judith is proof of that. I don't believe I've ever seen that woman smile. Ever. And as my father used to say, 'Smiles are important. They let the world know you're breathing.'"

He weighed her for a moment. "You look incredibly young but your way of thinking contradicts what I see. How old are you?"

She honestly didn't know what to make of him. One moment he was trying to leave, the next he was trying to stay. "Five and twenty, sir. And you?"

"Older. No longer in my twenties. I took a breath and here I am."

She lifted a brow. "You say it with such regret."

He averted his gaze. "Let us not get started on regret. England is the last place I want to be." Cold dignity overtook his features. "I will see you this Thursday. Don't be late." He stalked away.

His mannerisms were about as abrupt as thunder. He hadn't even introduced himself. She glanced at the card he'd given her and paused. Odd. There was an address but no name. "Sir?" she called out.

He swung back toward her, his dark hair falling into his eyes. "I'm trying to leave."

"Uh...yes, I know. And I don't mean to pester, but—" She held up the card and wagged it. "There is no name printed here."

He gave her a sidelong glance. "I know. Mr. Holbrook and I share cards given we reside at the same address. It saves money. Now if you will excuse me..." He skimmed her appearance. "I have to go."

"But I don't even know your name," she countered in complete exasperation. "You never gave me one."

He paused. "I didn't?"

A laugh escaped her. "No. You didn't."

He cleared his throat. "Oh. I...forgive me. I've been at sea too long and my manners aren't what they used to be." He inclined his head. "The name is Malcolm Gregory Thayer, the Earl of Brayton, after my late father." He hesitated. "If you hear rumors pertaining to my name and character, I ask that you come to your own conclusion based on what you see and not what you hear."

A knot rose in her throat. That sounded a bit too cryptic for her liking. Even worse, he was an aristocrat. And not just any. An earl. That was one less tier from a duke. Such elevated status in society usually created men who believed they had the right to do whatever they pleased with women. Her poor aunt had been abandoned at the altar by an unprincipled viscount who made a long list of promises he couldn't keep. Rot it all. She *knew* this was too good to be true. "And what rumors would they be, my lord? Would you care to elaborate? So I may think on this?"

"Gladly." He widened his stance. "According to the Bishop of Salisbury and all of Wiltshire, I compromised his daughter, Miss Dorothea Elizabeth Silverthorn. She was seventeen at the time of the incident and

I a mere eighteen. She was sent to Scotland, but eventually returned, lost all faith in herself, men and God and now works as birch mistress over on Charlotte Street. Any other questions?"

Her lips parted. She knew people well enough to say he wouldn't have admitted to all of that *or* given names and locations if he were guilty of it. Or...would he? "So did you actually compromise this Miss Silverthorn?"

He glared. "No. I was saving her from my own brother." He buttoned his great coat, patting it into place against his chest. "What little good that did."

He was quiet for a moment, clearly distracted by whatever he was thinking. He swiped his face. "If what I admitted is a concern, Miss Webster, and I imagine it would be, I can give you whatever money you need right now so we don't have to complicate this." He dug into his pocket and pulled out a few loose coins, counting out everything he had. He paused. "Unfortunately, I only have a few crowns left. Here. Take it. I'll find someone else to fill the position." He held it out.

It was obvious by his missing hat, the well worn leather of his gloves and the simple stitching of his clothing that he was being very generous with what he could afford. Bless him and his beating heart. She hesitated, then reached out and clasped his hand, which held the money, gently forcing his large gloved fingers around the coins.

He stilled, holding her gaze.

She smiled, sensing he needed it. "I'm not taking money I haven't earned, my lord. Just as you are giving me an opportunity to prove my worth despite my lack of references, I wish to offer you the same without judgment." She pulled back her hand. "I would very much like to take the position you're offering, Lord Brayton. Might I?"

A tremor touched his lips. "Of course." Lowering his gaze to the coins in his hand, he shoved them into his pocket. His brows flickered but he didn't meet her gaze. "I appreciate your level of trust given what I admitted."

She half-nodded. "And I appreciate your level of trust given I have no references. I consider us even."

They lingered, letting people on the street weave around them.

He lifted his gaze to hers and cracked his knuckles, the tension in his jaw hinting that he was debating something with himself. He inclined his head. "Good day, Miss Webster."

She also inclined her head. "Good day, my lord."

He veered around her, still heatedly holding her gaze and started walking backward to keep holding her gaze.

The tingling in the pit of her stomach turned to fire. She tucked his card into her apron pocket and held up a hand, trying not to let on that she was in any way affected by that stare.

He swung away, adjusting his great coat and disappeared into the crowd.

A shaky breath escaped her. The tingling in her stomach stayed. It. Stayed. She rolled her eyes, knowing she shouldn't permit tingles and marched herself back up into the tenement to clean up the mess the creditors left behind.

LESSON THREE

Curiosity did not kill the cat.

It only maimed it.

-The School of Gallantry

Two days later, late morning

Waiting for Thursday to come, which wouldn't be for another day, was like waiting for Christmas to come when it was only late April. She had become *obsessed* with thoughts of Lord Brayton. Those eyes. That scar. That massive frame. The way he had looked at her. No man had ever looked at her like that. No man had ever—

Leona puffed out an exasperated breath, adjusted her hands on the well-worn wooden handle of the broom and returned to sweeping the tenement stairs leading into the building. No one else in the building bothered to maintain the stairs that faced the street. So she always did it. And they let her.

Stepping down each stone step, she swept away debris the vendors always tossed when passing through. If only they would toss coins. Finishing up the last step and forcing the debris past the pavement and into the cobbled street, she sighed and swiveled to go back into the tenement when her gaze landed on the massive frame of the same man she'd been thinking about since Monday afternoon.

Her heart popped as their gazes met.

He veered in closer, his great coat billowing around him, displaying simple wool trousers, scuffed boots and a tweed waistcoat. Pausing before her, he inclined his head as if to announce he was not only present but expected full attention. "Good afternoon, Miss Webster."

She tightened her hold on the broom, wondering if her fingers would snap the wood in half. The pinch of the wood against her palm was beautifully grounding and calmed her. "Good-afternoon, Lord Brayton. I wasn't expecting to see you until tomorrow. Is everything all right?"

He adjusted his gloves and rumbled, "I was merely passing through. Mr. Holbrook had a book printed over on Paternoster Row a few streets down. I was checking in on it."

"Oh." And here she thought he couldn't stay away. "Mr. Holbrook is a novelist?"

"I'm afraid so."

She smirked. "Are you saying his book is that bad?"

"I'm afraid so."

A laugh escaped her. A real laugh. It was so nice to share in a laugh with someone other than her son. She nervously tapped her hand against the broom and eyed him. Maybe she could invite him up. He *was* her employer. And it wasn't as if they would be alone. Mrs. Henderson and Jacob were upstairs having whatever was left of the scones.

"Do you have a bit more time today than you did on Monday?" she ventured.

His blue eyes pierced what little distance was between them. "Maybe. Why?"

It wasn't a no. But it wasn't a yes, either. Perhaps a small nudge would make it happen. "I just finished sweeping, so I'm done here. There are still a few scones left from Monday. You're more than welcome to come upstairs."

He swiped his face, then shifted from boot to boot and gave her a pointed, agitated look.

She lowered her chin. "You don't have to come up."

The line of his mouth tightened a fraction. He looked around. "I have ten minutes. But nothing beyond that. So don't insist."

She bit back a smile. It was as if he didn't want the world to know he was interested. "Don't you worry. I'll ensure you're out the door in less than ten minutes."

A window swung open on its creaking hinges from high above, making them both look up.

Mrs. Henderson, who clutched her prayer book against her shawl-covered bosom, peered down at them with a perusing squint. Her eyes widened. "Leona." Her white ruffled cap fluttered with the movement of her gray head. "You know full well you aren't allowed to associate with any men. Are you wanting me to put this in a letter to your aunt? *Are you?*"

Leona sometimes felt she was being held hostage by a seventy-two-year-old canoness. Trying to be polite, she set the broom against the railing of the tenement and called back, "This here is the gentlemen who is hiring me!"

Mrs. Henderson paused and squinted again. "He doesn't look an earl. He doesn't look respectable."

Leona sighed. "I assure you, he is both."

"Prove it," Mrs. Henderson prodded. "Have the man prove it."

Oy. This had to stop. "The poor man is already proving it. Do you see him trying to touch or kiss me right here on the street?"

Mrs. Henderson gasped. "The Virgin Mary wasn't touched or kissed, and look how she ended up! Do you want another child out of this? Hell awaits you if you keep at it!"

Leona winced. Eyeing Lord Brayton, she let out an awkward laugh and thumbed toward the direction of the entrance. "Don't mind all the barking. Much like my aunt, she thinks men are a menace. She may ask you more questions than a jury at trial, but she nobly held my hand through the worst of it. And when I mean the worst, I mean...childbirth. For that alone, I forgive that woman anything. Shall we go in? Do you mind her?"

Lord Brayton held her gaze. "Why would I mind? I'm going in for your company, not hers."

Those husky words warmed the pit of her stomach. What was it about this man that made her very breath jangle? He wasn't dashing or beautiful. Not at all. He was overly large, rugged and his features were unpolished, especially with that scar fingering its way from his ear to his jaw. But his presence and those ice blue eyes dominated the space between them as if he were demanding she and every breath she dragged in be his and only his.

It was a bit overwhelming.

Frantically brushing off her apron from clinging flour in an effort to distract herself, Leona gathered her skirts. "It's been a while since Mrs. Henderson and I have had any guests. Please. Follow me. And mind each step. Some of the boards are warped."

She turned and hurried up the outside stairs of the three-level tenement through the open door propped open by a brick. Everything grew quiet. Trailing a hand against the uneven yellow wallpaper, she paused halfway up the narrow stairwell, turned and waited. As she stood waiting, it occurred to her that he was the first male she had willingly invited into her home since giving birth to her son.

She bit her lip knowing it.

Lord Brayton hulked his way up, using massive strides to take three stairs at a time. Coming upon her, he came to a quick halt, his large hand grabbing the wooden railing beside them. His firm hold on the banister was enough to make the black leather of his glove creak. He eyed the stairwell. "What? Are we eating the scones right here?"

A choked laugh escaped her knowing he hadn't even meant to be funny. "No. I was waiting for you."

"Were you?" He lifted himself a step closer. "How nice."

In the mugginess of the narrow stairwell, she could smell the crisp tonic that had been brushed into his dark brown hair. There was also another more distinctive scent that lingered. It wasn't cologne or anything a man would usually wear. Whatever it was, it reminded her of an orchard. He smelled like...apples. It clung to her very breath.

With him being only two steps below, the jagged scar that traced his face from ear to jaw had become distinctively visible. She could make out the small dotted white scars that originally had threaded the wound together. Her chest tightened. "Did it hurt?"

"What?"

"The scar on your face."

He shrugged. "I don't remember. I was a babe when it happened. The forceps sliced it open."

She swallowed. His mother must have cried. "Forgive me. I didn't mean to pry."

His hand trailed up higher on the banister, his muscled arm edging closer. "And yet you did pry." His gaze never left hers. "Why is that, Miss Webster? Are you curious about me?"

He had to be flirting. And yet that aloof expression said otherwise. She honestly couldn't tap a finger on the sort of man he was. "Don't mind me. I'm curious about everyone. And it always gets me into trouble. Which I don't need. Shall we go up?"

He stared. "Why? Am I boring you?"

His level of seriousness was a touch rattling. Men usually conveyed *some* sort of emotion during a conversation. But this one— It was a wall. "No, of course not. I was merely..."

He leaned in close, blocking all view of the stairwell. He sniffed.

Her heart skipped. She leaned back. He'd sniffed her. Much like a dog would sniff another dog's rear. "What are you doing?"

"I was noting your perfume."

She paused. "I'm not wearing any."

"You naturally smell like that?"

"Like what?" she echoed, trying not to be offended.

"Like sex and cookies."

Not expecting that answer at all, she almost fell against him.

He steadied her, his large hands gripping her hard.

She froze, noting both her hands were set on each substantial pectoral buried beneath his waistcoat. By gad, the man was a solid brick wall. Her fingers instinctively curled against the rough fabric of his tweed waistcoat.

His jaw tensed. "I would rather you not grope me."

She snapped her hands back toward herself. "I'm sorry. I...I didn't mean to—" Her heart raced. If she had known men could produce muscles like his, she would have never bothered with Ryder.

Lord Brayton edged down several steps back, putting more distance between them. He swiped his face and paused, his gloved fingers grazing the scar on his face. He dropped his hand, dug into his pocket and pulled out a watch. Glancing at it, he tucked it away again. "I actually have fifteen minutes to spare. Not ten."

She paused. What was that supposed to mean? Was she imaging it or was this getting serious?

"I could make it twenty," he rumbled out. "It depends on you."

She swallowed. Something told her he had just announced his interest. After he had just chastised her about groping him. "Twenty would be lovely."

"Good." He stared. "Did you know chess originated out of India?"

Where did that come from? And why was he staring? "No. I did not know that."

"Do you play?"

She shook her head. "No. I never learned."

He searched her face. "I'll teach you. I have a chess set I travel with. We can play at night after you tend to the house. I don't usually get much sleep. I'm incredibly restless whenever I'm not at sea. Are you interested in…oh, I don't know…playing?" A raw huskiness lingered in his tone.

He wasn't talking about chess anymore. He was advancing.

Her skin prickled at the thought of having so much muscle wrapped around her. And while, yes, she was genuinely intrigued by the thought of having sex with a man who physically filled up an entire stairwell, she wasn't *that* intrigued. She needed a father for her son first. A bed mate for herself second. Not last, mind you, but second.

She moved up a stair. Then two. "Whilst flattered, Lord Brayton, I ask that you keep all of your chess pieces to yourself. You and I both know your level of standing would never find its way down to mine. You're an earl, and I'm nothing more than the daughter of a deceased plantation owner whose finances went bankrupt. I also have a six-year-old. I'm not exactly a good investment for a man like you."

An inexplicable look of withdrawal overtook his gruff features. "I wish to assure you, Miss Webster, that I'm not in a position to make those sort of advances. Not that you aren't attractive. You are. I simply will have to return to my regular way of life at sea. I hope you aren't disappointed."

Annoyingly, her cheeks grew hot. "I'm not disappointed."

"Good." He tapped the banister with a fist, no longer meeting her gaze. "So who lives on King Street?"

She stiffened. He was referring to their conversation from two days earlier. When they first met. "Why do you ask?"

He kept tapping. "Why did you think this gentleman sent me to pay your debts? Who is he to you? Your brother?"

Heaven forbid. "No. I never had any brothers. Or sisters, for that matter. My father never remarried after my mother died. He was very devoted to her memory. Which, of course, my aunt always scolded him for, claiming such sentimentally only perpetuated pain. She was very bitter about relationships. She had been abandoned at the altar twice. By the same man, no less."

His brows came together. "You answered every question but the one I wanted to know."

Oh, for heaven's— Her mind these days. "Forgive me. I *always* say more than I should." She sighed. "Annoyingly, I've known him for a long time. His name is Ryder William Blake."

"And who is he to you?" he pressed. "Why do you associate with him? Any particular reason?"

For someone who wasn't interested, he was interested. "Yes. He is the father of my...son."

"I see." He hesitated. "Are you and he still together?"

"No." Thank God.

"Why aren't you and he together?"

This one just got curious. "I thought you weren't interested."

He gave her a withering look. "I'm not."

"Clearly you are. You're asking about my life *and* former lover. Why?"

He shifted his jaw, pulled out his watch again and glanced at it. "I have to go."

"Have to or want to?"

He tucked the watch away. "Both."

"And I thought I was wary of the opposite sex." She eyed him. "Who was she?"

His features tightened. "Pardon?"

She softened her voice. "Don't deny it. I know a broken heart when I see it."

He set a large boot on the stair between them with a glorified thud. "I appreciate your concern, Miss Webster, but I haven't associated with enough women to let them break anything. I'm too smart for that."

"Really? Then why are you so skittish?"

He lowered his chin. "I'm not skittish. I'm simply a touch confused as to how an attractive, self-assured woman like yourself would have permitted any man to seduce her. You don't appear to be the sort. You seem more intelligent than that."

He was accusing her of being stupid. "If you're interested in specifics, Lord Brayton, *which you clearly are,* you may be astounded to find that he and I were engaged at the time. So I don't appreciate you—"

She gripped the banister harder in a riled effort to remain calm. There were times when she surprised herself into not even thinking about what happened. And then there were times when she disappointed herself and thought about nothing at all. "If you've never suffered from a broken heart, my lord, consider yourself lucky. It's like watching yourself bleed to death, but for some reason, you keep breathing."

His harsh features softened just enough to reveal the real man beneath the jagged scar: one capable of genuine understanding. "I didn't mean to upset you. Forgive me."

Leona picked at the seam of her apron, shrugged and admitted, "There is no need to apologize. Because you're right. I was stupid. I was stupid to think his growing popularity as a pianist would have allowed us to ever marry. He and I were friends for a long time. Which was the problem. Friends first and lovers last. We used to get along very well. But the more popular he got, the more distance came between us. I wasn't as refined as he needed me to be, and soon, I wasn't even allowed to attend his concerts. I had cost him an audience with the duke of Clarence after I showed up in a shabby morning gown for an evening event. I simply wasn't raised entertaining the aristocracy and didn't realize everything about them was so petty and superficial. Which is what Ryder turned out to be.

"Because when he had an opportunity to play music for a wealthy, widowed and oh-so-stunning baroness in Bath, he called off our engagement as if it were a dinner party he couldn't attend. Three months later, I found out I was not only pregnant, but that he had already married his baroness in the name of progressing his career. And there you have it. My entire life laid out in forty-five seconds."

Those cool blue eyes grew more subdued. "I'm sorry."

It was nice to know there were still men in this world who cared enough to be sincere. She still wished she hadn't given so much of herself to a 'friend'. Knowing everyone in Shrewsbury would have made her life difficult, she traveled to London to stay with her aunt's cousin, Mrs. Henderson, until she gave birth. She was supposed to give Jacob over to the church, but when she saw his tiny face and those tiny hands...

She swallowed. "My aunt was angry with my decision to keep Jacob and altogether stopped associating with me. Fortunately, her cousin, Mrs. Henderson, has been very kind. She doesn't have much, but she ensures we don't starve. I plan to use the money I make from the position you're offering to take Jacob to Shrewsbury by summer. That way, my aunt will have no choice but to acknowledge him."

Lord Brayton held her gaze. "So what about this Ryder?"

She averted her eyes. "He's known about Jacob for some time but didn't seem to take an interest in our lives until two weeks ago."

Lord Brayton stilled his hand against the banister. "Two weeks ago? So are you associating with him now?"

"I wouldn't call it an association. I haven't heard from the man since I was pregnant. He appeared at my door fourteen days ago and pretends to have grown a conscience the size of Constantinople. I'm still trying to understand what he wants. It's rather strange. He is overly focused on my son."

Lord Brayton dropped his hand away from the banister. "Have him call on me. I'll do more than stuff a banknote up his nose."

She snorted. "I appreciate that."

Realizing they'd been lingering in the stairwell too long, she paused. What was it about this man that made her feel she could talk to him about everything? It was...unexpected. She hadn't talked to anyone so openly in a very long time. It was nice feeling as if her life mattered to someone other than herself.

She averted her gaze. "We had better get to those scones before they get any harder and we're forced to use chisels. They're from Monday." She turned and finished going up the stairs.

His heavy steps followed her up, informing her that he was far from done with their conversation. He rounded her and faced her. "I will look after you for however long I'm in London. It would be an honor."

She jerked to a halt and gaped up at him. He was serious. "I'm not looking for a benefactor."

"I know. But I admire how you chose to take responsibility for your child despite the hardship. It says a lot about you." There was an arrested expression on his face. "There are extra rooms in the house Mr. Holbrook and I are leasing. You and your son are welcome to take a room. It would be no cost to you."

Everything about him was so unearthly. She searched his scarred face. "There is no need to feel responsible for me. I am not your responsibility. I am my own."

His expression remained tight with strain. "You were heinously wronged, Miss Webster. And no one knows more than I how difficult life can be when that happens. I am here to help you. Whatever you require over these next few weeks, it is yours. All you need do is ask."

She leaned back. "I dare say, with a generous offer like that, we might as well get married."

He glared. "I don't appreciate being teased, Miss Webster. I'm being serious."

Oh save her. If she wasn't careful, she could end up liking this one far more than she needed to. He wasn't even trying to beguile her. It was like this was who he was. This. Reserved, gruff but...kind. "Do you always rescue every woman in need?"

He eyed her. "If I have time." He was serious.

She let out an exasperated laugh but quickly squelched it in an effort to ensure he didn't think she was so easily entertained. It was no use. She already liked him. It was terrible. Absolutely terrible. She didn't need this. She was *trying* to get her aunt to talk to her. And getting involved with yet another man would only prolong the bitterness the woman was known for.

"*Leona?*" a male voice echoed from behind them on the stairs.

Leona froze. It was Ryder.

LESSON FOUR

Men are born cynics, but women are, too.

Put them together and chaos will ensue.

-The School of Gallantry

Malcolm didn't have to be introduced to the gentleman in the stairwell to know that the dark-eyed dandy dressed in a knee-length blue velvet coat and snug black trousers was none other than the Ryder William Blake he and Leona had been earlier discussing. Annoyingly, Malcolm could see the attraction.

This Ryder had good, broad shoulders and was tall and lean, with enough muscle to fill out a satin embroidered waistcoat to the point of stretching. Beneath that expensive top hat, dark thick hair tapered neatly to the man's collar as if it were trimmed around it that same day. The man's smoothly shaven face was youthful in appearance and had clearly never seen hardship.

Despite wanting to knock all of the bastard's teeth out with the back of his elbow given what he already knew of him, Malcolm decided to be cordial. For Leona's sake. He extended a quick hand. "Allow me to introduce myself. I am Lord Brayton."

Ryder's gloved fingers tightened on the bouquet of flowers he held. "I prefer we not complicate this with civilized introductions. You and I both know aristocrats don't wander around these parts. So whatever your intentions, leave off. She isn't interested in associating with any men."

What a self-entitled prick. Malcolm lowered his hand. "Then why are *you* here, Mr. Blake?"

Those dark eyes flared. "Because she and I share a son. Is that a problem? Are you saying you want to take this outside?"

The man had no idea who he was talking to. Years in the Persian navy had made him lethal. Even he didn't trust his own strength. Not that it kept him from using it. "You want to fight?" Removing his black gloves to ensure he didn't get any blood on the leather, Malcolm shoved them into the wool of his coat pocket. "Lead the way. Be forewarned I will not be held responsible for whatever happens next. In my opinion, you deserve it."

Leona set a hand to Malcolm's chest making him pause. She lifted large green eyes to his. "Please don't."

He swallowed, those soulful eyes and that small, trusting hand making his chest squeeze. Unlike most women, she didn't appear intimidated by his physical breadth or the scar marring his face. She had even invited him to have scones at her table as if he were worthy of that honor. She made him feel like a gentleman. A real gentleman. Something he had always struggled to be in his mind and in his heart. "Do you want me to leave, Miss Webster?"

She shook her head, causing her pinned brunette chignon to sway. "No. But I don't want you encouraging him, either."

Malcolm inclined his head, letting her know he was at her command. "Of course."

"Thank you." Lowering her hand, she turned to Ryder and narrowed her gaze. "How dare you disrespect a man I wish to invite into my home?

You have no right even being here. Have I not made that clear to you the last time you came up to the door? Now leave."

Ryder pointed at Malcolm's face with the tips of the red roses he held. "Are you telling me my son is associating with this? *This?* Leona, for God's sake, someone *clearly* took a blade to his face."

Malcolm smacked the flowers away, sending petals scattering. "How about I take a blade to yours?"

"Lord Brayton, please. There is no need for threats. Allow me." Leona pertly pushed her way between them and angled toward Ryder, hardening her tone. "While you insult a man you know nothing about, I wish to assure you, I'm genuinely honored to be in his presence. *Honored.* This gentleman has shown me *far* more respect in the past two days, than you've shown me since we were ten, you worthless piece of...*tripe.*"

While Malcolm wasn't prone to smiling, her attempt to defend him made his mouth quirk. "Now, now, Miss Webster. There is no need to bite his arm off. I can do that myself."

Ryder lowered the flowers to his side and tapped them against his leg, sending more rose petals fluttering onto the stairwell. "Leona, what is this? Are you and he involved? Is that it?"

Leona folded her arms over her chest, crinkling her flower-patterned dress. "Yes. He makes love to me every afternoon. Do you care to watch?"

Malcolm felt his mouth go dry. He realized the woman was joking but wondered if perhaps she found him attractive enough to consider it. Not that he'd ever give himself permission to do *any* of that. Ever. Setting aside his religious upbringing, he recognized the raw and dangerous power of sexual instinct and that the only power greater than that instinct was that of self-control. Which, of course, was something his brother never understood.

Ryder whipped the flowers down the stairwell. "You haven't changed a bit. Hell, you might as well be wearing the same gown you wore the night we called on the Duke of Clarence."

Leona glared. "Go spit on someone else's life for a change. You're a married man. Have you no shame coming to my door? I knew you were stupid, but I didn't realize you were *that* stupid."

Ryder glared back. "Don't talk to me about shame. I'm a happily married man."

"Last I knew, a happily married man doesn't bring another woman flowers."

"I was attempting to be a gentleman."

"You should have tried that seven years ago," she bit out.

These two were relentless. It reminded him of the angst between his brother and Miss Silverthorn. This was *exactly* why he avoided relationships. It was...messy.

"Leona, I didn't come here to argue."

"Then what did you come here for? Go on. Entertain me."

"I—" Ryder paused, as if realizing Malcolm was still around. He adjusted his coat. "I prefer you and I share in a conversation alone. It's important we speak. I have a proposition and ask that you join me in my barouche. It won't take long."

She squinted. "Join you in your *barouche*? And what? Make the world think you and I are involved? God no. I'd rather be alone with a tavern full of other men and toss whatever is left of my reputation to that. If you have something to say, I suggest you say it now. Or better yet...*leave*. Because I'm not interested in what your piano fingers have to say."

"If you want me to say it, I'll say it." Ryder glared. "Claudia can't have children. She lost every babe we ever tried to have, including our most recent one. A boy. Which is why I'm here." Pulling out a folded parchment, Ryder held it out. "I hired a lawyer to reclaim Jacob given he is my rightful son. If you sign this paper, revoking your rights, you'll get ten thousand pounds and have the ability to see him once a month. If you don't sign it, my lawyer will file negligence charges against you, given the way my son is living, and I'll ensure you never see him again. Those are your choices."

Malcolm's lips parted. Was he serious?

Snatching the parchment, Leona unfolded it with frantic hands and in between visible breaths, read the words. Lifting her gaze, she stared at Ryder. "You want *my* child because your wife can't give you what *I* have? And here I thought I couldn't hate you anymore than I already do." She bared her teeth and ripped the parchment in half. Mashing it into a ball, she whipped it at Ryder's head. "*Get out!* Get out before I get arrested for murder!"

Malcolm tensed, more than ready to intervene.

Ryder's features stilled. "Think of the boy, Leona. What sort of opportunities can you provide for him? What the hell do you plan to turn him into? *A glorified farmer?* Like your father was?"

Leona jumped forward and smacked Ryder, snapping his head sideways. "Better a farmer than a worthless arse like you! My father was a good man. *Nothing* like you!" She smacked him again.

Malcolm didn't bother to stop her. The son of a tavern hag deserved it.

Ryder grabbed Leona's wrist and shoved her toward the edge of the stairwell, his top hat tumbling off to the side.

And this is where it stopped.

Malcolm grabbed the man by the coat hard, yanking him off Leona. Snapping a forearm up to that throat, he slammed Ryder against the nearest wall with the weight of his body, causing the walls around them to tremor. Digging his forearm into that linen-knotted throat, Malcolm fiercely met Ryder's gaze. "Don't *ever* touch her or go near her again. Or the hands you use to make a living, will be lying on the street where they belong. Do you hear me?"

Ryder's chest heaved against his own. "I'll *not* have my son raised in poverty."

Malcolm leaned in closer. "Then give his mother all the money she rightfully earned so she can raise him and get the hell out."

"Fine words those are! I've already— She is unfit to be a mother. *Unfit.* Which is why I'm sending a lawyer." Ryder shoved back at him, trying to break free.

Digging his forearm harder against that throat to keep the man from moving, Malcolm said in a barely composed tone, "Tell your lawyer to come see me at Thirty-One Prince Street. I'll be waiting. And given the long list of people I know, Mr. Blake, I can assure you, you aren't going to be a father any time soon."

Ryder hesitated.

The thudding of small boots came at them. "Let him *go!*" Little hands shoved Malcolm from behind, hitting the back of his knees. "Let him go or I'll call on all the angels to smite you!"

Realizing he had an audience, Malcolm instantly released Ryder. He edged back onto the landing, away from Leona and almost stumbled over the boy who continued to shove him.

"Jacob!" Leona tugged him back. "Enough. Now go to your room."

"I'll go to my room when I'm done. *And I'm not done!*" Jacob tore away from his mother's hold, darting forward again and kept hitting Malcolm, those swinging hands pounding his legs harder. "I don't care how big you are! *I'm bigger!*"

It was like seeing a miniature version of himself. It was...charming.

Ryder rigidly waved a hand toward Jacob. "Leona, rein him in. The boy is acting like a savage. Is this how you bloody raised him?!"

Glaring, Leona tried grabbing Jacob by the shoulders. "I raised him to know the difference between right and wrong. He simply doesn't know he came to the defense of the *wrong* man." She leaned down, trying to grab her son's arms and still them. "Jacob, I'm asking you to stop. You've made your point."

"But he was hurting Papa!" Jacob shoved her away and frantically continued hitting Malcolm, his breaths barely keeping up with his swings.

It was obvious the boy needed male guidance. Malcolm knelt and grabbed those fast moving hands. Hard. "Your mother said enough." He lowered his voice to lethal and met Jacob's gaze. "When I was your age, I *always* faced the wall when my mother asked me to. Whether I had earned it or not. Now no more of this, Mister Jacob. Do you understand?"

Jacob's hands stilled. His smooth cheeks remained flushed and his ragged breaths remained uneven as his narrow chest pumped beneath his silk-embroidered waistcoat. That furrowed brow remained tight and determined to annihilate him. "You were trying to hurt Papa. I saw it."

Malcolm knew nothing about children. But he did remember being one. It was a delicate time when every breath and every word mattered. When one could either be something or nothing. "Allow me to explain what you saw." Malcolm released those tiny hands. "Your father here came to the door, delivered very bad news, which rightfully upset your mother, and then he had the audacity to get aggressive with your mother by trying to shove her down the stairs. That was when I took your father to the wall to put an end to it."

Jacob's furrowed brow softened. He glanced at his father, his lips parting. "You tried to hurt Mama?"

Ryder threw his head back and after a long moment, leveled it and offered, "No. I'm sorry. I was upset. This entire situation is—" He glanced at Leona and offered in a strained tone, "I'm not doing this to hurt you. He simply shouldn't be living like this. I can give him a better life."

Leona coolly stared him down. "Like the one you gave me?"

Although her tone nobly attempted to conceal all emotion, Malcolm could still feel her pain. And it pierced more than his heart. It pierced his soul. Because he knew all too well what it was like to pour one's trust into someone only to find they were unworthy of it. "I think it time you leave, Mr. Blake," Malcolm said in an effort to remain calm. "The child has seen more than enough."

Ryder sighed and half-nodded. "Yes. I'll leave in a moment. After I speak to my son." Veering past in the narrow stairwell, he hesitated and hoisted Jacob up into his arms. He adjusted him onto his right hip, sweeping back Jacob's dark hair from his eyes. "I'm sorry we couldn't have met on better terms, Jacob. It isn't like I haven't tried." He angled his way into the tenement where Mrs. Henderson was lingering by the open door. "Can I bring him inside? I won't stay long. I have a concert to practice for." He disappeared into the flat.

Mrs. Henderson hurried after him. "Two minutes, Mr. Blake! *Two.* Anything longer and I'll take one of Leona's scones to your head. Don't think I won't!"

Hell and corruption. And he thought his brother's life was a mess. Malcolm fisted his hands and eyed Leona. "What do you want me to do? I'll do it."

She fell back against the wall of the corridor, just outside the open door. Her frayed chignon flopped to one side, threatening to come undone. A breath escaped her full lips as she stared out at nothing in particular. "I don't want Jacob seeing anymore than he already has."

The agony in her tone was like a blade twisting itself into his gut. He knew all too well what it was like to feel powerless and trapped. Malcolm set himself against the wall beside her, ensuring he kept some distance between them. She was so much smaller than him, he felt like an elbow in the wrong direction would break her tiny frame into twenty pieces.

Realizing his hands were bare, he dug out his gloves from his coat pocket and yanked them on, covering the roughness of each scarred hand in smooth leather. He didn't want her looking at the damage to his hands that whispered of days that went back well before the monastery. It wasn't something a woman needed to see.

He sighed, knowing he had to do something about this damn Ryder. Keeping her in London would only exacerbate this situation. "How much money do you need to get back to your aunt?"

She snapped her gaze up to his. "None of that." She untied her apron and bundled it beneath her arm. "I'm not going into hiding like some criminal. I'm his mother, and I've been a damn good one at that. No court can prove otherwise. I'm staying in London until this is resolved."

"Given how intent he is, staying in London is not a good idea."

She rolled her eyes. "Given how intent he is, going anywhere is not a good idea. At least with you around, he'll be mindful of what he can and can't do."

The woman did have a point. "I leave in eight weeks."

"By then, I'll no longer be your responsibility."

He didn't need this. Because he already felt responsible. Not to mention overly drawn to her. He hadn't *really* been passing through. Paternoster Row was an excuse. He simply found himself unable to wait until Thursday to see her.

She hesitated, searching his face.

Why was she looking at him? "What?"

"Can I genuinely trust you?"

His throat tightened. The last time a female had asked him that, he ended up in the monastery for a sin he didn't commit. "The real question, Miss Webster, is whether I can trust you."

She gave him an exasperated look. "You speak as if I were some rake."

"Some women can be. They make a man promises they don't intend to keep."

She lowered her chin. "I swear I won't molest you."

"That really wasn't my concern." He eased out a breath. "I suggest you and Jacob take the rooms I earlier spoke of. You'll be safer there. It will be no cost to you."

Her features flickered and then softened. "You are becoming the hero every woman dreams of meeting."

Oh, hell and whale bile. Trying to be a hero to an attractive woman was like stabbing himself in the neck. He knew full well having her around his house was going to cause problems. Holbrook loved women, be they married or not, and Malcolm himself wasn't always the saint he wanted to be.

He got lonely sometimes. Over the years, whenever his feet touched land, he'd been guilty of paying attractive women to run errands for him just so he could talk to them and...look at them. It was pathetic. "Be aware that I'm going back out to sea and I'm not coming back. So whatever you do, don't get attached."

Her mouth quirked. "I'll desperately try not to." She squeezed his arm. Hard.

His skin pinched beneath his coat, sparking the darkness of a desire he'd buried since he was eighteen. Her fingers dug into his coat as if she planned to initiate the sort of pain he wanted.

He swallowed and tapped at her hand. "Can you not do that?"

She instantly released him. "I'm sorry. I was only—"

"Touching me," he pointed out. "We're not married, Miss Webster. And even if we were, I would hope you would ask for permission. Which I didn't give you."

She blinked rapidly, her cheeks notably flushing. "It would seem you're more of a gentleman than I am."

Why did he want to kiss and bite her? Why did he want to go against everything he had learned to be merely because she showed up? He hissed out a breath and eyed her. "I'll talk to a few people regarding your situation." It would be easy. Nasser's grandfather would flatten this out of court with the snap of those revolutionary fingers. "No one is going to take your son. That I vow."

She smiled brokenly. "Thank you, Lord Brayton, I..." Her features twisted, a tear sliding down her face.

He edged closer, his throat tightening. "Don't cry."

She turned away, waving a hand at him, and sniffed. "I'm not crying."

"Really? Because we're inside and it's not raining."

She sniffed again. "All right, I'm crying. How can I not? Jacob is the only reason I survived what Ryder did to me."

How he genuinely admired this woman. She was strong, determined without being haughty, and more importantly, genuine. He could tell everything she said was exactly what she was thinking. And as if that wasn't impressive enough, she was...adorable. Almost doll-like. Her bundled brunette hair had strands that were sunlit, whispering of hours spent in the sun without a bonnet. Her small nose had freckles and her green eyes were so brilliant in color, they look painted.

He softened his voice. "I'll ensure he leaves quietly and doesn't startle your son." Malcolm gestured toward the doorway. "After you."

She nodded, swiping at her face several times, then breezed past into the flat, clearly determined to prove she was not intimidated.

With an exasperated breath, Malcolm lifted his gaze to the ceiling to get in a quick conversation. *Lord, I realize You have a tendency to do whatever You want, and that is Your right, but I need to know what is going on. I tried walking away from her twice when I first helped her on the street, but she wouldn't let me, and now I've stupidly agreed to move her into the house and my life. What are You doing? You can't trust me to this. You can't. Even I don't trust me with this.*

Leona reappeared and peered out at him from the doorway. "Are you not coming?"

Malcolm snapped his gaze to hers. "I am." Seeing Ryder's top hat, he puffed out a breath and snatched it up as a courteous Christian would. He followed her inside and closed the door, pausing in the narrow space leading into the small flat.

Mrs. Henderson grudgingly adjusted her lace cap against her white hair and plopped herself into a straight back chair at a linen-covered table across from where Ryder and Jacob were sitting. A large plate of scones were piled onto a chipped porcelain plate beside a jam bowl. Plates had been set before each chair.

Leona set her apron onto a sideboard and glanced at him, mouthing, "*He won't leave.*"

Malcolm inclined his head in silent acknowledgement. Knowing Jacob was watching, he casually walked up to Ryder and snapped out the top hat. "Yours, I believe."

Ryder hesitated and slowly took his hat, setting it onto his lap. "Thank you, my lord." He cleared his throat. "Did you want my seat?"

Now the man was overdoing it. "That won't be necessary, Mr. Blake. You and I won't be staying that long anyway." He gave the man a pointed hard stare. "Will we?"

Ryder glanced at Jacob and eventually murmured, "No. We won't."

"Good. Set an example by enjoying a scone in silence. Then you and I will leave." Malcolm set his shoulders and removed his gloves, shoving them into his pocket. He strode over to the table and chose a scone from the plate. He decided not to bother with any jam.

He closed his eyes and eventually said aloud in an effort to lead prayer, "Thank you Lord for this blessing. Without you, I would not be here to eat it. And without Miss Webster, it would not have been brought to this table. Amen."

"*Amen,*" Mrs. Henderson regally chimed in from beside him at the table. "My. 'Tis good to see a man giving a prayer without being asked to do it."

He'd learned from the best. His father. Opening his eyes, Malcolm held up the scone in everyone's direction in appreciation and bit into it. The overly hard, brittle and chalky dough made him pause. It was like biting into dirt and cardstock.

Knowing everyone was watching him, he slowly pushed the rest of the scone into his mouth in an attempt to be polite and tried to chew his way through it without breaking any of his teeth.

In between several well-labored chews, he eyed Leona. "You made these?"

She nodded, her green eyes brightening despite their earlier sorrow. "Yes. They're supposed to be made in an oven but we only have a hearth to work with. What do you think?"

He didn't have it in him to tell her. He swallowed what remained in his mouth, thankful he didn't have to eat anymore. "Not bad."

Her brows flickered. "Is it really *that* bad? Here. They're much better if you dip it in tea." She scrambled over to the table, as if to offer him the tea pot, but tripped on the uneven wood floor, sending a slipper off her left foot flying.

It skidded toward Malcolm and landed with a thud before him. He quickly lowered himself to pick up the worn leather shoe and paused in astonishment, realizing how small it was. Barely the size of his hand. It was also heavily scuffed and patched with various uneven strips of leather as if she'd been wearing the same shoes for years. He'd actually noticed that her son's appearance was rather lavish, with expensive new clothing and new leather boots. She was clearly a woman who put her son first. It was...endearing.

Her hand popped out. She sighed. "I'm always tripping on these floors. We have the landlord nail them down every few months, but annoyingly, they always come up. Much like my cooking, this whole building is falling apart."

An incredibly foreign sensation gripped Malcolm. It was like Eve had just landed into his garden and he wanted to keep her there.

Leona's hand hesitantly waved in closer. "Might I have my shoe, please?"

With his knee still on the floor and her shoe still in hand, he eyed her hand which hovered close. It was dainty and pale. And the best part? They weren't perfect. Those slim fingers were heavily calloused from years of labor. Like his.

She blinked down at him. "Is something wrong?"

He lowered his gaze to her grey-stockinged foot visible beneath her plain calico skirts and paused. Realizing he could see the slim curve of her ankle, his entire body grew obnoxiously hot. Her skirts weren't the length a lady's ought to be. It was obvious she had purchased her gown second hand. The hem was heavily frayed and the stitching was crooked. It reminded him of all the years growing up in which he had worn clothing the other boys would laugh about. Before he beat them into a wall with two fists.

He carefully tugged down her skirts to cover her ankle, then positioned the worn leather slipper before her on the floor, nudging it into place so all she had to do was slip her foot into it. "There."

She hesitated, then slowly slipped her toes and foot into it. Her voice softened. "Thank you, my lord. That was very kind of you."

He sensed she liked him. Which he wasn't really used to. Unlike his twin brother, who exuded nothing but too much charm since they were both old enough to recognize the power of females, Malcolm had always exuded the opposite. Even before his days in the monastery he'd always been too self-conscious and gruff around them. But this one made him feel capable of...

functioning.

He rose to his booted feet and blurted the nicest thing that came to mind. "Your scones were rather perfect, Miss Webster. I'm sorry I didn't emphasize that enough. Am I permitted to have another one before I leave?"

She smiled and set her chin, appearing content. "Of course. I'm so glad you liked them. Do take however many you want. Three, four or...more."

He wasn't going to be *that* nice. "Two is good." He grabbed two and tucked them into his pocket so that he looked incredibly eager but didn't have to chew through them in front of her.

Ryder sat up and stared. "Why not put the whole plate into your pocket?"

"Ey, now, at least I'm not taking her son," Malcolm said in between chews.

"Gentlemen, please. We have an audience." Leona leaned in between Malcolm and Jacob, preparing a scone with jam for her son. She set it onto the plate, making it clatter from its dense weight and nudged her son. "Don't you have something to say to Lord Brayton? About your earlier behavior?"

Jacob glanced up at Malcolm. "I behaved badly. Not at all as a gentleman should." His small hand popped out toward Malcolm. "Might we be friends? I'll never hit you again. Not ever."

Malcolm eyed that small hand, brushing off his hands against his great coat to remove the crumbs. He'd never shaken a hand that small. Reaching toward Jacob across the table, he carefully gripped those tiny fingers, giving it a gentle wag. "I accept your gentlemanly agreement and appreciate it. Friends."

Jacob's eyes widened as he leaned in to look at Malcolm's hand in between shakes. He poked at it. "Crickets on high. You have more scars than skin and your hand is the size of Goliath!" He kept shaking Malcolm's hand more and more enthusiastically. "You could protect us all from every last villain in the world with your hands, couldn't you? *Couldn't you?*"

It was the first time he'd ever felt worthy of a compliment. Malcolm smirked and released Jacob's hand. "Not to brag, but as admiral, these two hands once took on as many as five pirates at the same time. You should have seen it. There was blood everywhere. I was sliding in it."

Leona gasped. "Lord Brayton, really. That is hardly a thing you should tell a child."

Jacob's mouth dropped open as he gaped up at him. "Was it their blood or yours?"

Malcolm blinked. It was time to soften the conversation. For the boy's sake. "It was actually water from the ocean I was sliding on." It wasn't.

Ryder edged forward in his chair, his brows coming together. "An admiral? Are you in the navy, Lord Brayton?"

Malcolm paused, realizing he had put himself into a position he shouldn't have. Because joining the Persian navy wasn't exactly being a good Brit. "Uh...yes. It's a certain division of the navy that isn't well known by many given it's secret nature. I've been part of that division for over ten years. Prior to that I served at a monastery for a year. Over in France." That made him sound pleasant and less violent.

Ryder angled toward him. "So you went from reading the bible to fighting pirates? That is quite a dramatic change of vocation, wouldn't you say?"

Not in Malcolm's opinion. "On the contrary. Pirates are more merciful than you think, Mr. Blake. Unlike Christian organizations, they have a code of conduct even toward their enemies. I sustained fewer injuries at sea than I did in the monastery."

Leona stared at Malcolm, her lips parting. "Surely, you jest."

"I never do." He returned his gaze to Ryder. "I believe you have an appointment with your lawyer, Mr. Blake? Shall I escort you to the door? Or even help you into your...*barouche?*"

Ryder gave him a withering look. "That won't be necessary." He leaned over and tousled Jacob's hair. "I have to go, Jacob. I promise we'll see each other soon. You and I have a lot to talk about." Tapping on his top hat, he rose from his chair. "Leona, it is my hope you'll reconsider my offer. I think it to be incredibly generous."

She stared. "What happened to you, Ryder? What happened to the boy whose shoulder I once cried on when my father died? The one who used to be my friend?"

Ryder sighed. "He still exists. He simply wanted more. What you and I shared was pleasant. But pleasant doesn't inspire a man to create the sort of music that changes the world or his life. And it wasn't until I met Claudia that I realized that."

Ryder adjusted the curved brim of his top hat, his features clouding. "I tried to do everything to help you given I was already married, but you chose the tactic of war. I sent countless letters but you never responded. Not once. Not. Once." Staring her down, he angrily bit out, "I also sent money to your aunt every two months for the past few years. A good fifty pounds at a time. *Fifty.* Enough to have settled you, Jacob and your aunt into whatever bloody lifestyle you damn pleased. What the hell did you do with all the money, Leona? Why is my son living like this?"

Leona's eyes widened. "Whatever do you mean? I never got any of your letters *or* the money. I never—" Her chest visibly heaved. "Are you certain you were sending everything to the right address? Because my aunt never..."

Malcolm almost bit into his own fist. By God. Even her aunt was swindling her.

Ryder's features twisted. "Christ. Leona, I thought..." He winced and slowly shook his head and kept shaking it. "She kept telling me you received everything and that your bitterness was worse than hers. Which is why I stayed away." He muttered something to himself and murmured, "I suppose I can only blame myself for letting you love me far more than I loved you. And for that I'm sorry. I should have kept our association to what it had always been: friendship."

Leona said nothing.

Malcolm flexed his hands, trying not to get riled knowing how she had been so vilely taken advantage of by the two people she had trusted most. It reminded him of the way he'd been taken advantage of.

After waiting all afternoon at a garden party hoping to have a moment alone with the ever worldly and vivacious Miss Silverthorn, he cornered her, confessed his interest and then savagely kissed her in an effort to damn well prove it. The kiss lasted only long enough for him to realize she wasn't kissing him back. When he'd pulled away, she started sobbing.

He'd never forget it. He spent the whole day writhing in guilt and re-living that moment, thinking his method of forced seduction made her cry. A few days later, she used him to terminate the last of whatever relationship she had with his brother. A relationship James had never told him about because their association was too damn dark to speak of. That had been his first introduction to 'passion'. And needless to say, he'd been avoiding it ever since. For the safety of those involved.

Ryder veered his gaze to Malcolm. "I can't have my son living like this. I can't. And her aunt...that woman is— I'm done dealing with this. I have a right to my son. Do you have a calling card I can pass on to my lawyer?"

The bastard still wasn't letting this go. Even *knowing* about the betrayal. Ingrate. Malcolm shifted his jaw, dug into his pocket and pulled out his silver case. Opening it, he retrieved a card and snapped it out. "Direct all inquiries to me, Mr. Blake, if you're really that anxious to tear a boy from his mother. Until this is resolved, don't pester either of them. They have endured enough. Are we understood in this?"

Ryder took it and inclined his head. "Yes." He tucked the card away, and after a moment, offered his own.

Malcolm grabbed it, shoved it into his pocket and pointed at the door. "Good day, Mr. Blake."

"Good day." Ryder stiffly walked over to the door. Opening it, he glanced back at Leona, then stepped out and quietly shut the door behind himself.

Jacob stumbled over to Leona and braced her legs.

Mrs. Henderson sat up and wobbled her head, quivering the lace cap on her head. "I hope the floor opens up and hell grabs my cousin by the leg. I cannot believe Judith, my Judith, would do such a thing to her own niece. I knew she had grown incredibly bitter after being abandoned by that idiot but I never thought..." She glanced at Malcolm and then Leona. "I suggest you two create an alliance. Get married. That way no one will touch the child."

Malcolm choked.

Leona glared. "Mrs. Henderson, please. That isn't very helpful. After all, if Lord Brayton were at all interested, he would have proposed to me right now. And why wouldn't he? I certainly have *so* much to offer him and every man. A child that isn't his *and* a morally corrupt aunt who swindled her own niece out of enough money that could have very well sent Jacob into Eton alongside every last duke and earl!"

A breath escaped Malcolm. This bloody reeked of pandemonium. "We will resolve this, Miss Webster. But it won't be resolved if I stay here. I have to go. I'll see you this Thursday at three. I promise to do everything within my means to help you."

She lowered her gaze to the table she was tidying, her hands visibly trembling. "I don't even know what she would have done with all that money. She was never one to spend money on anything. She always wore the same dresses, the same bonnets and gloves for years and years. Even well before my father died." She paused, her features flickering with hope. "Maybe she plans to surprise Jacob and me. Maybe she bought us all a house in Bath, like I always wanted. Maybe..."

His heart hammered in his ears at the realization she was deluding herself. "Do you honestly think that?"

Leona let out an anguished sob. She closed her eyes, plastering a hand against her mouth. "I knew she and I were never that close, but I trusted her."

Damn people for being cruel. He strode toward her and refusing to think about what he was doing and why, he tugged her close and set her head against his chest, letting her sob against him.

Jacob's small hands frantically found their way around not only his mother but also Malcolm's leg.

They all stood in silence.

Leona sniffled quietly and lifted her head, swiping at her face. "I...forgive me for...crying all over you. I—"

"Don't apologize." Malcolm slowly released her and stepped back, letting her and Jacob's hands fall away. His chest tightened seeing them both lingering in tears. "I will right this."

Despite the tears, she met his gaze. "If only the world was more like you, Lord Brayton. So beautifully kind."

Beautifully kind? He damn well wasn't that. He made people bleed out of their noses for a living and thoroughly enjoyed watching it drip. "Let us not go that far. I'm an admiral. Not a saint."

Her anguished features became more subdued. Another tear traced its way down her smooth cheek. "I was merely offering you a compliment. I am and will always be eternally grateful to you for offering me a position and helping me."

And here it was. The tears and the sort of messy emotion and gratitude women were so well known for. The sort that made a man of steel snap in half and turn to rose petals merely because there was a damn tear tracing down soft skin.

There was a reason he surrounded himself with men at sea. So he'd never have to get attached to a female who would only send him down a path no rational woman was ready to embrace. Not willingly, anyway. "I don't need compliments to get me through the day, Miss Webster. This is about getting you through the day. So I humbly ask you do so."

She politely sniffed, set her chin and then forged a small smile, her tear-streaked green eyes struggling to brighten. "You needn't worry about me. I've gone through worse."

This woman was the sort of trouble a man could stub his toe on and still love whatever pain it brought. "I admire your fire. Keep that chin up. I'll see you tomorrow and will send someone over to pick up all of your belongings so you'll already be settled in." He inclined his head and then gave the older woman a pointed look. "Good day, Mrs. Henderson. Try not to marry her off to anyone. I know well-placed people who will resolve this." He turned and in passing Jacob, Malcolm leaned down and nudged the boy with an elbow. "Until tomorrow."

Jacob stumbled against the elbow and gaped up at him. "I almost fell because of you."

Malcolm grinned and nudged him again. "Good. The sooner you learn how to balance yourself, the sooner I can teach you how to throw blades."

Jacob straightened, eyes wide. "*Blades?* Truly? Who will we be throwing them at? Aunt Judith?"

Leona gasped and hit Malcolm's arm from behind.

His senses sparked to life. Grabbing her hand, he yanked her hard toward himself and spun her straight into his body. The pulsing softness of her bare hand and his instinctive aggression toward her astounded him into realizing just how dangerous their association could be.

Passion was the one thing that had drowned his own brother into becoming someone unrecognizable and if he wasn't careful, it would drown him next. "I wouldn't do that again, Miss Webster," he pointed out, trying to ignore her skirts bundling against his trousers. "As you can see, I have a tendency to overreact."

Her astounded gaze held his for a moment. "I'm sorry. I...Can you please keep my son out of the navy?" She leaned in, as if determined to set her nose against his chest. "He's only six."

That seductive scent of pepper and vanilla drifted from her skin again, taunting him. It teased him into wanting to rip clothing and scrape all of his teeth against her skin. Not. Good.

Malcolm instantly released her hand, the muscles in his body tightening. Digging into his pocket, he grudgingly pulled out his gloves and yanked them on, adjusting them around each finger. "The boy should learn how to defend himself."

"No blades," she countered. "He's too young. He'll hurt himself."

Maybe the boy *was* too young. Maybe if he and his brother hadn't been allowed access to so many dangerous things in their youth due to absolutely *no* supervision, their lives would have been different. Maybe. It was always maybe. "All right. Fine. No blades."

"Thank you." She hesitated and then patted his arm as if he were a dog who pleased her. "You may go now."

This woman was going to exhaust the hell out of him. Puffing out a breath, he left.

LESSON FIVE

If you have wings, why not fly?

The worst that can happen is you fall from the sky.

-The School of Gallantry

That afternoon

The double mahogany doors leading into the lavish private quarters of His Royal Highness, Prince Nasser as-Din Qajar, were swept open. Two dark-skinned Persians dressed in identical flowing emerald-green garbs bound by thick, red sashes around their waists pulled back doors on command.

Without waiting to be formally announced by the wigged butler in livery, Malcolm strode in, his boots thudding against the gleaming white marble. A line of servants departed the large receiving room and the doors he entered through closed, leaving him to address the prince alone.

He hadn't seen his dear friend in eight months. It was the longest they've ever been apart.

Malcolm paused in astonishment, realizing Nasser had abandoned his traditional style of Persian garb his father expected of him. Instead, the man was dressed in all black, save a blue silk cravat and a blue embroidered waistcoat.

Looking very much like any other upper-class European, Nasser was stretched out on a green velvet chaise in black wool trousers and polished boots. His favorite book, the *Kama Shastra*, was angled open just below his square shaven jaw. It was a new man. Even Nasser's black hair, which was usually finger-tousled was meticulously swept back with tonic, mimicking the latest French style.

"What the hell are you wearing?" Malcolm drawled, removing his gloves and tossing them onto a nearby table. "Did all of New York grab you by the turban? I don't like it. You look like everyone else."

"That is exactly the point, *Dalir*. I am *trying* to look like everyone else. I think I look dashing." Glancing up from his book, Nasser's dark eyes brightened. He tossed the book aside and swiveled off the chaise, rising. His mouth quirked. "By Allah, how I have missed you and your gruff ways. My time in New York City was worth *nothing* without you there. Nothing. Because you are and will always be the love of my life. The moment you tell me you are ready to be my man, I will gladly abscond from my crown. Then you and I can disappear into the Caribbean and share...*coconuts*."

Not in the least bit amused, Malcolm came to a halt before him. "You and I have to talk."

Nasser spread out both hands. "At long last. He wishes to have a conversation. I gather there is a perfectly viable reason as to why you never once wrote to me whilst I was all those months in New York. I am rather...how do you English say...*miffed* with you. You have no respect for my love."

"On the contrary." Malcolm stared him down. "I took a year leave from my position to help you with this mess. And if I may say, this is the stupidest idea you've ever had. Your association with Miss Grey is unholy."

"Pfah. You think everything is unholy."

Malcolm glared. "You sent me into London because you wanted me to look into Lord Banfield's life and give you an opinion you can trust. And I'm giving it to you. Lord Banfield has been in love with Miss Grey for years. According to Holbrook, and a few other more than reliable sources, she never once resisted their engagement. In fact, she has been enthusiastically replying to all of Lord Banfield's letters since she was fourteen, which means…she isn't telling you the whole story. Either way, I don't like it. Marriage is meant to be a sacred union of mutual respect. Not a means of hiding one's identity from the world. You're treating her like some monkey you plan to pet for the rest of your life. It's wrong."

Nasser was quiet for a long moment. "She told me she was dreadfully unhappy with the arrangement."

"I have seen nothing to support that. She probably only wants access to your crown."

"No. She has become family. So I ask you treat her as such. Something else must be amiss." Nasser squinted. "Forgive me for being shallow but is this Lord Banfield…unattractive? Do women scurry away from him? Does he have crooked teeth and bushy brows that wag like little fingers?"

Malcolm refrained from tapping Nasser's head. "No. Both brothers exude a little too much charm and could easily take advantage of women."

"Do they?"

"No. Holbrook has a tendency to play and flirt far more than he should, but he doesn't abuse or wheedle women. As for Banfield, setting aside what appears to be a single visit to a high-class brothel done in the name of education, he doesn't associate with women at all. He keeps busy with the estate and is completely and utterly devoted to Miss Grey."

Nasser blinked rapidly. "Why would my *azizam* try to escape a man who is devoted to her? That makes no sense. There must be something wrong with him. Is he the violent sort?"

"Far from it. The man hasn't gotten into a single scuffle since he left Eton. There isn't a person who has ever spoken ill of him. Not even his own servants. I have no idea what is going on, but given his affection for the girl, expect him to follow you into Persia."

Nasser swiped his face. "I did not realize this Lord Banfield was so attached."

"The man is more than attached. He sleeps with her portrait. And who knows what that means."

"*Ya weld elgahba.* If that is true, I am not touching this. My life is complicated enough. I went to New York for a reason. To see new things and escape my overbearing parents and the mess they are making of not only their lives but mine." Nasser pointed at him. "When Miss Grey arrives into town, which should be in the next week, I will talk to her and put an end to it."

"What about your father?"

"What about him?"

"Didn't you already tell him you were getting married to this girl?"

Nasser sighed. "Yes, but when he discovered she was an American, he threw a fit. He will be more than pleased by the termination, I assure you. I suggest moving out of Holbrook's house. The sooner we distance ourselves from whatever happens next, the better off we are. Would you like a hotel or would you prefer to stay here with me until we leave for Persia?"

Malcolm paused. Leona needed him. As did Holbrook. "I can't leave the house quite yet."

"Why not?"

If only he was more like his brother and didn't give a damn. "Holbrook had an argument with Banfield back in February about some girl who put him in debt. And I mean a lot of debt. He had to sell his townhouse and move into a place even rats consider beneath them. I've been more or less keeping him out of debt. Not that he knows it."

"*Dalir, Dalir*. Always a hero to everyone but himself."

Unfortunately. "Laugh. Because it doesn't end there. I also elbowed my way into *another* situation. I hired this...this...female to tend to whatever is left of Holbrook's house because the one servant Holbrook does have is useless and only ever sells lithographs from the back door. I intend to stay with Holbrook until it's time to leave London and was hoping you could actually help me with something."

Nasser lifted a brow. "I knew it was coming."

Malcolm retrieved Ryder's calling card from his pocket and held it out. "This is about the woman I hired. Her aunt swindled her out of a lot of money, and now this moron, Mr. Blake, is threatening to take her child away based on grounds of financial neglect. And believe me when I say, this boy is anything but neglected. I need you to get your grandfather involved. With him being one of the presiding judges overseeing cases at the Exchequer of Pleas, this should be easy. Just have him send someone of power over to Mr. Blake so his bollocks invert. Whatever your grandfather wants in return for his assistance, make sure he gets it."

Nasser sighed and took the card. He glanced at it, before tucking it away into his waistcoat pocket. "Your generosity is going to bankrupt me."

Malcolm stared him down. "It shouldn't cost you anything but a few words to a man you and I both know has England's right and left ear. But if it *does* cost you anything, take it out of my naval annuity. I don't mind."

"Keep your silver, *Dalir*. Everything will be fine. *Grand-pére* will ensure no lawyer goes near Mr. Blake. Now come here. We have not seen each other in a hundred and seventy-two days. I counted." Nasser grabbed the sides of Malcolm's face and grinned. "You look well for

yourself." He kissed Malcolm's forehead twice. "Was life incredibly difficult without me? It was, was it not?"

Malcolm lifted his gaze to the ceiling in a valiant attempt to accept
what he went through every time they spent time apart. "Oh, yes. I often
wonder how I survive without your kisses."

Nasser released him and gave him a pointed look. "You are usually
far friendlier than this. What is it? Are you still angry with me?"

"A little," Malcolm grouched. "I wasn't ready to come to London.
Why did you have to send me out? My life was what it needed to be.
Coming back was...I've helped so many damn people in my life except
for the one person who needed it most."

Nasser hesitated. "Is this about your father's death?"

Malcolm's throat tightened. Mourning for the loss of his father,
which had happened well over three years ago while he was at sea, had
actually been surprisingly easy. Whilst his poor father had always been a
good Christian man, they had never been close. He'd gotten more attention from governesses growing up than his father. And that wasn't saying much.

Malcolm was actually coming to terms with a much greater loss.
Knowing his brother was irredeemable. "No. I'm at peace with my father's passing. Well before his death, I wrote to him and disclosed the
truth about what really happened and why I never returned. I have no
doubt he shared the letter with my brother."

Nasser's voice softened. "What about your brother? Did you see him?
Did you try to?"

Malcolm flexed both hands in an effort to remain calm. "I didn't really want to, given he tried to stab me through the heart, but after thirteen
years of silence, I..." He hissed out a breath and raked both hands
through his hair before letting them drop. "I convinced myself to covert-
ly peer in on him a few days ago. His life is exactly how I had left it. In
shambles. In fact, he and Miss Silverthorn are associating again."

Nasser's eyes widened. "*Khak too saret.* Tell me they are not."

Malcolm tried not to be angry about it. He knew what it was like to fight the demon within. But after all he did to try to protect them from each other, this was his recompense: their reunion. "I made the other half of my own soul think the worst of me because I was convinced I was saving them both from darker things to come. So what does this female *bala* go and do in honor of my sacrifice? She abandons her monastic vows as a nun up in Scotland and prances back into London to work as a birch mistress. *A birch mistress.* Because apparently, nuns know even more about crucifixion than Jesus. And conveniently...*James* now frequents her establishment.

"At first, I decided I wasn't going to bother. Why would I? It isn't any of *my* business what the hell these two are doing to each other. But the more I thought about it, the more I felt I had a right to know how demented it really was. So I paid this mousy-looking scullery maid there at the brothel to tell me more and do you know what she told me? Do you? They don't kiss or have sex. They never do. All they do is drink brandy and dare each other to do odious things like taking turns pulling the trigger of a pistol while aimed at each other. Does that sound normal to you?"

Nasser gaped. "Are you certain that is what is going on?"

Malcolm sniffed hard. "Yes. I actually followed James one night when he carried in two pistols. One for her and one for him. Shortly after he left the brothel, I ploughed my way in to see Miss Silverthorn, but she refused to answer any of my questions. She simply sat there with her crop and told me unless I wanted to pay for a session, it was time for me to leave. My brother is a damn profligate looking to die. I warned him. I warned him to stay away from what they were doing to each other lest one of them end up dead. Those two are crossing lines."

Nasser averted his gaze. "Maybe your brother has learned to control it."

"That would be like saying the devil loves Jesus. Not true." A ragged breath escaped Malcolm. "It doesn't matter. I'm done. Seeing I announced myself to Miss Silverthorn and still haven't heard anything from my brother, it's fairly obvious he isn't interested in re-connecting. Which I'm fine with."

"Are you?"

No. But he also didn't want to find out what would happen if he and his brother ended up in the same room after thirteen years. They were too much alike. "It doesn't matter. He and I are better off not associating. We have only ever encouraged each other." He sighed, wanting to change the subject. "I thought you should know your father requested I arrive at the palace before September. He has 'questions' about your involvement with a certain ropemaker. Please tell me nothing happened between you and Rami. Please tell me your father is overreacting to whatever rumors he heard."

Nasser winced and edged back. "I drank too much."

"Which means...?"

Nasser whined. "I have created a mess. Rami and I...mounted each other. Even eight months later, I swear I am still having trouble walking. And the worst of it? He has been nagging me to return to Persia and do it again. Even though I am not in the least bit interested. Rami is an empty-headed boar. There is nothing remotely interesting about him other than his cock."

Malcolm lowered his chin. "Your lack of self-respect is going to cost you. Because your little ropemaker ended up bragging about your 'night' to one of the gunners and the gunner couldn't help but tell the purser who then told the whole ship. A ship that is under your father's jurisdiction. Not yours *or* mine. What the hell do you expect me to say or do now? *Lie for you?*"

"Yes. Lie for me. Bribe Rami with a few thousand, tell my father it was a misunderstanding and we are done."

Malcolm slowly shook his head. "No. I once lied for my brother and it cost me everything but changed nothing. I'll not do it again. You have to face this and tell your father. For pity's sake, when no child comes of whatever union you decide on, people will accuse you of making the throne vulnerable to invasion. *Beloochistan* has fifteen thousand men waiting to seize Persia."

"*Beloochistan* is hardly a threat. Those morons are still trying to figure out how to fire a cannon without blowing themselves up. It is the Russians who worry me. After taking Poland off the map, they recently started using their armies to take over other regions. As if their damn country is not already beyond the size it needs to be." Nasser was quiet for a moment. "If things progress, we will have no choice but to send you and the entire fleet to defend the Caspian Sea. Because if the Russians seize the Caspian, they seize us. Persia will no longer exist."

Motherless bastard. The Russians had a navy eighteen times the size of Persia. "The Russians would sink us and you know it." Malcolm let out a ragged breath. "They've negotiated various treaties with your father before and have kept a civilized distance. Why isn't your father negotiating with them now? Why insist on war?"

"Because my mother had an affair with a Russian officer shortly before I left for New York and now my father is trying to kill them all." Turning away, Nasser muttered something, strode over to an ornate side table arrayed with crystal decanters and poured two glasses of burnt wine. "I prefer not to talk about my parents. They are destroying far, far more than each other."

He glanced back at Malcolm. "Distract me with new conversation. What have you been doing with your time outside of the assignment? Did you go to the theatre?"

"No."

"The opera?"

"No."

"A coffee house?"

"No."

With a look of exasperation, Nasser eyed him. "What *did* you do?"

Malcolm shrugged. "Aside from going to church every Sunday, I kept Holbrook out of trouble, visited with Trent on a few occasions and walked around London."

"For two whole months?"

"My entertainment needs, as you know, are very simple." He smirked. "By the by, Trent wants an introduction. He rather fancies the idea of meeting a prince. Shall I arrange it? He might be a willing play mate."

Nasser gave him a withering look. "Oh, yes, put the two sodomites together. After all, we sodomites are so desperate for cock we will take whatever walks through the door." He glared. "No. I do not want to meet him. What are you proposing, *Dalir*? That I get involved with your own cousin? After you scold me for getting involved with the ropemaker?"

"The ropemaker had the intelligence of a turkey. Why not involve yourself with someone capable of more insight and sophistication?"

"Turkeys are far easier to lead, I assure you." Nasser rounded him and stared him down, his voice growing husky. "By the by, I, too, received a correspondence from my father. It concerns your duty as admiral."

Not good. "What do you mean? I relegated every flag and ship to the vice-admiral in order to take temporary leave. How else was I supposed to address the assignment you so rudely tossed at me? Are you telling me there is a problem?"

"Not in the way you think." Nasser angled closer. "My father delineated what was expected of you when he made you admiral. It involves *nikāh*. You had a birthday recently, did you not?"

Malcolm's eyes widened. "Codswallop. I'm not actually going to be forced into upholding *nikāh*, am I? I'm not Muslim."

A breath escaped Nasser. "If you plan to retain your position as admiral and continue living amongst my people, be you Muslim or not, you are expected to uphold our ways. Celibate life is against the teachings of the *Qur'an*. Every man in our kingdom is required to live in a married state and *must* be married by the age of thirty. As of fourteen days ago, you are *one* and thirty and therefore breaking Persian law. Which is why, setting aside my involvement with the ropemaker, my father insists you to return to the palace by September. The festival of *Eid-e qorban* is when everyone in the royal family weds. And you are very much a part of this family. You may not remember, but...you did agree to marry one of my sisters."

Malcolm swiped his face, feeling the blood pounding against his temples. He knew he shouldn't have drank so much burnt wine that night. He couldn't even remember half the conversation he had with the Shah. All he knew was that he ended up admiral and all four of Nasser's sisters started competing for his attention like female squirrels rifling through a barrel of nuts. "From what I remember, I was trying to be nice."

"*You? Nice?*"

"Yes. He was worried that none of them would ever be married. He was practically sobbing about it, saying they were too much like the queen. I felt sorry for him and told him if after five years no one wanted them, I would take one off his hands. I was drunk and didn't think he'd actually take me seriously. As you well know your sisters are overly needy. They only want to fill the palace with furniture, poodles and babies. None of which I need."

Nasser stared. "You better have someone in mind, then. Because my father wrote to say that he already redecorated the Harshini quarters for you and your future bride. He expects you to live at the palace in between assignments. You do know that, yes?"

Shit. Setting aside that he didn't *want* to get married, living at the palace was no different than living inside a zoo with animals who thought they were people. "Tell your father I'm not ready for either."

"You had better be. My father ordered an additional eight men into London specifically sent to ensure you board your ship in eight weeks. You will be detained and arrested if you do not follow orders."

Malcolm choked. "Detained and arrested? *For what?*"

"For not upholding the law of *nikāh*. You are an asset, *Dalir*. Since you became admiral, we have regained a stronghold on the Caspian Sea, which the Russians seek to dominate. Even if you are bold enough to relinquish your position and leave Persia, I assure you my father will not permit it for the safety of our country. He made it very clear that you either marry and uphold the law or you will be escorted straight to prison for your lack of subordination. Neither of which I can protect you from, because I am not king. He is."

God blind him. These Muslims were crazy. How did he ever get so attached to them and their way of life? "I don't even have time for women. You know my schedule. I only touch land long enough to remember my name before I go back out. What am I supposed to do? Marry and leave my wife the same night?"

Nasser scrubbed his head. "Most military men do. You may not want to hear this, *Dalir*, but you were given five years to find a bride and did nothing. No more time will be granted regarding *nikāh*. Not given your age. In eight weeks you will be escorted to Persia, and when you arrive at the palace, you will be expected to find yourself a bride."

"But—"

"Surely, if you are unable to find one at such short notice, one of my sisters would be more than willing to oblige. They are beautiful, are they not? Men crawl in their presence."

This wasn't happening. Malcolm walked past Nasser and sank down onto the velvet cushion of the chaise. He raked his hair back. "Beauty is overrated."

"My father keeps asking if you would at all be interested in one of them. Any of them. He is *praying* with a pillow tucked beneath both knees."

"Keep him on that pillow. Because if I'm forced to marry in the name of *nikāh*, I'm damn well not going to settle for one of your sisters."

Amusement now flickered in those dark eyes. "Let us play a little game, shall we?"

Life could be worse. He could be back at the monastery. "No."

"Yes. If there were no other women left in this world and you had to pick one of my sisters, which would it be?"

Malcolm snorted. "I would end my life well before that ever happened."

"*Dalir, Dalir.* Play along."

"Why would I—"

"My father and I have a bet going."

"*A bet?*" Malcolm echoed.

"Yes. He has to give up his concubine if I'm right. The old *boz* thinks he knows which of my sisters you would pick. I disagreed. Worry not. We will not hold you to it. This is between my father and me. We do these sort of things all the time. Now go on. Tell me. Which one?"

"If I had to?" Malcolm shrugged. "I don't know. I...maybe...Nahasti?"

Nasser grinned and snapped a finger toward the ceiling. "I knew it! I knew you had a twinkle for Nahasti!"

"I don't twinkle for anyone," Malcolm said tersely.

"Liar. Have you *never* wanted to grab a woman and show her the stars?"

Malcolm paused, a pulsing knot seizing his throat. Why was it Miss Leona Olivia Webster and her bright green eyes came to mind? He slowly raked his hair back again. He knew why. Because she was a *far* better option than Nasser's pouty-lipped, hip-shaking, jewelry-adorned sister, Nahasti. All of Nasser's sisters only ever giggled behind veils and whispered about how dashing he looked in a turban.

He didn't want an irrational giggling adolescent girl. He wanted a woman he could hold a conversation with. Something he doubted even Nahasti, at nineteen, could offer. He wasn't nineteen anymore. He couldn't relate to nineteen. Even at nineteen he couldn't relate to nineteen.

He could, however, relate to…five and twenty. Which was what…Leona was. Wait. She also had a child. A boy. Which meant he'd already have an heir. Which meant…he wouldn't have to worry about creating one. Which meant…

It would fulfill his requirement of *nikāh*. By law, a marriage and a son qualified.

He sat up and blinked. God save him. It was rather quite perfect. Leona would live in the palace, have servants, instead of being one herself, and be surrounded by a culture and paradise she and her son would endlessly enjoy. He wouldn't have to worry about physical *complications* in the bedchamber because he'd be at sea most of the time anyway. Months and months at a time.

It was…*brilliant.* "Tell your father I already have someone in mind. It's done. All I have to do is ask her."

"Who? *Nahasti?*"

"I'd rather gouge my left eye out with my left toe. No. Not her."

Nasser's brows went up as brought over the two glasses of wine. He held one out. "Whatever is wrong with my Nahasti? She has been in love with you for years."

Which was exactly the problem. Love only made women crazy. Miss Silverthorn and crop sort of crazy. And he was crazy enough. Crazy atop of crazy equaled unending menace. No.

Sensing Nasser wasn't pleased, Malcolm took the glass. "Nahasti is stupidly young." He gulped down all of the wine in his glass and set it onto the table with a chink. "I don't want or need a kitten jumping into my lap, meowing at me every two seconds for attention or panicking the moment something goes wrong. I need a strong, dependable woman. A leopard capable of facing anything and handling me and my life. I'm not the easiest person to get along with."

"You do realize leopards have to be kept well fed and satisfied. Or they rip throats apart."

"Exactly. I know how to defend my own throat, thank you. So the rest is easy."

Nasser lifted the glass he held to his lips and after a few swallows said, "Now I am beyond curious. I never thought I would see the day. Who do you have in mind? This is absolutely marvelous. When did you and she meet? Who is she?"

Malcolm's body felt heavy and warm remembering how she had touched his chest in the stairwell. "Her name is Miss Leona Olivia Webster. I met her on the street a few days ago."

Nasser snorted. "*A few days ago?* You— Oh, yes, this sounds promising already. Toss aside a princess and take a peasant from the street instead."

"Cease. She isn't a peasant. She is well-spoken, very intelligent, very articulate and incredibly honorable. I offered her a position at the house Holbrook and I are leasing." He blankly rubbed the hand she held when assuring him of her trust the very first day they met. It was what made him want to stay and get to know her. She made him feel like the gentleman he always wanted to be. The uh...normal sort.

Nasser lowered his gaze to the hand Malcolm rubbed and smirked. "Apparently, she makes you want to touch yourself."

Dropping his hand to his side, Malcolm rolled his eyes. "Your humor annoys me sometimes."

"At least I have a sense of humor. Is this the same woman you are having *Grand-pére* assist?"

"Yes." Malcolm cleared his throat. "She has a boy named Jacob. He reminds me so damn much of myself at his age. You should have seen how this halfling took me on in the name of defending his father. It was adorable."

Taking another gulp of his drink, Nasser paused. "*His father?* I am confused."

"About what?"

"Are you saying this boy's father is alive?"

"Yes. She never married the man."

Nasser choked on his drink. "*Dalir,* what in Allah's name is wrong you? You plan to take care of some other man's child? *Why?* Never mind that you and she just met *on the street,* never mind that transitioning a foreigner to accept our ways is next to impossible, why would you be interested in marrying a woman with no self-respect?"

Malcolm refrained from poking him. "Don't be so judgmental, Nasser. A woman's immodesty cannot be blamed for a man's lack of control. Somehow you can get drunk and defile yourself with a turkey in the cellar of a ship, but a woman betrayed by her own fiancé has no self-respect? Damn you and that. She has self-respect. Too much, in fact. She made it very clear she isn't interested in men because of it. Which I fiercely admire. I can relate to her."

Nasser took another sip and squinted. "Is she attractive?"

"Is that all you ever think of?"

"Attraction is the spark that ignites the fire. Without the spark, there is no fire. And with no fire, you will freeze come winter. Now is there a spark? For I will not begin to support this if there is no spark."

He knew there was. Malcolm let out a slow breath. "There was plenty of spark. So much of it, I felt it in my teeth. But it went beyond that. It was the strangest thing. I kept trying to leave, but couldn't. I kept talking to her, and the more we talked, the more I realized I wanted to get to know her beyond the physical attraction I was feeling. It was like we were having a real conversation outside of her being female and me being male. I've *never* had that happen before."

Nasser slowly set his drink onto the table and sat beside Malcolm. He stared at the vase on the table. "In Persia, they say the soul recognizes one's destiny even when our minds do not."

The back of Malcolm's neck strangely tingled at the thought.

"I envy you," Nasser continued, his voice growing miserable. "You can meet a woman on the street and decide she suits you without being punished for it. Whilst I? Whoever I deem suitable, *will* be punished."

Malcolm glanced at his friend, his throat tightening. "Talk to your father in the same way you talk to your mother. Maybe he will embrace what you are."

"Or maybe he would shove a brick through my skull and name my younger brother the next king. Which is more likely." Nasser was quiet for a long moment. He smoothed his coat sleeve. "I will write to my father and tell him you found a bride. He will be pleased knowing you are finally upholding *nikāh*." He sat up, becoming more cheerful. "I have an idea."

"*No.* All of your ideas are the equivalent of a boat sinking."

"You exaggerate. My ideas are brilliant. Now. I suggest you go get this peasant of yours an expensive bauble from Rundell, Bridge and Rundell over on Ludgate Hill. That is where all the aristocrats go. Romance her and when you are ready, gift it to her." Nasser smirked and nudged him. "Maybe she will reward you before the wedding night. Why wait for Persia?"

He'd rather have his soul fried in hell than find out what such a night would bring. "If I'm to be honest, and I want to be honest, I'm not turning this into the Piccadilly Circus by giving her trinkets *or* a wedding night. I'm keeping this simple. Respectable. Civilized. Confined to an iron box that has thirteen keys buried around the world. Because I can't have her going into this thinking I'm a normal man. I can't. Our wedding night would be...I don't even want to think about the horror."

Nasser hesitated. "The horror? I thought she was attractive."

"She is."

"Then what is the problem? What are you talking about?"

"I'm not ready to bring a woman into my bed. Nor will I ever be."

"*Shāk dar āvordam.* Are you *still* holding onto that blessed virginity?"

Malcolm shifted his jaw. "Maybe."

Nasser's features now twitched in amusement he attempted to restrain. "You poor, poor *Bisho'ur*. How do you survive? Do you masturbate on an hourly basis?"

"A real man only uses his hands for three things: defending others, defending himself and praying to God. And I adhere to all three."

Nasser leaned back. "I find it *very* difficult to believe you never entertain yourself at night."

Malcolm dropped his hand and leveled him with a stare. "Prior to going into the monastery, I used to do it all the time. But after spending a full year surrounded by degenerates who openly masturbated and sodomized each other when the luminaries weren't looking, I decided to make a conscious effort to be what my father wanted me to be: a Christian gentleman. Because if I can't master my own desires, it will master me, and the moment I give into it, I become a menace. Like those degenerates *and* my brother. I won't *ever* touch a woman in that way. Not even if I marry. My wife will simply have to accept that I will never share her bed. And that is exactly why Miss Webster is perfect. Because she already has a child. I'll raise him as my own and have the boy follow in my steps as admiral."

Those eyes widened. "You do not actually believe what you just said, do you? How can you rationally justify not bedding your own wife?"

"*How?* Nasser. I'm already overly aggressive in nature. I enjoy beating the blood out of people and am not interested in finding out what I'm capable of when the doors close at night. What if I can't control it? What if I start making women run for Scotland in fear? Like my brother did? What then?"

Nasser swiped his face. "Twin or no, you are not your brother."

Malcolm stirred against the chaise, his throat tightening. "Am I not? I was drawn to the same damn woman he was. I was heading down that same damn path. Pain, as you well know, doesn't bother me anymore than it bothers him. I savor getting it *and* giving it. Between the two, I'm a walking cannon."

A tense silence enveloped the room.

"This is serious, *Dalir.* How will you ever marry?"

"Marriage is not the problem. I never saw myself living alone. A companion would be nice."

"A wife is more than a companion. If you do not oversee her desires, she will suffer."

"She will also suffer nine months later giving birth. What is your point?"

Nasser sighed. "Do you not like women, *Dalir?* Does your cock not respond to them? Is that what you are saying?"

What a question. "Of course I like women. Too damn much. I used to pinch the bottoms of every female servant in my house as early as ten. I simply *won't* let my cock overrule the responsibility I have toward the safety of the women around me. What if a woman ends up dead because of me? What if—"

"Dalir—"

"*No*," Malcolm bit out in an effort to remain calm. "Your father may damn well expect me to uphold *nikāh,* but that doesn't mean I have to uphold anything else. Because you're not the one who has to live with whatever happens when I lose control. *I* have to live it. And this is how I live with it. By staying *in* control."

Nasser slowly drew up a leg, wrapping an arm around it. He eyed him. After a long moment, he digressed, "When my mother was fifteen, she met a very interesting woman in Paris during the rise of the revolution. This woman specialized in...*men.* Very rich men, in particular. Surprisingly, my mother and this woman became close friends during a turbulent time when the bourgeois and aristocrats were not even allowed to share the same road. My mother and *Grand-pére* were forced to flee France due to the danger and valiantly did something for this woman. They assisted her lover to escape Paris with them. He was severely injured after his house was torched. This French woman has long since relocated here to London to be with her granddaughter. My mother asked that I visit her and deliver a gift. Which I did yesterday. What was supposed to be an hour turned into eight. The life this woman has lived is...*beyond words*. I will have her call on you. Did you know her first lover was a profligate dedicated to the art of pain? She knows quite a bit about it. Maybe she can help you."

Malcolm felt his face flush. "Help me? With what?"

"We all have fears that make us incapable of embracing ourselves, *Dalir*. She will help you."

"*With what?*" Malcolm got up and glared. "I'm *happy* being celibate. I'm *happy* keeping away whatever the hell swallowed my brother. I don't want it."

Nasser rose and leveled him with a stare. "I do not think it wise you compare yourself to your brother. You are *not* your brother. You will *never* be your brother. Do you not understand that?"

In his head, Malcolm knew that. But in his heart, he hadn't been able to connect the two. Ever since he was old enough to breathe, he and his brother had always shared too many of the same interests. And when he'd forcibly grabbed and savagely kissed the same woman his brother enjoyed physically torturing, that was when it became obvious their souls were connected into wanting *too* much of the same thing. Not to say he wasn't curious about exploring that side of himself with a woman. He was. But how could he even begin to... "What if I unleash something I'm not prepared to embrace?"

Nasser set a hand gently against Malcolm's cheek. "You are too good to hurt any woman. Trust yourself more. Talk to her, *Dalir*. If you do this, I will go to Persia and embrace who I really am. As you have always wanted me to. I will tell my father the truth and kneel to whatever happens in your honor. That way, we face our fears together. Like brothers. Shall we do this? Shall we become the men we have always wanted to be?"

Malcolm gaped at Nasser, his heart pounding. "You're willing to tell your father?"

"Only if you are willing to embrace who you are. You have isolated yourself long enough. I know you want a family, *Dalir*. I have seen the way you look at mine. It is time you accept yourself in the way I accept you. This woman will help."

Damn. "You have that much faith in this woman?"

"No, *Dalir*. I have that much faith in you."

LESSON SIX

Allow me to introduce you to the

only friend you have: trouble.

-The School of Gallantry

Thursday afternoon

At least it wasn't raining.

Tightening her hold on Jacob's hand, Leona bustled them down the narrow, cobblestone street doing her best to keep her flapping bonnet in place against the wind tunneling through the buildings. She only paused on occasion to make note of rusting iron gates, cracked windows, chipped stairs and unpainted houses. Everywhere.

Jerking to a halt, she glanced down at the calling card Jacob held and squinted down at it. "Are you certain we're supposed to be on this street? Let me see that."

Jacob angled it toward her and tilting his head, also squinted at it. "It reads...P-R-I-N-C-E and S-T-R-E-E-T. That spells Prince Street together. Does it not?"

"It certainly does." She glanced around. There weren't even trees. The neighborhood looked like a row of workhouses rammed in together.

An older gentleman with a frayed morning suit strode past, coughing up a gargling, crackling wad of phlegm. He leaned over one of the rusting gates and squirted a thick clump of spit before wiping his mouth against the sleeve of his coat and trudging past.

Leona made a face she couldn't hold in. "One has to wonder how the city even names a street. Because there are no princes here. Not one."

Jacob glanced around. "Maybe they're all dead."

She coughed out a laugh she almost choked on. "Let us try and be a little more optimistic, shall we? Let us assume they are all sleeping or...hiding." She nudged him onward. "We're only a few houses away. If we move fast enough, we'll only be a few minutes late."

Jacob hustled close beside her and glanced up several times, his wool cap shifting against his head. "We would have been on time but you kept going back to the mirror. Do you like looking at yourself?"

She tsked and kept moving. "No. But I couldn't very well show up in a top knot and an apron, could I?" That was what she wore yesterday. "It's very important to be presentable when dealing with the aristocracy."

"Is that why you borrowed rouge from the neighbor?" he continued.

It would seem her son was onto her. "Yes. I ran out of my own." She did.

He jerked them both to a stop. Leaning back, he used his weight to make her stay.

She turned and gently tugged on his arm. "What are you doing? Jacob, I don't have time for this. We're already fifteen minutes late. Which is what happens when you take directions from people you don't know."

He stared up at her. "Do you like him?"

She blinked. "Who?"

"The man with the scar?"

Her heart jolted. Even at the age of six they clearly understood the power of attraction. "Well, I…yes. Of course I like him." A lot. "He has been very kind to us." He had the most beautiful, beautiful eyes. And his well-muscled, massive frame was something worth dreaming about. After he tucked her so protectively against him when she found out about her aunt's betrayal, she *still* inwardly melted and reveled in his concern. Was it incredibly forward of her to yearn for a man she had just met because he was kind? Was it also incredibly shallow of her to admit she wanted all that muscle wrapped around her for more than a night?

Jacob shook her arm in reprimand. "It wouldn't be right for you to like anyone else. What about Papa? Aren't we going to live with him now? Isn't that why he came back?"

A breath escaped her. Feeling the strength in her legs fading, she lowered herself to his level. Releasing her son's hand, she cupped his soft, freckled face. "Dearest?" she whispered, knowing it was time he hear it.

Green eyes that were the exact shade of her own met hers.

She swallowed. "Your father is already married. You know that. Which means he and I could never be a family. He has a whole other life, and although, yes, he wants to make you a part of that life, if I let him, we would no longer be together. It's therefore up to us to create our own family. And I promise, even after what Aunt Judith did to us, we won't be in London much longer. You'll be playing in fields, not streets. I'll work very hard to ensure we have at least a garden. It'll simply take some time. We won't be able to afford much, either, but I promise we'll be happy."

He lowered his gaze. "Is Papa a bad man?"

She would be a horrible mother if she made her son believe such. "No. Of course not. I used to love him very much."

"But you don't anymore?"

Her throat tightened. "No. I don't. All of my love went to you."

He eyed her. "If you don't love him anymore, it means he isn't worthy. And if he isn't worthy, I don't want to see him anymore. He made you cry. I want a new Papa. One who won't make you cry."

She often wondered how she ended up with such a beautiful child. She must have done something right. She gently squeezed his hands. "I thank you for thinking of me, as always. Do tell. If I remarry one of these days, what would you like in a new papa? So I may know what to look for."

His eyes brightened. He dabbed at each finger on his hand, using every one as an example. "He has to be nice. He has to be able to carry me down the street. He has to play with me. He has to teach me how to ride a horse. He has to be nice."

She bit back a smile "I'll ensure he is not only nice but that he *stays* nice."

Jacob excitedly continued, "He'll also have to take us on carriage rides, buy us whatever we want, including big pieces of toffee, and teach us how to swim, so we can board a ship without drowning and visit America. Mrs. Henderson says there are Indians there, you know. I would very much like to meet an Indian. They hunt buffalo! Oh. And maybe when we're there, you can pray to Jesus and ask that he give me four brothers." He paused. "No. Not four. Five. And a sister. I want a sister. But only one. I'll have to see if I like her first before I ask for more."

Sometimes she envied her son's ability to dream. She missed that about herself. She used to have a lot of dreams. So many, she couldn't keep up with them. Ones that included dancing on stage on pointe at Her Majesty's Theatre and riding up in an air balloon over France while sipping champagne and kissing the lips of a good-looking, rich gentleman. Now her dreams included trying to sleep six hours. "A big family would be divine, wouldn't it? I know I never had any brothers or sisters. I would have liked that."

Jacob paused. "Is the man with the scar married, Mama? Do you know? Would he be interested in being part of our family?"

Oh, dear. "I'd rather you not marry me off just yet. Lord Brayton is very highly placed. If he were to ever marry, I doubt he would settle for a mere Miss like me. I barely own a shoe." She adjusted his cap, rose and took his hand again with a sigh. "Now come along. Or we'll be *so* late, he won't even open the door."

Hurrying down the street, they eventually paused at their destination. A small wooden plaque with the address of **31** was crookedly hanging beside the door, attempting to cling to the single nail that adhered it to the house.

It was obvious Lord Brayton was financially ruined.

Her heart squeezed. Damn him.

Unlike the other houses whose stairs had at least been swept, there was debris scattered on every step from passing peddler carts that included wilting turnip tops, parsnips and cabbage. A rolled-up newspaper had been unceremoniously shoved between the rusted railings, clearly having been read and disposed of by someone passing by.

And this was only the outside of the house.

She released Jacob's hand with an exasperated breath, yanked out the newspaper from between the rails and proceeded to use the end of it like a broom, clearing away the debris down toward the pavement. She owed the man this much. Whether he was able to pay her was a whole other mess she wouldn't think about until forced to.

Veering in beside her, Jacob used his bare hands to scoop up two large handfuls of soggy, rotting vegetables covered in dirt. He turned and whipped it, hitting a well-polished carriage parked in the street.

She gasped. "Jacob!" She frantically grabbed his arm to keep him from throwing more. "Try not to hit the carriages." She paused, realizing his hands were completely covered with...dog excrement. She groaned. "Jacob. There was a reason why I was using the newspaper."

He gaped. "But you didn't give me one."

Unable to resist his adorable little logic, she burst into laughter and shook her head. "You're right. You're absolutely right. I should have given you a newspaper. How irresponsible of me. Now hold still. And please don't touch anything. Not yourself and most certainly not me."

He pinched his lips and stiffly stuck out both hands before himself, waiting. "It smells."

"Of course it does. It came out of a dog's rear." With a shake of her head, she unfolded the newspaper and separated the pages in a makeshift attempt to create napkins. "Give me your right hand first."

He angled it toward her. "Why not my left?"

"Because your right is dirtier than your left. Now stop arguing." Leaning closer to him, she was about to wipe off the thick brown muck on his hand when a male figure leaning against the open doorway of the house made her pause. Her pulse lurched, realizing who it was. Her fingers instinctively crushed the newspaper.

Lord Brayton tilted his dark head, his blue eyes intently observing her. "That newspaper could make it worse. Who knows where it's been."

She gave him a pointed look. "Oh, come now. It can't be any worse than what is already on his hands."

"Oh, yes, it can. Someone rolled it up and abandoned it for a reason. Get rid of it."

Leona cringed and frantically shoved the newspaper back in between the railing.

He smirked, pushed away from the door and wagged his fingers at Jacob. "Come inside. What you need is soap and water."

Jacob jogged past, holding out both hands, as he went up toward him. "Your stairs are very dirty, Lord Brayton. Very dirty. Look at what they did! I'm a mess!"

Brayton's mouth quirked. "Don't blame the stairs for your folly, Mister Jacob. They may take offense." Grabbing Jacob by the head, he carefully turned him and guided him inside. "Whatever you do, don't touch anything. All right? Or your poor mother will have to clean it."

Haha. Leona puffed out a breath and followed them in. Closing the door behind them with a foot, she swiped her hands against her skirts. She could feel the grime on her hands. She hated London. Everything was so dirty. At least in the country, one always knew where to step. "I'll have to wash my hands, too. Then you can show me around and I'll get to work."

Still guiding Jacob by the head, Malcolm glanced back at her from over a massive shoulder. "There is water and soap in the kitchen."

Oh, thank the heavens. There was a kitchen. She was worried she'd be forced to cook everything by the fire of a chimney like she did back at Mrs. Henderson's. Not that a stove would improve her cooking.

Leona hurried after them, glancing about the narrow space of scuffed wooden floors and tarnished brass sconces that threatened to tip the half-melted wax stubs of unlit candles. Strips of cheap, beige and blue, flower-patterned wallpaper bubbled in certain places of the walls where the glue refused to stick.

She was not taking five pounds a week from this man. He couldn't afford it.

When they entered a small, but well equipped kitchen, she paused.

A young gentleman in a ratted, powdered wig slept with his cheek mashed against the wooden table and his boots wrapped around the legs of the chair he was propped in. One arm was wearing an evening coat and the other had been pulled out of it, leaving the coat to hang off his broad back. A half-empty bottle of wine touched his fingers as if he had fallen asleep in between guzzles and removing his coat.

"Do assure me that isn't one of the servants I'll be working with," Leona half-whispered. "It's three in the afternoon. Is he a drunk?"

"No. He merely stayed out late." Lord Brayton sighed. "Surprisingly, Mr. Holbrook comes from good stock. His older brother is Viscount Banfield. The two had a fight back in February and the poor boy has been like this ever since. He is overly sensitive about everything and in my opinion, too young to be living on his own."

Releasing Jacob, Lord Brayton muttered something and walked up the table. Using his large boot, he hit the chair twice. "*Holbrook*. For pity's sake, wake up. Miss Webster and her son are here. You were supposed to be helping me find more of those lithographs. Fine help you've been. For all I know you've been stashing them into your back pocket."

The gentleman startled awake. He slowly, slowly lifted his head, pushing the wig back with a bare hand to expose messy brown hair. Dark eyes met Jacob's. With a slow lopsided grin, Holbrook managed to sloppily shove his arm into the sleeve of his coat and bring it back over his shoulders. He leaned far forward in his seat and stuck out his bare hand. "I've heard a lot about you and your mother. A pleasure to meet you, Jacob. It'll be good to have another man in the house. Show me that grip. Go on. Make it worth my while."

Jacob grabbed that hand, adhering excrement to it.

They all paused.

Holbrook peeled away his hand and glanced at it, his smile fading. "How fitting. My life just got shittier."

Leona choked on a laugh and then cringed knowing it was terrible for her son to think foul language was funny.

"*Holbrook*," Lord Brayton bit out in exasperation. "There is a lady *and* child present. Or didn't you damn well notice?"

"I could have said worse." Holbrook rose to his full height and upon seeing Leona, swung toward her and let out a whistle. "Now I know why you hired her, Brayton. Hell, she can scrub my floors any time. Have her start in my room."

Lord Brayton shoved Holbrook by the head. "Leave off. You're too young to even know what women are for."

Holbrook smirked. "Unlike you, I'm not interested in wasting my youth. You also seem to forget that this here is my house. Not yours."

"Yes. A house you haven't paid rent for since I moved into it," Brayton countered.

Holbrook winced. "Don't remind me. The latest sales of my books are dismal. Absolutely dismal. For some damn reason people only ever want to read Jane Austen. And she's been dead for thirteen years. How is that fair? She doesn't need the money. I do." Striding over to a large water basin set atop a wooden side-table, he grabbed the soap and started grudgingly scrubbing his hands.

Leona was about to pick up Jacob but to her surprise, Lord Brayton leaned down and hoisted Jacob by the waist, carrying him over to the basin like a wet dog. "Move over. The boy needs it more than you do."

Holbrook sidled away, making room. "Have at it. And here. Take the soap."

Positioning Jacob's lifted body before the basin, Brayton leaned in from behind Jacob, took the soap and carefully nudged the top of Jacob's head with his shaven chin. "Do you know how to wash your hands? Or do you need me to help you do it?"

Jacob glanced up. "I'm six. I don't need help. I wash my hands every day."

"I'm glad to hear it." Brayton kicked out a foot toward Holbrook. "You see. At six, he knows more about hygiene than you do." With one hand, Brayton rolled up each sleeve for Jacob to keep him from getting wet. "Try not to get water everywhere, all right? We don't want to drown everyone."

Jacob giggled. "You're being incredibly silly. This isn't even enough water to drown Jesus."

Brayton paused. "Jesus?"

"My bear. I didn't bring him. Mama said our things will follow later today."

Brayton rumbled out a laugh. "Right. Keep scrubbing."

"I am." Jacob scrubbed and splashed while sitting up on Brayton's knee.

Watching them interact, Leona's throat tightened. It was like they had always been father and son and she was merely realizing she was looking at her own husband for the first time. The sort of husband she had always wanted. One who was generous, strong and kind. One she could tuck her head against during a good cry and depend on for anything when life turned into a mess.

As he had already proven.

It was tragic that Jacob had already spent six years of his little life without a father or much of a family at all. She had been too busy earning a living and too proud to admit Jacob needed anything more than her. But he was getting old enough to notice that something was, in fact, missing. It wasn't the first time he had asked her why she wasn't married or why he couldn't have brothers or sisters. Pride aside, she didn't want Jacob to grow up without a father. Not given she herself had been forced to grow up without one.

Her own aunt had nagged and nagged about the evils of men, about the evils of Ryder and how none of them cared, when the woman herself had given into the very evil she preached against by tucking away letters and money that might have saved Leona from being so bitter.

And this is where it stopped.

Brayton glanced back at her. "There is plenty of room for you, Miss Webster. You said you needed to wash your hands. Do join us."

She smiled and walked over to the basin.

Bumping Holbrook over with his shoulder to allow for more space at the counter, Brayton re-positioned Jacob and met her gaze.

The man was so darling. How was it he wasn't already married with three children? What was wrong with him? Something had to be wrong with him. After all, a million women would have honed in on him by now. Wouldn't they? "Thank you for tending to him."

He inclined his head. "'Tis an honor."

Maybe there were a million stupid women. It was possible. Squeezing in beside him and her son, she smiled and was about to dip her hands into the water but noticed it looked a bit muddy. Or rather...a lot muddy.

Ew. She wrinkled her nose. "We need a fresh basin. In fact, I suggest we go outside to do this."

Holbrook leaned in. "There is nothing wrong with this here water, Miss Webster. What are you? A princess? You'll be fine. Dip and go, I say. Dip and go. The soap takes it all off. No matter what the hell it is."

She stared him down dubiously. "Despite what you seem to think, Mr. Holbrook, there are some things not even soap can clean."

Holbrook snorted. "Are we even talking about water anymore?"

Brayton set Jacob down with a breath, turned back and jabbed an elbow into Holbrook. "*Enough.* The water needs to be changed, and you damn well know it. Now go. Fetch her a fresh basin and take the child with you so he can wash his hands properly."

Swiping his wet hands against his evening coat to dry them, Holbrook lowered his chin. "The pump is four streets away. Isn't she the new hire and I the master?"

Brayton glared. "Be a gentleman for a breath, will you? Let her settle in before we put her to work. If you had more money, you might have more say. But you don't, do you? Now go. Before I make you *drink* whatever you're looking at."

Holbrook muttered something, then turned, snatched two empty tin pails and trudged toward the door. "I'll be back. *In two bloody hours.* The lines at the pump are outrageous. You would think the city would install more pumps. Parliament only ever thinks of itself."

Jacob scrambled after him. "Can I get the water with you and wash my hands again at the pump? Mama and I do it all the time. I can carry buckets heavier than myself. Look." He flexed each scrawny arm.

Holbrook choked on a laugh, shook his head and glanced back at Leona. "I like this boy. Can I borrow him? I don't mind tending to something this adorable."

Leona eyed Brayton. "Is he trustworthy? He won't leave him there, will he?"

Brayton smirked. "No. He knows I'd kill him."

She sighed. "Do you know how long you'll be gone, Mr. Holbrook?"

A bucket went into the air. "Please. Call me Andrew. There are no formalities here. I've had enough of that growing up. I'm an independent man now." Andrew lowered the bucket and lifted a brow. "As for how long I'll be gone, that will depend on how many people need water. The last time I went, there were forty-two people in front of me. In Jacob's defense, it'd be nice to have a bit of company, even if he can't carry his own weight. I don't mind looking after him. It would give you time to settle into tending to the house. Which it damn well needs. And I promise I won't let your boy out of my sight. I plan to one day be a father, myself, and this here is what I call practice."

Sensing it would be all right to trust him, she puffed out a breath. "Fine. I'll expect you both in two hours." She pointed. "Or I'll come looking for you."

"Oh, I'd like that." Offering a wink, Andrew opened the door and called out, "Mr. Jacob, we are on a mission to find clean water. And if there are any attractive women waiting in line with us, make sure you tell them I'm a renowned novelist and worth a fortune."

"*Yes, sir!*" Jacob hustled out the back door, adjusting his cap.

Andrew grinned down at him and then used his scuffed boot to slam the door behind them.

Silence now pulsed.

Leona glanced up at Lord Brayton. "A renowned novelist worth a fortune? Are you certain I can trust him?"

"Upon my honor. I've gotten to know that boy a bit too well. If he could learn to stay away from money-grabbing women, he'd actually be very respectable." He averted his gaze and crossed the room to the table where Andrew had been sleeping. He nudged the half-empty bottle of wine. "I'm afraid you'll be overworked. For which I apologize."

She blinked. "Overworked? What do you mean?"

"I was forced to dismiss the last remaining servant we had. He was running a business out of the house that would not have been conducive to you or your son. It was best."

Oh, no. "What sort of business was he conducting?"

He swiped his face. "Nothing overly nefarious, but it needed to be addressed. He acquired a ridiculously large collection of lithographs by Achille Devéria from a cousin who had gotten arrested and therefore started selling them at three shillings a piece, attracting men to the door at all hours. Holbrook kept coming to his defense, seeing it brought in extra money, but it was getting out of hand. These lithographs were being stashed everywhere. And I do mean everywhere."

She squinted. "Achille Devéria? I don't believe I know the name."

"You're better off."

When their eyes met, she knew *exactly* what he meant. "I see."

He threw back his head and stared up at the ceiling as if to avoid further eye contact. "If only nudity were the problem. It was so obscene it might as well have been happening."

A giggle escaped her. It was hilarious knowing a man of Lord Brayton's size was avoiding eye contact while saying it. "I didn't realize you were prone to blushing."

He leveled his head and stared. "I'm not. This face wouldn't even blush if I dangled it over a fire. I basically spent the last three days scrambling to dig these damn lithographs out from every corner and crevice of this house. Holbrook and this idiot had so many, between the two, they couldn't even remember where they stashed them all. The only reason I'm even telling you any of this is because I'm worried that during any extensive cleaning you'll be doing, you'll find them. I don't want you thinking they're mine. Because they're not."

Oh. Now she understood. The gentleman in him was protective of his reputation. She bit back a smile. "I promise I won't hold anything I find against you."

"Good. Thank you. I'm hoping there isn't anything left, but the reality is, Holbrook was paranoid about getting arrested." He rolled his eyes, set his shoulders. "Allow me to formally introduce you to your new domain. I ask that you forgive its dire state."

He swept a hand toward the kitchen around them. "The rust on the stove has to be scoured and black leaded. If you require more coal than we have on hand, inform me of it, and I'll have more delivered. According to Holbrook, the last cook ended up taking some of the pots and pans, so I apologize in advance for the few that are left. I'll offer you a weekly allowance of half a guinea for the kitchen. That will permit you to purchase whatever you need."

"No. That won't be necessary. I'll pay a third of it out of the weekly allowance you give me, seeing Jacob and I will be taking from the kitchen." She paused and knowing she had to say it, regardless of his pride, she blurted, "I won't take more than ten shillings a week, Lord Brayton. I simply won't. You can't afford it. I naïvely assumed with you being an earl you had some money. I refuse to accept your generosity knowing you live like this."

His expression grew somber. Almost brittle. He searched her face. "You think I'm poor?"

She blinked. "There is no need to be embarrassed. I don't think any less of you. I'm as rag poor as they come. I simply...You've been so kind to me, please know that I don't need all of the money you earlier spoke of, because I'm not going to Shrewsbury. I'm not interested in listening to my aunt's explanation as to why she let me and my son struggle all these years. I plan to stay here for however long you need me and will gladly work for whatever you can afford."

His features softened. "You honor me."

Leona tried not to linger on how he made her stomach flutter. "Don't get soft. It's only money."

His features remained soft. "I have more than enough to get me through the world. So you needn't worry about me."

"Looking around this house, it's hard not to worry." Smoothing her hands against the sides of her calico gown, she glanced toward the open cupboards that held empty sagging burlap sacks of what used to be sugar and flour. "When was the last time this kitchen was serviced?"

He still regarded her. Intently. "I don't know."

She tried not to get nervous given the way he kept looking at her. "How can you not know? You're living here."

"I've always eaten at other establishments. Never here at the house. I've only been in London for a little over two months, so I really don't know what was and wasn't done with the kitchen prior to my arrival."

"I see." She sighed. "I'm not familiar with this area. Will I have to go far to find shops or vendors that will make it possible to stock the kitchen?"

"No. There are several shops within close vicinity and various vendors come through with their carts all the time. You won't have to walk beyond anything more than a block."

That was nice. There were very few vendors by Mrs. Henderson's tenement. She usually had to walk over two miles to find anything worth buying. And it was almost always all gone by the time she got there. "Good. That is one less thing for me to worry about." She hesitated. "Aside from all the cooking and cleaning, given there are no other servants now in the house, am I expected to answer the door?"

"You needn't worry. No one ever comes to the door."

"But what if they do?"

"Then they do."

"Does that mean I'll be answering the door? Do you want me to?"

He stared her down. "You don't have to."

It was like talking to the door itself. "If you don't tell me what to do, Lord Brayton, I may end up taking over the house."

He hesitated. "I don't mind."

"You say that now. Until you realize my cooking will send you *and* Mr. Holbrook back to the pubs where you belong." She walked up to the small iron stove and hefting the lid off one of the heating vents, she peered inside. Nothing but piled ash which had never been cleaned. A rat scrambled out of the ashes, making her jump. "*Ah!*" She let the iron lid drop, clanging it and frantically wiped her hands against her skirts at the thought of that thing crawling on the food she was supposed to make.

Lord Brayton rumbled out a laugh. "At sea, they become your friends."

She paused and glanced back at him, her heart pounding. "You mean you let them stay on your ship? You don't throw them over?"

He eyed her. "You only throw over the ones that cause trouble. In the twelve years I've been at sea, I've only ever tossed out a few."

"*Twelve years?*" She turned and made her way toward him. "You've been at sea *that* long?"

"Yes." He half-nodded. "But I enjoy it."

How fascinating. What made a man isolate himself from the world by staying at sea? "I'm rather the opposite."

"Are you?"

"Yes. I won't dip a toe into any water larger than a bathtub. Not to say I'm not intrigued. Where have you travelled?"

He shrugged. "Anywhere I was needed. From the Caribbean to India." He averted his gaze. "Private matters of business."

The Caribbean? *India?* It sounded so exotic. Something her father would do. "I've always been curious about seeing the world, but I've had an irrational fear of water well before my father died. My aunt tried to take me to Germany to visit relatives who offered to pay for our trip, but when I saw that water, I refused to let go of the port dock. I sprinted halfway into the next town to avoid it."

His brows went up. "Why?"

She unraveled the frayed ribbon on her bonnet and grudgingly admitted, "I don't swim." She removed her bonnet and set it onto the table between them. "Not that learning how to swim ever helped anyone aboard a sinking ship. My father knew how to swim incredibly well but that didn't save him. My aunt and I buried a set of his clothes and boots in his honor. They never found his body."

His voice softened. "I'm very sorry for your loss."

She half-nodded, her throat tightening. "Thank you. I was twelve when he...well...when it happened. He chartered a small ship to visit his tobacco investments, which were failing due to droughts. He had me stay behind given Aunt Judith wasn't feeling well. She was still recovering from being abandoned at the altar and was treating the whole affair like a disease. Men being the gravest of disease in her very bitter opinion."

He observed her for a long moment. "You don't share in her way of thinking, do you?"

She paused. His tone had changed. "After Ryder, I did. But it's obvious he wasn't intentionally trying to hurt me. Which eases my discomfort given I always considered us to be close friends. And now, after meeting you, I'm beginning to realize that—"

What in blue skies was she doing? Announcing her interest? Why? So he can laugh and admit that raising another man's child was not in his nautical book? "Forgive me. I have a tendency to ramble. Might I ask what India is like?"

Shifting his scarred jaw, he stared. "Hot. Very hot. I never felt rested." He still stared.

She swallowed, wondering if he was even referring to India.

He skimmed her appearance before returning his gaze to her face. "You look very different from when I last saw you. What did you put on your face?"

Her cheeks started to feel warm knowing he had noticed the rouge. Given she was blushing, she probably looked like she had slathered twice the amount needed. "Rouge. I was a touch pale this morning. Why?"

His steady gaze bore into her. "You don't need it. You're rather perfect without it."

An ache rose within her, and she wondered if the years of loneliness she felt were the same years of loneliness he felt. What sort of women had he associated with? Could a man like him cast an anchor for a woman like herself if tempted? Surely his lack of finances and her lack of finances made their association a bit more...plausible. Didn't it?

She lowered her gaze to her bonnet and traced her finger along the edge of the straw rim. "Being at sea must be lonely."

He dragged the bottle of wine toward himself and wrapped his fingers around its neck. "It can be."

She continued tracing her finger along the edge of the straw rim. "Do you ever try to make time for relationships? Or are you solely devoted to the sea?"

His fingers stilled on the neck of the bottle. "What are you asking, Miss Webster?"

Her hands felt moist. Flirting with an admiral *and* an earl was not the brightest idea she'd ever had. Setting aside that she was a shunned woman with a six-year-old, he was leaving in a few weeks.

Oh, God. What was she doing getting attached? She needed someone willing to stay. "I wasn't asking anything."

She quickly turned back to the stove, removed all the iron lids, setting them aside and opened the oven and side warmers. Grabbing the small, handheld broom crookedly hanging beside the stove and the dust pan, she bent and carefully swept all of the ashes into the dust pan. She continued to silently focus on cleaning out the stove in an effort to prepare it for cooking.

He strode toward her and lingered, his hand grazing the edge of the stove. "I think you were asking if a relationship between us is possible. Am I right?"

She cringed, turned and seeing a rubbish bin, emptied the charred ashes of coal into it. Frantically tapping the small handheld broom against the soot covered dust pan, she turned back to the stove and hung both onto their appointed hooks beside the stove. "I'll wait until fresh water arrives before I try to clean anything."

He said nothing.

She had certainly made things awkward. How could she be so stupid? He'd been so kind to her and here she was not only taking money he didn't have, but was also trying to insist on a relationship. What made her so special? She wasn't.

She had no real talent that might impress a man. She couldn't sing. She couldn't dance. She fell asleep at the one and only opera she ever attended. Her sewing always came out uneven. She couldn't cook without turning everything to cardstock and couldn't even put on the appropriate amount of rouge without making a man point out she needed less.

And yet…she wanted to be special enough to be loved beyond her very own breath.

Was that too much to ask?

Pinching her lips in an effort to pretend she was occupied, she started going around and opening cupboards throughout the kitchen to better understand what was where. Nothing was organized. Plates were stacked on top of bowls and cups were shoved in between dented lard bins. Pots and pans had forks and spoons in them and a whisk had been forcefully bent to fit in beside a tea-pot. "This kitchen reminds me all too much of my life. Maybe I should only try to organize everything and clean. Cleaning is the one thing I can do well. Stains and dirt fear me."

Stalking toward her, he shut the cupboard before her with a bang, making her jump.

He faced her. "You didn't answer me. Are you interested in progressing this or not?"

Her heart skidded. Why did he make her feel like a toe-dragging girl of thirteen? She lifted her gaze to his and eeked out, "But you leave in a few weeks."

A muscle flicked in his jaw. "I'm fully aware of that. It's up to you to decide if you want to follow me to Persia. Do you?"

She gaped. Was he insinuating that she...get on a boat? She wouldn't even do that if she were madly in love with him.

Hoping she wasn't overreaching, she chose her words carefully. Very, very carefully. "Even if you and I were interested in progressing this – *and I'm not saying either of us are* – my son has very fragile expectations. Ones I don't intend to crush by introducing him to a father who won't stay. My son needs a father more than I need a lover. Not that a lover wouldn't be amazing. It would. I'm simply waiting to be ready."

"Are you saying you're ready?"

She froze, uncertain of whether their conversation was progressing or flailing. It had been too long since she had associated with a man. So long, she had probably forgotten how to pucker her own lips. "Well, I...I've been waiting for the right man to come along."

"Have you?"

"Yes. More than anything, I need someone capable of embracing my son as his own."

"I would be honored. Genuinely honored." His voice was deep with sincerity. "I'm far from perfect, Miss Webster, but I always do my best to be honorable. Which is what every boy needs."

Leona tried not to panic knowing it was *finally* happening. A father. For Jacob. One willing to take him as his own. One willing to— This couldn't be real. It couldn't. It was happening too fast. Too soon. But...what if it was real and she let this pass? What was considered too fast or too soon anyway? She'd known Ryder since she was ten, which was well beyond fast and well beyond soon, and *that* ended miserably.

Maybe a new strategy was better than an old one. "Well, I...Jacob certainly likes you." She hesitated. "When he and I were making our way over, he even asked about your marital status."

"Is that so?" Lord Brayton smirked. "I admire the way he stood up for what he believed was a wrong and would be proud to mold him into the sort of man this world needs. As for his mother..." His smirk faded. He held her gaze. "I'm having trouble breathing around her, but I think she and I can work around that."

Leona could feel her *own* breath waning. Their interaction was surreal and felt so, so different from what she and Ryder had shared. Her life with Ryder had been...comfortable. Much like Ryder himself had pointed out. She'd known him from the time they were ten. When he'd *finally* kissed her at eighteen, she'd been incredibly disappointed with his lack of genuine passion. He'd only pecked her on the cheek. Even during their short-lived six-month engagement, he treated her more like a sister, which wasn't very flattering to a girl.

When she finally insisted on a full-mouthed kiss one evening after his concert, he had awkwardly smeared his lips against hers as if forced to. And when they had *finally* undressed and made love several times leading up to his abandonment, it had always been the same. Awkward. Overly tame. Overly polite. The blowing out of a candle to ensure she didn't see anything, the gentle lifting of her skirt followed by the careful rolling of hips and reserved breathy sighs. Pleasant, yes, but nothing really exciting.

As for *this*? She sensed this man was inwardly pacing like a lion, merely waiting for permission to unleash something that went far beyond tame and polite. It was damn nice. Because she was tired of being seen as a sister to men. She hesitated, knowing there was only one way to see if this man was even capable of making her and the city burn.

All she had to do was throw a match. "You can kiss me if you want."

He gaped. "*Now?*" he rasped.

She almost tsked. He was *too* much of a gentleman. Which was as surprising as it was disappointing. She *wanted* a kiss. "Later would rather defeat the point, don't you think? Now go on. You have my permission. Kiss me."

Edging back and back, he swung away. Slowly raking back his hair with scarred hands several times, he stalked across the kitchen and paused when reaching the doorway that led to the rest of the house. He crossed himself, as if speaking to God, and then glanced back at her. "I don't think either of us are ready. I was just thinking about ripping your clothes off and breaking all of the furniture here in the kitchen with our bodies. Is that what you want? Sex, blood and bruises?"

With that, he disappeared.

Her eyes widened. Sex, blood and…bruises? She brought her hands together, noting that they were trembling. Was he waiting for her to follow? And if she did, would the ripping of clothes and the breaking of furniture commence?

She swallowed, her entire body pulsing and fluttering with anticipation.

Despite all common sense, she trailed right on after him.

LESSON SEVEN

No matter your struggle, or your doubts,

or your vice, you will be wise not to let

your unsung passion turn to ice.

-The School of Gallantry

P eering down the narrow corridor, only to find it empty, Leona grazed her bare hand across the expanse of the uneven walls she passed and lifted her gaze to the narrow stairwell she now rounded. She glanced into the darkened parlor which held very few furnishings along with a leather trunk.

He wasn't there. He'd gone upstairs where the bedchambers were. He was announcing his intentions and it was now up to her to respond.

If she was bold enough to do it.

She doubted it would be tame.

She doubted it would be polite.

And yet for some damn reason it felt...*right.*

She frantically swiped and rubbed at her cheeks to try to smudge off whatever rouge was on her face, knowing he didn't like it. She then pertly arranged her skirts, patted her hair to ensure the pins were in place and even checked her breath by cupping her palm before her mouth.

All was good.

She dragged in several breaths and squarely faced the stairs. Too many years of sleeping alone with a deflated pillow challenged her into embracing whatever was about to happen next. Gathering her calico skirts, she made her way up the stairs. They creaked beneath each step as if scolding her into recognizing her folly. She winced at each creak that announced to Lord Brayton she was coming.

On the landing, she pushed out another breath and turned to find only one door was wide open. The second door to her right. She entered the room and paused beside a lumpy mattress and coverings that were unceremoniously laid on the floor without a bed frame. She blinked and was astounded to find Lord Brayton had already removed his coat, exposing the bulk of his muscles that strained his linen shirt and waistcoat.

It took her a moment to realize the removal of his coat hadn't been done in the name of seduction but to allow for better movement of his arm. He was carving strange, squiggling symbols into the wall.

He scraped and dug into the wall with the tip of his blade, his features tight and focused. "You shouldn't have followed. I'm *trying* to restrain myself."

She knew that. "I'm afraid I've been alone too long to listen to common sense." She edged closer, noting the archaic symbols he carved. "What are you doing?"

He tightened his hold on the blade with a rigid fist and curved the blade to finish one last marking. He lowered his blade and smoothed a large hand over it, scattering the shavings from the plaster and wallpaper. "In Persia, a man is not allowed to speak to an unmarried woman. Courtship is reduced to signals. Signals that allow each side to decide whether to move forward or fall back without the consequence they will be bound to once real words are spoken between them. I never fully understood its power until now."

Leona drew in a half breath, wandering closer.

Everything about this man was so real and soul provoking. It made her wonder if perhaps there was such a thing as reincarnation. Maybe once upon a time, they had been more than lovers. Maybe they had been each other's better half, meant to prod each other into remembering how important it was to be sincere.

When she was finally beside him, she reached out and traced the unknown markings he had made before letting her hand fall away. She glanced up at him, captivated by the unknown world he seemed to be luring her into. "What does it say?"

He punched the blade into the wall, leaving it impaled, and dropped his hand to his side. He turned toward her, setting his massive shoulder against the wall beside it and captured her gaze. "I'm not ready to tell you."

This just got interesting. "Why not?"

"Because I'm still struggling to accept that I've allowed for this much."

A hazy veil of unspoken intimacy settled between them. It was obvious he was the sort of man who didn't seduce a woman with his body, but rather his soul.

She set her own shoulder against the wall, closing what little distance was left between them and tilted her head to better look up at him. "Why are you allowing it?"

His gaze drifted to the wall he leaned against. "Maybe I'm doing it for the same reason you are."

Such honesty. "Are you saying you're lonely?"

His blue eyes now held hers and had a burning, faraway look to them. "Maybe."

Her heartbeat throbbed in her ears as her body grew faint at the thought of being touched by him. She wanted those large hands in her hair, on her breasts, on her buttocks, and yes...in between her thighs so she would never have to resort to doing it herself again.

A part of her was *so* relieved to know she wanted to have sex with him. She thought it would never happen. She thought she would never be physically attracted to a man after the intimacy she had shared with Ryder. "I'm willing to explore this if you are."

His features tightened. "I'd be very careful. Because when I dig my teeth into something I like, I don't let go. I skip right over chewing and just swallow. Be aware of that."

It was like he was trying to scare her into thinking he would shred far more than her clothes. It was *incredibly* provocative. A whispering shiver of want *and* need ran through her body and mind as she sidled closer, attempting to no avail to even her breaths. Chanting to herself not to faint, she lifted her hand to his face and grazed a finger across the uneven indentation of his scar.

He stilled.

She traced her finger to his hair and brushed it away from his forehead, her heart pounding at the realization she was touching this...*feral animal.* And he was letting her touch him. A tendril of power laced itself around her.

"What are you trying to do?" he hoarsely asked, still not moving.

She could feel her fingers trembling. "I'm showing you that I trust you, Lord Brayton."

His broad chest rose and fell more notably. "Malcolm."

She dragged in that distinctive scent that clung to the heat of his skin. "Malcolm," she softly repeated, honored that they were no longer lord and miss. She leaned in, drawing her lips upward.

He lowered his gaze to her lips, the warmth of his breath fanning her face becoming all the more ragged and uneven.

Like her own breath.

They lingered.

He silently edged in, signaling he was ready for whatever she would permit.

And oh how ready she was to permit.

Lifting herself on her slippered toes, she gently touched her lips to his. The warmth of his soft masculine lips made her almost spill into his arms. Everything about him made her want to shatter like shards of glass glittering in sunlight.

She slowly parted his lips and let the tip of her tongue slide across his.

He staggered but otherwise didn't move or touch her or even try to return her kiss. He remained eerily still. So still, one would think he was a statue set in the middle of a bursting fountain.

She had never met a man so determined to resist. But then again, she doubted he had ever met a woman so determined *to* insist. She dragged her hands up the breadth of his solid chest, reveling in its impressive expanse and further dragged her hands up into the softness of his smooth hair, which she had earlier mussed. She yanked him down toward herself, demanding he cooperate, and deepened her kiss, determined to melt that veneer of ice.

She was more than certain it was all veneer. It had to be. He had to be more than ice.

Melt, she inwardly whispered to him. *Melt for me like I'm melting for you. Show me you're different from Ryder. He never once tried to throw himself into sharing his passion or his heart with me. Show me what beats within you. Show. Me. That. Beat.*

Malcolm staggered and groaned against her mouth like a deprived man who just realized he needed it even more than she. He widened her mouth with his, now frantically tonguing her.

Leona clung to him, her fingers pressing into those tense, massive shoulders in disbelief.

Grabbing the sides of her face with rough, rigid hands that dug and pressed into her skin without mercy, he crushed her body against his own, whooshing the breath out of her and bending her backward. Angling his head in an attempt to open her mouth even wider, he drew her entire tongue into his own hot mouth so brutally and viciously hard, she squeaked from the unexpected sharp pain that pinched her to the jaw.

He froze, his chest heaving against hers, and released her tongue and her face. He jerked back.

Her eyes snapped open and numbly flicked her sore tongue in an effort to recover. By gad. It was like he had tried to eat her. Whole. The base of her throat still pulsed, making her feel as if her heart had risen from its usual place. Ryder, even in his most riled amorous state, had *never* kissed her like that. Ever. This man had kissed her as if his soul depended on convincing her he was worthy of more than what she had in her mouth.

It was everything she could have ever wanted in a kiss.

She dragged in several astounded breaths, composing herself from the excitement of knowing what they had just shared: *real passion.* In his eyes, it was obvious she was no sister. It had actually nudged itself closer to outright prostitution. "That was...quite a kiss," she breathed.

"I'm sorry." He swiped his flushed face with a large hand. "I'm so sorry I did that."

Sensing his distress over the fact he had hurt her, she quirked a brow. "I'm fine. Fortunately, my tongue is still functioning and attached."

He stared. "I hurt you. And that is unacceptable."

Bless his ever magnificent heart. He was like a benevolent giant who realized his size made it impossible for him to be delicate. "I'm fine. More than fine. I..." A shaky breath escaped her. "That kiss was so perfect, I still can't breathe. Nor do I want to. It made me feel like the woman I always wanted to be. Do it again."

"No." He edged back. "Once was enough."

She swallowed, her cheeks slowly burning in humiliation knowing after one kiss he was done. It would seem she, as a woman, had clearly failed to meet his expectations as a man.

It hurt. But at least he had the decency not to have let it go as far as Ryder had. "I disappointed you, didn't I?" she managed, trying not to convey any emotion.

"No," he rasped. "You didn't. Believe me when I say you didn't. This isn't about you. This is about me."

She stilled. "Ryder said the same exact thing to me when he called off our engagement. That his disinterest wasn't about me. But obviously, this *is* about me. How else can two very different men end up saying the same thing to the same woman? Am I not attractive enough? Am I not—"

"*Leona.*" Malcolm's blue eyes intently held her gaze. "Stop overreacting. Ryder was and *is* an idiot. I'm not calling off anything. In fact, you're going with me to Persia. Both you and Jacob. And I promise, you'll never have to be a servant to anyone again."

Her lips parted, her heart pounding in elation *and* confusion. Persia aside, he had just called her Leona. As if he were already the master of her heart. "I don't understand."

His voice broke. "I don't expect you to. I'm simply asking that you and I keep this civilized. All right? It's important. You have to help me."

"Help you?" She blinked. "With what?"

"We need to control this."

"Control what?"

"Our attraction to each other."

"Why would we want to control that? Isn't attraction good?"

"No. Not given what went through my head when I kissed you."

She paused. "What went through your head?"

"If I answer that, you would take your child and run. And I don't want that. I rather like you. Simply know that *this* can't end up in a bed. It's never going to happen."

She swallowed. "Why not?"

"Because I'm overly aggressive in nature."

Now she was morbidly curious as to what falling into bed with him *would* bring. Bruises from too much touching? Or broken bones from falling through the bed and onto the floor? The very thought of all that muscle unleashing *that* much passion only made her want him more.

Maybe she was stupid wanting to poke a lion with her bare finger, but she had learned to set aside the sweet, naïve girl who used to wait for the crumbs others would give her. In the name of her son, she learned to be more ruthless and seize what she wanted. Right down to a bear toy. And this was no different. Because waiting for what she wanted only led to disappointment and heartache.

She was done with that.

She stepped toward him. "I'm not scared of you. And I'm more than willing to prove it. We have at least an hour. I say we make use of it." Holding his gaze, she undid the small hooks at the base of her throat and kept opening it, determined to show him far more than a corset. "If I can survive giving birth standing up, I can survive you."

His gaze fell to her fingers, his chest rising and falling. "I wouldn't do that."

She stopped unfastening the hooks just above the ridge of her corset beneath. "Would you rather do it?" she asked, uncertain as to what he wanted.

"No." His gaze was still on her fingers. "I've seen enough. Put it away."

Put it away? Was he worried he'd see something he shouldn't? Like...sagging breasts? "I assure you, my pregnancy didn't destroy *that* much. Everything is still fully functional and—"

"Stop arguing with me, Leona, and hook yourself up."

"But—"

He glared. "I'm not interested in seeing your damn breasts or anything else. Not now or ever. Is that too hard for you to understand?"

Not now? *Not ever?* What on earth was this? He was making her feel so unattractive. Which she damn well didn't need after Ryder. "No. I don't understand. And I'll not do *anything* until you tell me what this is about. I've met plenty of men who demand a woman undress, but I've *never* met a man who—"

He snapped up a hand and then rigidly sliced the air with it to demand cooperation. "Stop talking, Leona, and just hook yourself up. All right? I'd do it myself, but I'm not touching you. So I suggest you hurry up with those fingers and get everything in place."

The audacity. *No* amount of talking was going to help this or him. He was delusional if he thought he could insult her and then expect her to be polite about it.

Knowing it was silence he wanted, she decided to give it to him.

Hooking herself up almost to the point of tearing the seams, she glared at him to ensure he knew she wasn't pleased. When she finally finished adhering the last fastener into place, she pointed a single finger at the now covered throat. A throat she planned to protect right along with a heart that had been through too much to make any of this acceptable. "I don't plan to *ever* show you anything *ever* again, *Malcolm*. So you needn't worry in that. It's fairly obvious you aren't interested in what I have to offer, and I wish to assure you, I not only regret offering, but will *never* offer it to you again. So don't ask."

His earlier dark mood lifted. "Please don't get annoyed with me. I'm only doing what I think is best. Now listen up. Because I'm only going to say this once."

Setting both hands behind his back, he paced back and forth, back and forth, like any military man would, occasionally glancing at her in between his trooping which shook the room. "Given you and I already kissed, and that I respect you and admire you with genuine sincerity that goes beyond anything I have ever felt for a woman, I now have a moral obligation and responsibility toward you as a Christian *and* a gentleman. We will therefore write up a contract for *nikāh* in the presence of a lawyer so it can be delivered well before we get to Persia. Expect several ceremonies that will bore us both beyond mental tolerance. The good that will come of it is that you and Jacob will live the sort of lives few get to touch. I will do my best to see you both whenever I can and extend my stay when permissible, but I'll be at sea most of the time, which cannot very well be helped. Persia may be going to war with Russia."

She bit down on her lip until it throbbed right along with her pulse. If she didn't know any better, she would think he was asking her to marry him. Already? Noooo. Why would he— Their kiss must have rattled her brain *and* his. "Pardon my ignorance, but...what are you talking about?"

He stopped trooping. "Isn't it obvious?"

"No. And while we're on the subject of my confusion, are you actually admitting to me that you're an admiral for the Persian navy?"

"Yes. I've been with the Persian navy since I was nineteen."

She squinted. "But that doesn't make any sense. You're a British earl."

He sighed. "It's complicated. I fell into it when I was young and quickly realized England doesn't need the sort of help Persia does. England will always have my love and eternal respect, but Persia has become more than my home. It is my way of life. I'm connected to the land and the people. They welcomed me during a time when I wasn't even willing to welcome myself."

That sounded a bit arcane. "But isn't serving another country outside of your own considered...oh, I don't know...*treason?* Don't people hang for that?"

"Damn right they do." He pointed at her. "And that is why you will tell *no one* outside of these four walls I'm working for the Persian government. No one. Not even Jacob. I'm putting my very breath into your hands, pigeon. I expect you to be infinitely flattered."

She tightened her lips. "*By what?* That you are now assigning me with an endearment that has only three letters *more* than the word 'pig'?"

He tsked. "I happen to like pigeons. They can fly through enemy fire and still deliver a message. Now stop nagging me and embrace the fact that I revere you enough to tell you all of my secrets. The sort of secrets that get a man killed. For that alone, I expect to be fully rewarded."

She straightened and adjusted the collar of her gown. "I was trying to."

He lowered his chin. "That wasn't what I was talking about. Respect the fact that I respect you enough to keep this civil. Now. I'm already a year beyond the age most men enter into *nikāh*. So the sooner we do this, the better off I'll be. Traditionally, contracts are signed before a family member representing each side but given you aren't talking to yours and I'm not talking to mine, we'll keep it to us and a sole witness, and whatever we both agree on, we agree on. It shouldn't be that complicated. We like each other, don't we?"

What...? She squinted. "What are you talking about?"

He dropped his hand to his side. "Marriage. *Nikāh* is a legal contract between a groom and his bride. We agree on certain terms, I pay you the *mahr*, and then we fulfill those terms by way of ceremony. It's essential to upholding an Islamic marriage. It's the whole 'your foes and woes are mine and mine are thine' mentality."

She choked. He *was* asking her to marry him. Holy— "Whilst flattered well beyond breath knowing I was able to get you to propose so quickly, I'm not Muslim."

"Neither am I. But these Persians get offended if we stay in their land and don't play along. Consider them family. For they are. You and I will have our own Christian ceremony here in London before we leave. That way, it will be legal in our eyes and that of our God. Not just theirs. Now what is your *mahr*? Name your dowry and I will acquire it."

She hesitated. "My dowry?"

"Yes. What sort of dowry do you want? How can I get you to accept my offer of *nikāh*? Name your price. It can be money or any other physical item you want."

This was...unusual. "I set a price? And *you* pay it in return for *my* hand?"

"Yes."

"I'm confused. Doesn't the female usually pay the dowry to a man?"

"No. Not in Persia. A female is worth far more there than she is here in England."

Imagine that. She'd been living in the wrong country all her life. "Well, I..." She paused. What was she thinking? He didn't have much. And if he was going to marry her and provide for her and Jacob, she really didn't need much else. Not financially, at least. "I accept your offer without this *mahr*. I waive my right to it."

He lowered his chin. "It doesn't work that way."

"A good husband more than satisfies the price I want paid. There is no need for us to throw money at it. I find that incredibly vulgar and not in the least bit romantic."

"*Romantic?*" He said the word as if trying to swallow a jug full of vinegar. His aloofness showed. "Leona, I'm not a...*rendez-vous romantique* sort of man. Or is that not obvious?"

She met his gaze, sensing his wariness. "It's obvious."

"Good. Because I dislike having expectations placed on me. I place enough on myself." He hesitated. "Our agreement won't be binding unless I offer you a physical gift of *mahr*. So what will it be? What do you want?"

The one thing Ryder never gave her. "An engagement ring. One that denotes a real promise the world can see. It doesn't have to be expensive. It can be out of tin. As long it's mine."

He rolled his tongue on the inside of his mouth before finally saying, "Done. Only it won't be tin. If we're going to do this, it's going to be done right. You want something that won't bend or fall off your finger. Is a ruby acceptable? Or did you have another stone in mind?"

Her brows went up. "Aren't rubies expensive?"

"They certainly aren't cheap."

She clasped her hand over her ring finger already feeling its weight. "My father once gave me an expensive ring and I lost it. I'd rather not live with the guilt. Maybe I can have just a simple gold band. That is, if you can...afford it."

"Stop thinking I'm poor. I'm not. I simply don't like to flaunt what I have or live in extravagance given all the people who struggle in this world." He inclined his head. "Consider a gold band yours. In the meantime..." He widened his stance. "Here are my terms. They're really quite simple. I want and need a companion. Someone I can attend gatherings with and whose presence I genuinely enjoy. You've already proven to be intelligent and entertaining and I like that. I like you."

She smirked. "I'm glad you like me. I rather like you, too. Maybe we'll be madly in love with each other by the end of this."

He stared. "Let us not get ahead of ourselves, because I'm not done giving my terms. At night, I ask that you respect the physical distance I require. So don't come knocking on my door half-naked with some excuse. Because unless you're being chased by Russians, I won't open it."

Her lips parted. "I don't understand. Are you saying you and I won't ever—"

"I'm not done. During the day, you and I will be the family Jacob needs us to be. The boy will want for nothing and will grow up to be an admiral. Like me. Which means by the time he is sixteen, he will be sailing on every last outgoing ship with me and will be earning a damn good living. You will naturally be permitted to join us at sea whenever you like, unless of course, we are at war or on assignment. I will expect you to be faithful, as I will be to you, and whenever we're apart, you will stay indoors at all times. For your safety."

"*For my safety?*" she echoed.

"Yes. Aside from the fact that more than a few Russians and well over a dozen pirates want me dead, if you think British men are incapable of keeping their trouser flaps buttoned in the presence of a pretty lady, Persian men are the equivalent of fish needing to put their heads into water. Which means, once we marry, and you begin wearing traditional garbs and veils, you aren't allowed to go anywhere into public without me. Not even a walk around the garden. A woman wandering alone in public is a signal to all the men that she is a prostitute and available for sex. So if and when I am at sea, you'll be expected to stay indoors at all times until I return. No exceptions. If Jacob wishes to go anywhere or play or see the sights during a time when I'm unavailable to take him, he will be assigned a guard that will escort him outside instead. Because you won't be able to do it yourself."

It sounded like a prison sentence. "If the men in Persia are *that* incapable of control, and given that the Russians and pirates don't like you, either, I insist we all stay right here in England. In London. Which is the middle of the country and far, far away from shore. In fact, I'm not giving you a choice about it. Because even if you were promising me paradise in its truest and bluest form, I'm *not* getting on a ship. And Jacob most certainly will *not* become an admiral. War aside, ships are incredibly dangerous. I didn't bring a child into this world to see him leave it before his time."

The thought of it made her feel like water pressing itself against her throat and squeezing every last gagging breath out of her lungs. Which is exactly how her poor father died. In water.

She swallowed. "If we're going to do this, we will lead our lives right here. On land. In England. Away from shore. Yes?"

"No." His voice notably hardened to emphasize his point. "I resume my duty as admiral by the end of September. Which means, if I'm not on that ship in eight weeks *with a bride*, I'll have eight Persian guards escorting me to sea with enough chains wrapped around me to sink whatever vessel I'm on. Which is why you and Jacob are coming with me."

"No. We're not. We're staying here. Because I'm not stepping on a boat. I'm not—"

"You most certainly are. Aside from the fact you know my greatest secret – meaning, that I work for the Persian government – I also kissed you. Both of which make you officially mine. Not only in *my* eyes, but the eyes of God." His voice continued to be laced with depth and authority. "You are now mine. And you have no further say in this."

Her eyes widened. Whoever thought this daydream could turn into a nightmare? "No further say in this? *Really*? So in your vast nautical opinion, I now *have* to marry you?"

He set his shoulders. "Yes. And why wouldn't you want to?"

She snorted. "Why, indeed. Let us set aside the fact that your ego has *magically* inflated beyond the size of your chest, Jacob and I aren't getting on a ship. Our feet stay on land. My father *died* at sea. Shall I repeat that for you? He died. Why? Because humans weren't meant to crawl onto pieces of nailed wood and float about a large expanse of water. It isn't natural. Which mean Jacob and I are staying right here. His two feet and my two feet *will* stand on land. I'll not be convinced otherwise. And if it means we don't marry because of it, then we don't."

He stared her down, his blue eyes flaring. "Allow me to repeat what I earlier said, pigeon. I'm taking what is mine on a ship. You are cargo that goes on my shoulder and you aren't leaving my side."

He did not just call her pigeon *and* tell her she was cargo.

She glared. "I know you're probably used to giving orders and having them followed, but I'm not part of your naval fleet, *Admiral.* Aside from the fact that your marriage proposal falls short of making me feel like I'm a piece of furniture you plan to move across England, I'm not about to face my greatest fear of getting on a ship for a man who insists I live in a country where the natives assume all women are prostitutes. I'm *also* not about to marry a man who isn't interested in kissing or touching me. That-that...isn't normal. I *want* to be kissed. I *want* to be touched. After all, if I were *that* interested in sleeping alone at night, all I have to do is introduce myself to the life I'm already living!"

He scrubbed his head in exasperation. "Why are you complicating this? I'm offering you far more than I've offered *any* woman."

She snorted. "That may explain why you're still available."

He glared. "The last time I even *allowed* myself to touch or kiss a woman, was when I was eighteen. *Eighteen!* Everything I've ever done, I've damn well done by choice. And you made your choice, Leona. You made it. Because if you didn't want to get involved with me, if you didn't want me to be your man, you shouldn't have damn well followed me into my *bedchamber* and kissed me! That is *unacceptable.* Because I'm a Christian man."

Bwuh. She pointed at him. "So says the man who talks about sex and cookies. Don't you dare give me the Christian talk."

He still glared. "Why? Are you not a Christian, Leona? Do you not believe in God?"

"It isn't that I don't believe. I simply haven't been all that impressed."

"Faith is *meant* to be tested."

"No. Not this much." She stepped back, her eyes burning. "I still haven't forgiven God for taking my father. Of all the ships He could have drowned, He chose the very one I needed Him to save. I'm *also* bitter knowing the leaders of His so-called church refuse to baptize my child. A child who has every right to the same privileges as other children. Because my sins are *not* his sins. As I said...I'm not impressed. *At all.*"

"Leona. You can't hold God accountable for simpletons. There are churches that will baptize your son. None in London, mind you, but there are some in Essex. We could ride out and have him baptized within the next week if that is what you want."

She pulled in her chin. "Are you my pastor all of a sudden?"

He stared. "If you need one, I consider myself well-trained for it. How often do you pray?"

"I don't. I have no need for a God who *never* listens. I already get that from the rest of the world."

His lips parted as if astounded. He intently searched her face, and after a long moment, said in a hard, removed tone, "No wonder you don't put your feet into water. You have no faith. Which *will* haunt you. I'm giving you an opportunity to give Jacob more. And if that isn't enough for you, do remind yourself that you had the boy out of wedlock. Who do you think is going to genuinely accept you and that boy, Leona? Ask yourself that. *Who?*"

She stared, feeling as if he'd slapped her. And he had. For while a part of her knew he was right, given very few men would *ever* accept her or Jacob without judgment, she wanted more. More for herself and more for her son. Because she had already once settled for less.

But not this time. She was done letting a man dictate what she did and didn't want out of life. "Don't you dare speak to me about offering whatever you can, because the only offer I'll take will be the one that permits me to lead the sort of life Jacob and I deserve. I don't expect sweeping gestures of romance from a man who punches blades into the wall, but I'm not about to let you treat me like cargo, either. The way you treat me is the path I set for my son. Which is why, if you want me, and I'm more than willing to give you and this a try, we're going to go into this like normal people do. *Without* contracts. *Without* limits. That means...when I come to you, no matter the hour, no matter the reason, you had better be ready to show me I'm the only woman you ever want in your arms and in your life. Am I understood in this?"

His expression stilled and grew serious. "You want too much."

She could feel her breasts rise and fall under what felt like labored breaths. She was tired of everyone telling her that. Maybe she was a mere miss, maybe she had no money, maybe she wasn't special to anyone but herself, but to her son, she was a queen. And she was going to damn well live up to that. For Jacob. And more importantly, for herself.

"No," she bit out, pointing at him. "*You* want too little. For while you dare offer me marriage in the guise of wanting to be a father to my son, the reality is I'm nothing more than hired help to you. A hired help you conveniently need to fill some *Islamic* contract I want no part of. I have trouble accepting my own God. What makes you think I'm going to accept theirs? Which is why I'd rather we continue with what is already in place. That is: you be Lord Brayton who leaves in a few weeks, and I'll be

Miss Webster, your servant, who takes whatever measly shillings I earn so I can invest it in a life worth living. A life where I'm not limited to someone who refuses to give me the one thing I not only deserve but want: *everything*."

His features tightened. He said nothing.

Which she expected. What man would ever offer her and her son *everything*?

The loud chime of a bell from down the corridor made her pause.

"So much for no one coming to the door." She set her chin and took on the respectable tone of a servant. "It appears you have a visitor, my lord. Shall I find a tray for the calling cards? And will you be accepting any visitors today?"

He averted his gaze. "No tray," he muttered. "I'm not interested in seeing anyone."

"No surprise there," she tossed out. "Why let anyone into your life but God?"

He kept his eyes averted. "I suggest you leave."

His lack of emotion was disturbing. "After I answer the door, I most certainly will. You needn't worry in that. Jacob and I will be gone."

He kept his gaze averted. "I didn't mean in that way." His face cracked and became somber. "You kissed me, Leona. And I wholeheartedly kissed you, too. That makes you mine. Regardless of whether I ever touch you again or not, you are mine. And I will not let you walk away."

She swallowed. Despite wavering and refusing to let this man into her mind and into her heart, she did. In that moment, she did. For she could see it in his face and his eyes that he wasn't trying to hurt her. This was about something else. Something she couldn't understand because he wasn't letting her. "Malcolm, if there is something I need to know, tell me. Tell me before we hurt each other. You've been...so amazing to me. I've never met a man so beautifully dedicated to being honorable. From the moment you yanked that creditor out of my face and stepped into my life, I finally feel I have a chance to touch something few women do. I foresee nothing but amazing things for us. So why are you insisting that we not share in what men and women usually do? Explain it so I may understand. Because I don't."

His rugged features twisted and eventually gave into anguish. Setting a heavily scarred hand to the back of his neck, he squeezed his eyes shut. A slow and well-controlled breath left his lips. "I'm not like other men, Leona. I would tell you more, but—I stayed at sea for a reason. I didn't want to meet any women because I didn't want to do something I would regret. Be aware, that the more you ask for and the more you want from not only my body but my heart, the less I'm able to control."

What was she getting herself attached to? Whatever this was, whatever he was not saying, it wasn't something she was willing to expose her child to. She would rather hug a damn pillow for the rest of her life than live in the shadow of whatever he was talking about.

"I can't do this," she finally choked out. "I don't know what you are or aren't saying, because you aren't giving me enough to understand. The kiss you and I shared in, the one you insist that now makes me yours, obligates me to nothing. Because I have a child to raise, Malcolm, and forgive me for even saying this, but I don't need a man to raise, too."

With that, she walked out of the room to answer the door.

LESSON EIGHT

You appear to be so obsessed with demonizing your

desires, you are destroying what you really are: human.

-The School of Gallantry

Whoever thought so many insults from a woman could make a man want more.

Leona, Leona, make me bleed and suffer in unending bliss, Leona. Malcolm plastered a disbelieving hand to his mouth, his body still pulsing from so much want and so much need. A cavernous yearning he'd been struggling to bury since he was eighteen years old gripped him. For he had finally met *the one.*

She was the leopard he'd been waiting to embrace. The one whose spots were all visible, for her nature refused to let her hide it. The one who growled when angry and purred when content for her nature refused to let her hide it.

He knew he had wounded more than her pride. He wounded her heart. A heart she tried to foolishly place into his hands without fully understanding how much he lived in fear of crushing it. Over his lifetime, his greatest sin was living with a need to feel *so* much until it became *too* much. What she considered to be a mere kiss, was him actually wanting to bite down and take her tongue right out of its socket to ensure she felt what he did: *everything*. And when she had flinched against him in pain in response to his yearning, he reveled in it.

Which he knew was wrong. Very, very wrong.

Letting his hand fall away from his mouth, he slowly turned to the wall where he carved the word *deltangam*. Which meant: 'My heart is tight'. It was a Persian expression for longing. It was how she made him feel.

Shifting his jaw, he yanked out the dagger he'd stuck into the wall. Angling the blade, he was about to gouge out the Persian word he wished he hadn't written, when a flurry of two female voices, one belonging to Leona and the other to one he did not recognize, drifted toward him.

He paused, lowering his blade and intently listened to what was going on.

"He was told I would be calling," a female voice lectured in a refined, but heavily French accented tone. "It is imperative I tap a finger to this head that reminds me all too well of a man I once knew. A man who rattled himself to pieces in the same way."

Leona interjected. "Whilst I wish I could understand, Madame, he simply isn't accepting any visitors right now. Nor is this a good time. He isn't—"

"*Absuridté*," the woman tossed back. "When a man is in need, the time is always right. And I assure you, I am not just *any* visitor. I am *Madame de Maitenon*. Back in France, not even the National Assembly would have turned me away. No one puts dirt on my bonnet like this. *Non, non, non.* I will find him myself. Try to be useful elsewhere, *mon chou. Excusez-moi.*"

The clicking of determined steps made him realize that the female voices were coming up the stairs and heading down the corridor toward him.

His throat and chest tightened. It was the French woman Nasser mentioned. The one who was supposed to help him. He doubted she could. He'd been this way a very, very long time.

But if he wanted Leona and Jacob to be part of his life, if he wanted to be part of a real and normal family, he had to try. He'd *always* yearned to be normal. He'd always yearned to be able to gently kiss a woman's hand without thinking of nipping or biting it. He'd always yearned to be able to bend a woman backward without breaking her back.

This was his one and only chance. It was this or nothing. And he was rather tired of nothing.

Malcolm swung toward the open doorway and waited. *With the holy thou shalt be holy: and with a perfect man thou shalt be perfect. Help me, Lord, in understanding how to expel this evil from within me.*

An elderly woman wearing an oversized bonnet trimmed with too many feathers and lace and ribbons breezed into the room.

He awkwardly lowered the blade he forgot he was holding. He tossed it, letting it clatter. She looked like an elegant version of his grandmother who died when he was ten. And here he was greeting her like a sea hoodlum. "Forgive the dagger."

Bright blue eyes that could have put the sky to shame pertly skimmed the blade and then Malcolm's appearance. She puckered her full, pink lips during her perusal, and although it appeared to be disapproving in nature, the merriment that glittered in those eyes after seeing the blade, contradicted said disapproval.

With the sweep of gloved fingers, she unraveled the length of the ribbon belonging to her flamboyant bonnet and removed it, revealing silver hair elegantly bundled in perfect ringlets. "Lord Brayton. A pleasure. I am Madame de Maitenon." She regally held out her bonnet to Leona, letting the feathers wag. "This will take a while, *mon chou.* Leave us and do not linger by the door or I will give him permission to toss you on your pretty little ear. This will require utmost *discrétion*. Are we understood in this?"

Leona hesitated and slowly took the bonnet.

How fitting she was here to see what he'd been trying to hide all along: the truth.

After years and years of denying it, he was done. He was done fighting it. He was done pretending the other half of his dark soul didn't exist. It did. It always did. No matter how many good deeds he tried to plaster over it, it was always there nagging him. Once in a while, when he couldn't stand it, and he'd be lying alone at night, unable to sleep and refusing to stoop to the level of masturbation, he'd take a blade, dip it in gin and poke himself. Just so he could stop thinking about having sex with a woman who would not only leave marks all over his body but would let him leave marks on hers, as well.

It was a bit of a problem.

He puffed out a breath, not wanting Leona anywhere near this conversation. "Miss Webster, can you please close the door after you and go downstairs? Mr. Holbrook and your son should be back soon. It's important this is addressed before they return. It is my hope you will forgive my earlier behavior that led to our argument. I wish to progress in sharing something more meaningful with you. I would like us to move forward."

Leona's lips parted as she edged back with the bonnet. "I'm moving backward, right now. I'll go...clean something downstairs."

Madame de Maitenon turned to Leona, a silver brow going up. "Am I to understand you and Lord Brayton are involved, Miss Webster?"

Leona winced. "I...well...oooo...I'm merely a glorified scullery maid. I'm no one."

Malcolm swiped his face, the taste of Leona's tongue against his own still making it hard for him to focus. "Leona, this woman is here to help me. So don't play games with her or me." He leveled his gaze at the

French woman. "I leave to Persia in eight weeks. If you can help me bed Miss Webster well before then and have her willingly follow me out of the country, I would appreciate it."

Leona gasped. "Have her help you bed me? *What?* I'm not—"

Malcolm pointed at her. "Don't pretend you don't want what I do. *This* is happening whether either of us are ready for it or not. You want everything? Fine. You're going to get it. And given you want me in your bed, you're going to get that, too. In fact, I'll be in your bed so damn often, you won't have time to leave it."

Leona's mouth dropped open.

The French woman chimed out a laugh and swept back toward Leona, her viridian morning gown rustling in the silence of the room. Pausing before Leona, she tugged back her bonnet from Leona's hand and pertly set it atop of her hair, angling it. Madame tied the ribbon around Leona's chin, fluffing the ribbon. "This stays on until he keeps his promise."

Leona dropped her hands to her sides and puffed at a large ostrich feather that fell over its rim. "Oh, yes, and how will I sleep with it?"

Madame de Maitenon smiled. "I am hoping you will not have to." Turning Leona around by the shoulders, she gently nudged her toward the door. "Peer in on us in exactly two hours. By then, he will need you."

Leona swung back around. "Need me? For what?"

Madame tsked. "If I answer that, you will be long gone. Which would defeat him and the point. Now go. *Go, go, go.*"

Leona blinked rapidly from beneath the angled rim of the oversized bonnet, then awkwardly turned and left, closing the door behind her. Harried steps indicated that she was not only leaving, but had no interest in staying *or* listening in.

Malcolm shifted from boot to boot and after a long, awkward blanket of gnawing silence, he set aside all common sense and blurted, "Given you're here to help me, help me. I almost pulled her damn tongue out of her socket when I kissed her. *And* I thoroughly enjoyed knowing she was in pain. I *enjoyed* it. What do you have to say to that, *Madame?* How can anyone even begin to help...*that?*"

Turning toward him, Madame de Maitenon tugged on the wrists of her gloves, as if that entertained her far more. "What was her reaction?"

He lowered his chin. "What do you mean?"

"When you almost pulled her tongue out of her socket. What was her reaction?"

He hesitated. "She stupidly wanted to do it again."

"And did you let her?"

"No, of course not. Why would I— I was scared I'd..."

"Hurt her."

He swallowed. "Yes."

A delicate breath escaped Madame. She was quiet for a long moment and eventually walked toward him, the click-click of her slippered heels drawing closer. "Prince Nasser was very concerned about you. And rightfully so. These tendencies can lead to very dangerous situations. No one knows that more than I. It can be frightening to a young woman who has never been exposed to it and equally frightening to the gentle-man who only yearns to fulfill the dark fantasies in his head."

She sighed. "Prince Nasser told me everything, but there are too many things even he could not answer. If I am to help you, I must better understand the depth of these tendencies. For I am not about to prod you into a relationship if you are a danger to yourself and whatever woman you wish to get involved with. I am therefore asking you to be incredibly honest and filter *nothing*. Even if you think the answer may disturb me, I want that answer. I need that answer. Can you do that? Because I cannot help you without your honesty."

Malcolm became uneasy. Not even Nasser knew the extent of what he was. No one did. No one but his brother had ever truly known.

"Lord Brayton?" she prodded.

He puffed out a breath. He could either move forward or backward. And his back was simply too far up against the wall to go anywhere. "Yes. I can do that. I can be honest."

She inclined her head. "*Merci.* I appreciate your attempt to face this."

Hell, he appreciated his own attempt. "I just want to be a normal man."

"Let us not run with the dinner fork quite yet." She hesitated. "Do you remember a time when you were not drawn to pain?"

Malcolm puffed out another breath and scrubbed his head with both hands, knowing it had started a long time ago. In his youth. He and his brother only ever had each other. His parents were too damn occupied with their social lives to bother with two boys who needed far more attention than even God was willing to give.

He was about nine when he accidentally slammed the door on his fingers. He'd done it many times before, but something was different about it that day. Although he had cried, he was fascinated with the way his heart had pounded and the way his fingers had trembled as the pain ebbed away, giving him peace. So he placed his fingers in the door and slammed the door on them again. Harder.

It had been a little too hard, and he wailed loud enough for all of England to hear. The governess scurried over and yanked him onto her lap, kissing and kissing his fingers and begging him not to cry. In between those full-lipped kisses, which she *never* bestowed on him, given she was usually too busy yelling or spanking him, he realized the pain had been well worth the reward.

He'd been obsessed with the power play of pain ever since.

A breath escaped him. "I think I was young when I purposefully started slamming doors on my fingers," he admitted. "It was the only time the governess ever gave me the attention I wanted. Even worse, I fancied myself to be in love with her. So I went out of my way to...hurt myself. My brother liked my approach and started doing the same. Only he wasn't using doors to slam his fingers. That was mere – pardon the expression – 'child's play' for him. He was obsessed with breaking glass, and we basically competed with each other to see who the governess would run to first. Blood won out over bruised fingers every time, so I had to get more creative. The governess eventually figured out what we were up to and stopped responding. So despite our love for her, we…got her dismissed. We soon had a new governess every Season doing the same damn thing. Our parents never thought anything of it. They were too busy with their lives and thought we were merely being boys. It wasn't until our mother died some of those habits changed, seeing our father was more intent on interacting with us."

Madame de Maitenon traced a finger across her bottom lip in thought. "What you are describing goes far beyond sibling rivalry. How is it your brother shared your same tendencies for pain? That is unusual. You are two separate people with two separate desires."

Ha. "In the eyes of the world, yes, we are two separate people, but James and I have always viewed ourselves as one. He is my twin. And he is very much the darker half of our darkness."

Her eyes widened. "*Mon Dieu.* Twins. I understand." She rounded him, searching his face. "Your scar is rather prominent. Was that done during your attempt to gain attention?"

He snorted. "No. I was never *that* stupid when it came to getting attention. The forceps sliced my face at birth. I almost died."

She continued rounding him. "Were you born first?"

"Yes. Although one wouldn't know it. James always sought to lead. Always."

"And do you still associate with your brother? With this James?"

He rolled his eyes. "I prefer to stay away. I've learned to live a life separate from his."

"Why?"

"James is overly comfortable with the idea of hurting not only himself but others. There isn't a line he won't grip or cross. He isn't…mean-spirited, but…he expects everyone to kneel to him every time, no matter what it is. Even if it isn't safe. Whilst I? I've learned to enjoy more of a...oh, I don't know...a softer approach. I don't like to impose on others. Especially women. They're...*delicate.* You can't just...rough them up and leave marks all over their bodies. I also can't ask them to return the favor, because I know they would think I'm touched in the head. So I've avoided it, because I've always wanted women to like me. Not dread and fear me. I already dread and fear me. I don't need them doing it for me."

Her mouth quirked. "You are fascinating. What is even more extraordinary is you are unaware of how special you are. Very few men who have your tendencies can exercise *such* control over their minds and bodies as to will themselves to lead a chaste life. You should be very proud. The respect you have for women is to be commended. Applauded. *Hailed.* It is rare."

He slowly adjusted his waistcoat, utterly baffled. "Applauded? *Hailed?* Madame, I am *admitting* that I enjoy pain and that I want a woman to enjoy it with me. How the hell is that to be commended?"

She held up a hand. "You are looking at yourself through the eyes of society, Lord Brayton. Not through your own eyes. Society's definition of what is and is not acceptable is a guideline, and oftentimes, is an overly strict guideline that prevents us from respecting what we know to be true."

Leaning in, she delicately tapped his shoulder. "I was worried this was going to be complicated, but it is rather obvious this is merely about teaching yourself to be comfortable with your tendencies. You need to accept them and safely apply them. Nothing more. Once I assist you to fully embrace what you have long denied, I foresee nothing but rainbows in the sky."

He stared at her. There had to be something wrong her. Maybe the French Revolution made her bloodthirsty. "You plan to help me *embrace* it? Are you...*mad?* I'm trying to get rid of it. I don't think you understand the severity of the situation. I don't see rainbows when I look at Miss Webster. I see crops."

She smiled. "I am well aware of that. Unfortunately, I am no magician. I cannot erase your tendencies and neither can you. It would be too much *aggravation* to try to dig out something that has always been attached to your heart since childhood. It would murder everything you are and have come to be. Pain and pleasure are the two things that remind us we are connected to our bodies. Give yourself permission to think of yourself as being so overly connected and that is why you take pleasure in both. The more attainable method of approaching this is not to murder everything you are but to *live* with what you are. Which means...you must share your fantasies with Miss Webster and explore them."

He choked. "Explore my— Share my— She would run."

"Then let her run. For that is how you will know she is not the one. Honesty is the first step to intimacy, Lord Brayton. If what you share with this woman is real, she will do her best to understand and embrace not only you but your fantasies. And when and if she does, you will learn how to negotiate your fantasies against hers. You will negotiate what sort of pain *you* want and let her negotiate what sort of pleasure *she* wants."

He paused. "I can do that?"

She laughed. "*Mais oui.* When in bed, there are no limits as to what defines pleasure as long as both sides agree."

"I...*Truly?* So you mean as long as she agrees to what we're doing, we can..."

"Yes. As long as she agrees. There is nothing wrong with what you desire as long as she understands and accepts your desire."

He straightened. "Well, how the hell do I get her to do that? What do I have to do? What do I have to do to get her to—"

"Calm yourself, Lord Brayton. Calm. That is not up to you. That is up to her."

He swiped his face. "Then this is where it ends. Because she will think there is something wrong with me."

"No. There is nothing wrong with you. 'Tis very important you understand that. There is nothing wrong with you or what you want from Miss Webster."

A wave of apprehension gripped him. "That is a lie."

She glared. "I never lie." She reached up and flicked his ear. "Are you not listening? There is nothing wrong with you or what you want from Miss Webster."

And he thought Muslims were crazy. The French apparently were, too. "My moral ethics don't appear to be same as yours."

"Set aside your distorted way of thinking. You are a gentleman who knows how to exercise the one thing few men do: *control*. How else do you think you remained a virgin all these years? By being an irresponsible rake who tortures women? *Non*. You understand pain is something that needs to be respected. Which is *very* important when you embark upon playing with pain. You are compassionate and therefore will not be a danger to yourself or whatever woman you wish to involve yourself with. You must simply learn to give yourself permission to share your desires with another. That is all."

He paused. "How can I impose such dark desires on a woman who has a child and seeks to lead a normal life? I can't. I...what I would be asking of her wouldn't be...*normal*."

She tilted her head. "What defines normal in this world, Lord Brayton? The real question here is whether you can take this woman into your bed and apply *your* definition of normal. Intimacy is the only time when we are able to be real with those we love. And if you cannot be real with her in bed, knowing the world is not even watching, when *can* you be real? Never, I imagine. You are simply wasting not only her time but yours. Do you understand?"

The more he listened to this woman, the more he realized he had been looking at his life the wrong way. Just as his brother had always told him. Because it didn't matter what the world thought when he was in the arms of a woman he wanted to be with. All that mattered was that the woman in his arms remained there *willingly.*

He swallowed. "So how do I tell her? How do I tell her what I am and what I will expect from her without scaring her?"

Madame lowered her gaze to his hand and wagged her fingers. "Show me your hand."

He held out his right hand, displaying the scars marring his outer hand, palm and fingers. He felt awkward. He'd never had a woman ask to look at his hand. He usually wore gloves to prevent them from seeing what he had always considered his shame.

Taking his hand, Madame turned it over, inspecting all of the scars with a dainty squint. "It certainly has seen its share of pain. My Andelot had hands like these."

"Andelot?"

Her features tightened. She slowly released his hand and averted her gaze. "He was like you," she murmured. "Only...he was dedicated to solely giving himself pain. I was too young and too scared to understand him in the way I understand things now." She was quiet for a long moment. "Does the rest of your body look like your hand?"

He flexed both hands. "Unfortunately. Although it was hardly my doint. When I went to the monastery my body became unrecognizable. I don't like looking at it. It's too much. Not at all what I wanted."

Her features softened. "Show her your body and do not allow *poompoom* to happen when you do it. For you cannot do it as a means of seduction or you will scare her. Do it as a means of unveiling the truth by explaining to her what it is she is seeing. It will have a more profound effect and will reveal her true heart. You need a woman willing to accept who you are, because it *is* who you are. Do you understand?"

Panic gripped him, realizing something. "What if – *and I'm overreaching here, so don't judge me* – what if she *agrees* to be with me? What then? I'd be unleashing things I never— What if I hurt her? What if—"

"You will not hurt her."

He glared. "How the hell do you know that? You don't."

A pert sigh escaped her. "Prince Nasser tells me you are a religious man, who believes in God, and that you always rise to the occasion of helping others, even at the cost of yourself. Not even normal men can claim that much. Take pride in knowing that even while you explore your darkest desire, your *compassion* will be the light to pull you away from the darkness every time." She leaned in. "Your *compassion* is what helped you end that kiss that *almost* made you pull her tongue out of her socket. Am I right? Did you rip her tongue out? *Non*. You did not. You stopped yourself. Why? *Compassion*. That is all you need to ensure she will be safe. Because you will keep her safe. *Oui?*"

It was like a heavenly golden light *finally* glittered from above and shone down on what he always thought to be nothing more than darkness. She was right. She was...right.

Malcolm crossed himself in honor of God for finally speaking a truth he could understand. He hadn't recognized that in himself until she said it aloud. For while yes, when he kissed Leona, his Leona, and submitted her to his desire and his need to give her pain, he hadn't forced her to continue with it. Her pain become his pain and knowing it, that gave him the power to stop, which had *always* been his greatest fear. Not being able to stop.

But he had. He put Leona's well being before his darkest desire.

And that was how he was going to keep her safe.

Drawing in a slow, disbelieving breath, Malcolm let it out, feeling as if he were *finally* being given permission to...breathe. Because he *was* compassionate. He'd always been. And nothing, not even his darkest fantasies, not even his own damn brother, had been able to rip that out of him or the rock he had molded around his life.

Madame gently patted his cheek. "I can see you opened the first door. Now you must enter the house and live in it without destroying the furniture."

If there had been a vast green meadow before him, he would have set aside being a man for a breath and skipped in it. Still in disbelief, he grabbed Madam's hand and fiercely pressed his lips to her hand, squeezing it hard in an attempt to convey his gratitude. "I feel like I can breathe. Which I never even thought possible. I can finally—"

"*Oui, oui.* But it will not be enough. You will have to learn how to continue breathing. There is more you will have to learn if you plan to be a master of all pain and pleasure."

He released her hand and slowly straightened. Master of all pain and pleasure. Ey, now. He rather liked that. It was a subtext to his position as admiral. And that was what he damn well was. An admiral. He had led men through battle, raging waters, had faced sabers and fists and broken bones and pirates. Facing an adorable, five-foot woman with green eyes and freckles was fucking easy. So fucking easy, all he had to do was aim and go click.

Malcolm pushed out a determined breath. "I thank you for the new title, Madame. I think I can manage. I know *exactly* how to approach this."

"Do you?"

"Yes." Stepping back, he set a hand to the back of his neck, pinching the muscles on it hard in an effort to remain calm. "I'll have Holbrook keep Jacob out of the house for the rest of the afternoon tomorrow. After that, I'll call her up to my room, strip, explain, she and I will agree on terms, then I strip her and we get to it. Simplicity at its finest."

Madame let out a bubble of a laugh. She quirked a silver brow. "Lord Brayton, whilst I am incredibly pleased with your miraculous progress and assertive military nature, I suggest you *slow* the beat of your heart down a tick."

He lowered his hand. "If I slowed it anymore, Madame, I'd be dead. I've *finally* found the woman I want and I plan to damn well seize what is mine before someone else comes around and takes it. Have you seen her? I'm surprised there are *that* many stupid men walking around London. I'm pulling out the artillery. I'm doing this. Right now."

Madame tsked. "Unfortunately, a woman's heart is not a battleship you can blast your cannons at. What you are proposing to do will only scare her. You must wait."

"*Wait?*" he echoed. "For what?"

"The perfect moment. A moment when you are *guaranteed* full cooperation. You do want her to accept you for what you are, *oui?*"

That would be helpful. "Yes. Of course. I...so what constitutes a perfect moment?"

"Only you can define that."

He paused. "But I just defined it. Tomorrow afternoon. Perfect moment."

"*Non.*"

"No?"

"*Non.*"

His brows came together. "I'm confused."

"Men usually are." She sighed. "The perfect moment is unplanned. It is a moment similar to seeing a shooting star. You blink and it happens. Give yourself time to wait for that *perfect* moment. You cannot rush this or you will break the bond you are seeking to create."

He puffed out an agonized and rather annoyed breath. "Are you saying I have to—" He couldn't believed he was saying it. "*—romance her?*"

"It depends on whether you think it would be helpful."

Damn it. "She did mention romance. So I guess...I— Do I buy her flowers?"

She rolled her eyes and waved a hand about. "*Non. Pas de fluers.* Gifts, such as *flowers,* come later. When you have already given her everything else."

His brows came together. "Explain what you mean by everything else."

Her lips puckered. "*Romance* is lending a quality to her life. How are you lending to that quality? You seem like a very gruff man. And there is certainly nothing wrong with that. Women are drawn to gruff men. You are strong, confident and do not feel the need to prove that strength or confidence to anyone. Or...do you? Yes, you do. *To her.* Being a good, noble and gruff man is exciting, but imagine if this same gruff man can surprise her with tokens of affection she does not expect. Fall on your knee for her and announce your affinity."

He stared. "Announcing one's affinity I understand, but how does falling on my knee prove anything other than the fact that I'm on my knee?"

She leaned in and tapped at his forehead. "Falling on your knee is the ultimate act of submission. It amplifies the words you are conveying and announces you are willing to be vulnerable enough to remain beneath her. Such tokens allow her to recognize she is the glory of all you want. And is that not what *you* want? *Her?*"

This just got complicated. He wandered over to the wall and sank against it. "What if my tokens aren't enough?"

Her voice softened. "If they come from your heart, Lord Brayton, they will be more than enough. They may almost be too much."

He swallowed. Leona was the one and only chance he wanted to take. She and those soulful green eyes and that giving heart that insisted on being loved, was the closest he would ever feel to being...normal. "I will wait until I believe she and I are both ready."

Madame's features brightened. "You listen beautifully and apply what is necessary with no resistance. I admire that. Whilst I do not believe you will require too much cultivation or guidance, as you are impressively well grounded, I still wish to invite you to apply to my School of Gallantry which will be opening its doors soon. You will meet other men who struggle with their own understanding of...women and such. It may prove useful over these next few weeks prior to you leaving to Persia. Are you interested in applying?"

A school for gallantry? Huh. He could...use that. Would he be pathetic to admit that he—"Well, I..."

"Prince Nasser insisted and already paid for it. He will send you any and all information."

Malcolm bit back a smile. Leave it to Nasser to take over his life when he needed it most. "Thank you. I will be there. Fortunately for me, I have a Persian friend who seems to think I have time to burn."

Bringing a hand to her bosom, Madame theatrically patted it to her heart. "And burn you shall."

Quick booted feet and the slamming and opening of doors made them both pause and turn.

Someone frantically pattered over to the door, the knob turned and a small hand banged open the door. Green eyes brightened mischievously as Jacob grinned and ran in. He skidded around Madame de Maitenon and stumbled over to Malcolm with booted feet.

"Is this your room?" Jacob glanced around, his eager grin fading to distress. "Where is all the furniture? And why is the mattress on the floor? Did you use the bed frame for firewood?"

Malcolm smirked. Leona wasn't going to be the only one keeping him busy. "No. I'm afraid the rats ate everything."

Jacob gaped. "And you let them? *Why?*"

Malcolm coughed out a rough laugh. "Remind me not to joke with you and your freckles. If you want the truth, all of my real furniture is on a boat at sea. And given I don't want to take anything more than a few trunks back with me, I'm keeping my life real simple. Now." He grabbed the boy's head and turned him toward Madame. "Don't be rude, Jacob. A gentleman always acknowledges other people in the room. Introduce yourself to an incredible lady who is going to ensure we become a family."

Jacob's eyes widened. "By all that is blue. She looks like she could be married to Father Christmas."

Madame de Maitenon let out a breathy sigh. "I do believe the boy just announced I am old. My hair went entirely silver by the time I was forty and I assure you, I am not even sixty. Unacceptable. I am done here. It is time I go back to Father Christmas before he notices I am gone." From behind a raised hand, she winked playfully at Jacob and then gathered her skirts. "Lord Brayton, it was a pleasure." She turned away and then paused, glancing back at him. "I suggest reconnecting with your brother."

He winced. "Uh...no. No. We encourage each other too much. My language gets foul, I get into even *more* fights and—"

"He never denied that part of himself, my lord. While *you* always did. You can both learn from each other."

"Or kill each other," he drawled.

"If you can allow yourself to embrace him again, you will be able to embrace yourself. Which is what you need. Do you understand?"

Malcolm's throat tightened. Who was he to deny he missed his brother? He'd been missing him since that very first day he left for France. "I will call on him when I'm ready."

"*Bien.*" She held up a finger. "I leave you with your first lesson. It is this: *Le moment parfait.*"

The perfect moment. He sighed. How hard could it be? Malcolm inclined his head. "*Oui, Madame.* The perfect moment. *À la prochaine.*"

Running feet echoed, making them all pause.

Leona skidded into the doorway, the oversized ribbon and feather bonnet flopping forward. She removed the bonnet from her head and cringed. "I'm so sorry. Jacob and I were playing a bit of hide and seek, and I...Jacob, dear, I told you not to—"

"Worry not, Miss Webster," Madame de Maitenon regally announced, sashaying up to her. She took the hat and set it on a perfect angle onto her coifed silver hair, tying the ribbon into place beneath her chin. "Expect nothing but full cooperation, Miss Webster. He is ready and willing. The real question is...*are you?*" Madame smiled. "As the bible says 'Love each other deeply, because love covers a multitude of sin.' Be patient with him, Miss Webster. He needs it. That said, I will see myself to the door. *Au revoir* and...*viva l'amour.*" She disappeared with a pert, click-click-click of her shoes.

Silence pulsed.

Dread gripped Malcolm. How the hell was he going to tell Leona he wanted to spend the rest of his life letting her bruise him so he could bruise her? It wasn't a romantic sentiment.

Leona met his gaze. Her green eyes prolonged the moment. "You and she spoke for some time."

He awkwardly nodded. "Yes. There was a lot to discuss."

"What were you two discussing?"

He wasn't ready to say it. *Especially* with Jacob in the room. "I need more time before I—"

"Mama, *look!*" Jacob held up the dagger Malcolm had earlier tossed onto the floor and started running with it, slashing at the air. "I'm a pirate! A real pirate!"

Leona's eyes widened. "Jacob, for heaven's sake, don't—"

Jacob stumbled beside Malcolm.

Malcolm's heart popped as he lunged and grabbed the boy hard to keep him from falling onto the blade or the floor. A searing burn punched into Malcolm's thigh. Deep.

LESSON NINE

Dare to be yourself.

-The School of Gallantry

L *ord, I do love You, but Your timing isn't always the best.*

A choked scream escaped Leona. *"Malcolm!"*

He staggered, realizing the blade was embedded into the muscle of his upper thigh, and used the other hand that wasn't holding Jacob to keep the dagger firmly in place, lest he bleed out. His throat tightened against the skull-pounding pain that was as lethal as it was euphoric knowing Leona had cared enough to scream.

Was this the perfect moment? Probably not. "Let go of the blade, Jacob," he rasped. *"Slowly.* We don't want to move the blade."

Jacob, who still dangled frozen from his arm, slowly released his small fingers from the handle of the blade. An anguished sob escaped Jacob as Malcolm's blood oozed from the blade, soaking the area around the trousers.

"Shhhh. It's okay, Jacob. I'm fine." Malcolm carefully set the boy down, then edged back and winced his way over to the mattress on the floor. He lowered himself onto it and hissed out a long breath as fire-piercing pain dug deeper into the core of his muscles. He knew wounds well enough to say it was going to get worse. "Leona, I need three bottles of gin and a doctor. I would rather not stitch this up myself. Go have Andrew take care of it."

Leona nodded frantically, her chest heaving, and ushered Jacob to the door. "Jacob, let's go downstairs to Andrew. Hurry! We need to—"

Jacob let out another sob and grabbed at his mother's leg. "I didn't mean to hurt him, Mama. I didn't— *Is he going to die?*"

Malcolm hissed out another breath, recognizing that the child was more traumatized than he was. "Jacob, no. I'm not going to die. I'm fine and can I assure you I've survived worse. Now go to Andrew. Tell him I need three bottles of gin and a doctor and stay with Andrew until the doctor arrives. Can you do that for me? Can you be brave? Like a pirate?"

"Yes, sir! Like a pirate!" Stumbling out of the room, Jacob sprinted out of sight.

Malcolm tried not to move knowing it was best to keep the blade in until the doctor arrived.

Leona lowered herself to the floor before him, her skirts playing across his booted feet. Her chest heaved as she clasped a trembling hand against her entire mouth. "Only the handle is sticking out," she said through her hand.

"I know, pigeon, I can feel it," he said through his teeth. "There is no need to elaborate."

She winced. "I'm sorry. I— What do you want me to do?" She leaned in and frantically searched his face, her hands hovering but not touching. "What can I do? Tell me what to do and I'll do it. What do you need?"

He breathed in and out, in and out, trying to control the pain raging through coiled muscles. The fact she was staying with him and was panicked and concerned was a very good sign. It meant she...cared. She cared enough to do *anything* for him given he was in pain. *Anything.*

It was a game he had played since he was nine-years-old.

This just got dangerous.

He cleared his throat, trying to raggedly focus on her and only her as opposed to the raging pain rolling up the length of his thigh. Because if he focused too much on the pain, knowing she was watching him in pain whilst on both of her delectable knees, begging him to instruct her, the perfect moment might not be so perfect. And he wanted it to be perfect. For her. For them. For whatever future—

"Malcolm?" she choked out, still searching his face. "What can I do? Please. I want to help."

His eyes burned to restrain his aching need to savor the beautiful concern in those green eyes that were focused on him and only him. What if there was no perfect moment? What if he revealed his morbid need for pain and became nothing more than a freak in her eyes? A freak she would never trust to take care of her child or whatever child they brought into this world.

He'd never know more than that single glorious kiss she'd given him.

He'd never hear her say 'I love you' in the dark or feel her hands on his skin.

It would all go to another. She and that wit and that laughter he wanted to swallow and keep chained to his heart would go to another. Not him. Another.

"*Malcolm?*" she choked out again, sounding a touch more hysterical. "I need you to look at me and talk to me. Keep talking so I don't think you're fading. *All right?*"

His heart hammered knowing, that in this moment, she was his, all his, without prejudice. She was merely waiting to serve him and wouldn't think any less of him, because she didn't know.

He'd be her version of normal. He'd be excused anything merely for being in...a lot of pain.

He caught her gaze and leveled his breathing. "Leona, I need you to do something that is going to make all of this damn pain worthwhile."

She lowered her hand and searched his face, her green eyes panicked. "Of course. What? Anything. What can I do?"

"Close the door and lock it. I need you to lock it."

She paused. "Lock it? But the doctor will be—"

"It'll keep Jacob from seeing something he shouldn't." He was all about being honest. "Close and lock the door for me."

Her lips parted. "Maybe you're right. Maybe— We'll keep it closed until the doctor comes." She jumped to her feet, stumbling, and slammed the door and locked it. She skid back toward him, landing back at his feet. She paused. "Wait. Should I go get the gin first?"

"No. No gin. Not yet." He wanted to feel everything that was about to happen. He shifted his jaw, digging his trembling fingers into the straw mattress beneath him. "Now come here. I need you to kiss me."

She pulled in her chin. "Kiss you?"

"Yes. Kiss me."

She choked. "*But you have a dagger sticking out of your leg!*"

He wet his lips and nodded. "I know. Believe me, I damn well know." He dragged in several uneven breaths. "But this pain...it's...it's killing me. And I keep thinking to myself...what if I die?" He wasn't in *that* much pain, but, how else was he going to get this woman to kiss him while he still had a dagger in him? "I need *something* to distract me while I'm waiting on the doctor. Do you know what I'm saying?"

Leona glanced toward the locked door and then scrambled onto the mattress beside him, toward the side of his good leg. She scooted close, kneeling so as to get more to his level, then grabbed his face and kissed his cheek. She leaned back. "There. Is that better?"

He gave her a withering look. "What the hell was that? Do you want me to die?"

"No, I—"

"Make this pain worth my while. Give me your tongue. *Lots of it.*"

She stared. "Are you— How can you even think of kissing at a time like this? *What is wrong with you?*"

"I'm in pain. A lot of pain." He was.

He leaned toward her and winced as the dagger rudely reminded him he had company. All he had to do was make her feel sorry for him. "If this is the last time you ever see me alive, pigeon, what sort of kiss would you want to remember me by? Show me. I'd love to see it."

Her cheeks flushed as an exasperated breath escaped her. "*Must* you call me pigeon and talk about death at the same time?"

"*Must* you make me suffer and resist at the same time?" he breathed. "Don't make me pull out this dagger. If I pull it out, blood will go everywhere and we'll both faint. Now kiss me."

She glared. "You're insane. But because I feel *incredibly* sorry for you right now, I'll set aside all common sense and entertain it." She seized his face with both hands and savagely kissed him, her hot velvet tongue dominating his.

Malcolm almost fainted. Closing his eyes, he grabbed her head and worked his tongue against hers, digging his mouth harder against hers until he couldn't breathe. Knowing he was making love to her mouth, his cock grew hard.

He wasn't a practicing Christian gentleman anymore.

This was the woman he wanted to spend the rest of his life with. A woman willing to kiss him because he insisted, even though there was a dagger buried in his thigh. He gripped her hands and, while still kissing her, shoved them toward the flap of his trousers.

She broke away from their kiss. "What— What are you doing?"

His eyes snapped open as his chest heaved. "Avoid the blade and we'll be fine."

She choked and leaned back. "Malcolm, how much blood have you lost?"

"Not enough." He tried to focus on the throb of his hard cock despite the fact that the entire left side of his leg was as equally numb as it was on fire. He grabbed her hands and bringing them to his lips, kissed them. Her palms were soft while her fingers were calloused and rough. He kept kissing and kissing them, wanting and needing her to give into his need. "I'm never letting you go. Not ever. This is just the beginning, do you not realize that?"

Her fingers trembled as she watched him. "You're delirious."

"The pain is incredibly bad," he choked out. It was actually getting bad. So bad his cock wasn't quite as hard as he wanted it to be. He gripped her hands in between more kisses. "Do you mind if I bite down on your hand? To help?"

A shaky breath escaped her. "My hand?"

"Yes."

"Will it help?"

"Yes."

"Then...do it."

This fantasy just kept getting better and better.

He squeezed her hands tightly, swallowing hard. "I'll only bite down once, but I will warn you, it will amount to the same amount of pain I'm feeling. Are you capable of handling it?"

She gave him a withering look. "I gave birth standing."

Damn. "Good. That means you can handle it." He dug his teeth against the side of her hand, savoring her warmth and softness and then bit down forcefully hard until he could feel his own chest tighten, watching her expression.

She winced, her chest heaving. "Ow!" She yanked her hand away, glared and smacked his shoulder twice. "How is this even helping you?! You're getting out of control!"

"You have no idea." She would have looked exactly the same if he pounded his cock into her. He grabbed her face and kissed her again, only this time, he slowed the pace and the pressure. He moved his tongue delicately against hers as a reward for the pain she took for him.

She moaned against him and her mouth softened.

He slid his hands down her neck to her shoulders and curved them to her breasts. Breasts. Beautiful breasts. They were his. At long last his. They were so full and soft even with the material in his way. He was never going back to 'normal' after this. Ever.

Knowing he couldn't fully undress her, seeing the doctor could arrive at any moment, he savagely shoved up her skirts. Forcing her onto her knees in between kisses by tugging her into place beside his good thigh, he slid both his hands up the smooth length of her thighs, reveling in how soft she was. He opted not to pinch or scrape her skin in need given she was responding to him without knowing what he was capable of.

Lord, I vow to protect her. For in doing this, I make her mine. Forever.

She broke away from their kiss, her chest heaving and managed, "For heaven's sake, you're injured and the doctor—"

"You're my doctor right now," he insisted, dragging her closer and sliding his finger into the folds of her wetness beneath her gown. "I need this. I need you." He stroked his finger against her, blindly looking for the proverbial nub he'd heard of. "Writhe for me."

She gasped and used one hand to steady herself against his shoulder. "I can't...I...Malcolm

...I..."

He buried his head against her corseted waist, biting into the material that separated them and fingered her harder. The pain in his thigh amplified his senses beyond tolerance as he flicked her. The nub controlling her gasps and the involuntary jerk of her hips was so delicate and so small against his large finger, he refused to believe it was capable of giving him *this* much command.

She bowed her head forward against him, fighting against what he knew her body wanted.

Withdrawing his finger from her folds, he smeared her wetness against his mouth and tongue, wanting to know what it would taste like. Salty and sweet. Like her. His hands trembled as he unbuttoned the flap of his trousers, shoved down his undergarments and pulled his rigid cock out, only exposing what was needed to make her his.

He laid back against the mattress and tangled linen, wincing against the blade that was oozing more blood. He didn't care. If he made love to her and died from blood loss, his life would at least be what it needed to be: real. Heatedly holding her gaze, he held up the length of his stiff cock at its root with both hands. "I'm yours if you want it."

Her chest heaved as her gaze went from his exposed cock to the dagger in his lower thigh, the wool of the trousers around it blood soaked. "Malcolm," she choked out, her features twisting in anguish. "I wouldn't deny you in any other circumstance, but I can't do this. I can't—"

He hissed out a breath, recognizing she had gone beyond what he had even hoped for. "Just watch me then. It's all I need to get me through this." He wet his hand with saliva and did something he hadn't done since he was eighteen. He masturbated.

Holding her stunned gaze, Malcolm used one large hand to hold the root of his cock and the other to jerk its midway to tip. He writhed in pain *and* pleasure as he worked his hand faster, his chest tightening against sensations he had long forgotten were worth feeling.

Knowing she hadn't once averted her gaze but was still watching him, he breathed out, "Your eyes haunt me into wanting to do things I swore I'd never do."

A shaky breath escaped her. Leona lowered herself to his side, carefully setting her body against the better half of him, and with trembling hands, touched his face.

Her submission was all his heart needed to burst. Fiercely burying her head against his waistcoat with one hand, he sped up stroking his cock beyond his own breath and control until he yelled out against the blinding glory of pulsing pleasure that was laced with pain. The pleasure of his cock became greater than the pain streaking through his thigh, making his breath catch in reverence of how the two battled for his senses.

His seed leaked from the tip, warning him its warmth would soon cover his entire hand and cock. He refused to stop stroking. He refused to give into knowing it was almost over. He gritted his teeth, prodding and jerking his cock into giving his entire body more spiraling spasms and enough seed to fill Leona's womb beyond holding.

Malcolm stiffened, knowing he was about to— "Leona, take me into your mouth," he choked. "If you feel anything for me, anything at all, I need you to—"

Her mouth was already on his cock, her hot wet mouth pressing down on whatever length she could fit into her mouth.

Jerking against the velvet of her tight mouth, he held her head and buried his cock into her throat as far as it would go. He tensed as his seed pulsed and filled her mouth. She gagged. He groaned in blurring disbelief that he had spurted so much into her mouth.

His hands fell away from her and onto the mattress. He drifted, his head and his body and his heart feeling as if it no longer existed. It didn't need to. It had experienced too much.

Leona sat up and using the linens wiped all of his seed from her mouth into it.

In between ragged breaths, he blindly shoved his cock away into his trousers and buttoned the flap then adjusted himself. He winced, realizing the dagger had moved with him. He pushed himself up on shaky arms and grabbed Leona, kissing her on the mouth hard. He refrained from nipping her lower lip.

To his surprise, she scrambled out of his arms and jogged over to the door. Unlocking it, she banged it open. Uneven breaths escaped her. Lingering by the door, she set both hands against flushed cheeks and made her way back over. "Why did you do that? Why did you...?"

Malcolm lifted his gaze to hers, feeling lightheaded. Everything was beginning to catch up to him. His arms trembled in an effort to hold himself up. The room swayed, and he didn't know if it was because of how Leona made him feel or because blood had been trickling out of the sides of the blade for too long.

He staggered, reaching out a heavy hand to her. "Would you believe me if I said you make me delirious? Now come here."

She was quiet for a moment, then slipped her hand into his.

Using whatever strength he had left within him, he yanked her down toward himself, forcing her to sit beside him on the mattress. He grazed the softness of her face with his fingers, watching his thumb edge along her cheek and then her lips. "If you haven't already guessed, I'm yours, and I'm damn well hoping you're mine. You better be mine."

She searched his face, confusion clouding her pretty features. "Malcolm, why did you—"

He curved his hand around the back of her neck and gently gripped it. "Because I wanted to ensure this was real. I needed to know you and your concern were real. Was it real?"

Her brows came together. "Of course it was real. What sort of stupid—"

He jerked her toward himself and covered her mouth with his, not wanting to talk. He worked his tongue against hers, refusing to stop until the doctor came or until he lost consciousness. Whichever came first.

"I hate to interrupt what appears to be an application of modern medicine—" Holbrook called out, "—but the doctor will be here in a few minutes thanks to a neighbor, who let Jacob and I borrow his carriage. We just got back."

Though not wanting to let Leona go out of fear he'd never get a chance to touch her again, Malcolm released her, still breathing hard from everything they had done. "Thank you for the kiss, Leona," he rumbled out. He needed that. He'd been waiting his whole life to feel...loved.

Lurching back, she frantically swept back hair that was falling into her eyes.

Striding toward them, Holbrook veered his gaze to Malcolm's leg. He let out a long whistle. "That certainly gives a whole new meaning to taking it in the leg, Brayton." Nudging Jacob who lingered close beside him, Holbrook prompted, "Give this poor man some gin, Jacob. Oh and uh...*Miss Webster, Brayton*...I just wanted to say...I kept this boy from hearing things that would have aged him by at least twenty years. So...*you're welcome.*"

Malcolm and Leona both cringed in unison.

Thumping his way over to Malcolm in silence, Jacob held out a full bottle of gin, his small chest lifting and falling in confusion.

Shit. "Thank you, Jacob." Reaching out for the bottle with a dignified flinch ignited by pain that was exhausting him beyond what he liked or wanted, Malcolm accepted it. He met the boy's gaze, trying to even his breathing. "Your mother's kisses make me feel better," he sheepishly offered.

Andrew snorted. "I bet they do."

Malcolm glared. "Make yourself useful, Andrew, and get more gin. I need to get drunk before the doctor gets here."

He hated needles and pins. It had the *opposite* effect of what he considered euphoria. They reminded him of the old tailor who used to come out to the cottage when he was fifteen and prick him with too many pins in all the wrong places. The old tailor smelled like urine and in between pinning wools and tweeds to Malcolm's body for measurements, the old man's cock would grow visibly hard from all the touching. The old man never did anything, but it wasn't a memory he liked. No needles or pins. "Bring two more bottles of gin. This first one here will be going mostly to the leg."

"More gin it is. I'll be right back." Saluting him, Holbrook jogged out.

Jacob openly gaped at the blade still sticking out of Malcolm's leg. He pointed. "Is that going to stay in your leg from now on?"

Malcolm coughed out a rough laugh and then winced from the exaggerated movement. "Uh...no. Not if I can help it, Jacob."

Jacob blinked. "Oh."

"You've seen more than enough," Leona interjected. "Don't look at it, Jacob. It's— Let's go back downstairs. Lord Brayton is a touch delirious." Scooting toward the edge of the bed, she picked Jacob up into her arms with a large breath and staggered. "Oh, for the love of butterflies. You're getting heavy." She winced and then stared down Malcolm, her cheeks and mouth visibly flushed from their kisses. "Hopefully the gin will remedy whatever I couldn't. And when you *do* recover from the doctor and the gin, *my lord*, you had better start talking. Are we understood in this?"

How was he even going to begin? He cleared his throat. "Yes, Leona. Perfectly."

"Good." She made her way to the door with Jacob, but gave up and set him down with a puff. "You're too heavy. Go on. We'll wait downstairs for the doctor."

Jacob darted out.

Leona finished walking to the door, hips swaying and skirts rustling.

Tilting his head, Malcolm enjoyed the view knowing it was his all his. "Leona."

She paused and glanced back at him.

He held up the bottle of gin. "To us. I thank you for that kiss. I needed it."

She gave him an exasperated look and left.

He smirked, gulped down several hearty mouthfuls of gin, letting it burn his tongue, throat and senses, and then merrily poured the rest of it onto the dagger and wound, letting it sizzle a breath out of him.

In that moment, it wasn't the pain he savored. It was knowing Leona was his. And he would damn well ensure she stayed his. Even if it meant he never told her the truth.

Even if it meant the '*le moment parfait*' never came.

LESSON TEN

Too many men have an invigorating

lack of decorum. Slap it out of them.

-The School of Gallantry

Early evening

Gently closing the door behind herself, knowing Jacob was *finally* asleep, Leona grudgingly folded the incredibly detailed lithograph. A lithograph with a trouserless young man splayed unceremoniously on a chair while being pleasured by two young women facing outward who used the friction of their bare bottoms to rub his cock into a squirting fountain while he looked out toward the observer in a glowing daze from in between them. Jacob had found the lithograph in their room hidden behind loose wainscoting he had been trying to push back into place. The cheap paper had been well folded when Jacob had padded over and handed it to her an hour earlier. His pinched lips and overly big eyes forced her to sit him down and explain everything.

Fortunately, she wasn't a prude and more than managed.

She turned to tip toe away from the door with it and jumped at see-ing Andrew standing behind her in the corridor. "You scared me," she choked out, almost smacking him in exasperation. She glared, unfolded the lithograph and snapped it out toward him. "My child bloody saw this. *He saw this!* You're fortunate Lord Brayton explained your little *business* in advance. Not that I forgive you."

Andrew's dark brows went up. "I was looking for that." He grabbed it, merrily folded it and tucked it into his pocket. "The paper isn't the best quality, but Achille Devéria is incredibly popular. It's worth five shillings."

"I'm surprised it's even worth that much."

He smirked. "So says the woman interested in fucking Brayton."

She gasped. "*Don't—*" Glancing at the closed door of the room she and Jacob were now sharing, she tapped a finger to her lips. "Do watch that tongue and be quiet. It took Jacob a whole hour to settle into bed. Aside from the lithograph, all he kept talking about was the blade sticking out of Brayton's leg. I feel like a horrible mother."

"You aren't a horrible mother. You've just involved yourself with horrible men. It happens." Andrew chuckled and kept his voice low as he slung on a wool cap and yanked on leather gloves. "Speaking of Brayton, I suggest you go see him. He has been asking for you since the doctor threaded him up. I have someplace to be, and don't know when I'll be back, so I'm afraid you'll be tending to him all night. I've already helped the poor bastard piss into the chamber pot, so no worries there. I also changed the dressing, so all you need to do is give him a cap full of lau-danum if he needs it. Fair warning...he is still royally tipped. Not as bad as he was earlier, but I've never seen him so damn helpless. So whatever you do, don't take advantage of the poor man." Andrew smirked, swiv-eled on his booted heel and strode down the corridor, disappearing down the candlelit stairwell.

Leona let out a soft breath, dreading the idea of facing Malcolm. He had certainly followed through on his whole sex, blood and bruises warning. And they hadn't even *had* sex. Maybe there was something wrong with him. Just as he said. That silver-haired female who had visited him asked her to be patient with him.

Which meant...the woman knew something Leona didn't. So what was it? And why did Malcolm fear telling her? She was almost scared to know.

Quietly making her way to Malcolm's bedchamber, she hesitated before his closed door and delicately traced all five of her fingers across its surface, desperately wishing she could better understand the man who was on the other side. She already knew she adored him. She also knew she would only be ripping her heart apart by pretending she didn't want to be with him. She did. He made her feel...special. Something she had always wanted to be in the eyes of far more than herself.

Swallowing back her own angst, she tapped on the panel of the wood, announcing herself. "Malcolm?" she quietly called. "Are you awake?" She paused. "Might I come in?"

There was a prolonged moment of silence, followed by an overly drawn out and delighted, "I *insist*, pigeon. Did you...*miss me?*"

This ought to be entertaining. Edging open the door, she stepped inside and purposefully left the door wide open. Lest either of them had any ideas.

A lone candle lit the dark room, set by a small bottle of laudanum on a crate. The unevenly nailed crate was tucked beside a lumpy mattress on the floor that had been shoved up against the wall. Malcolm was propped up against well-piled and well-fluffed pillows, his dark hair scattered across his forehead. A plain grey-wool robe was well bundled around his large frame, covering the oversized linen nightshirt that exposed his throat and small V leading to a a glimpse of a smooth upper chest. Fresh linen she delivered earlier to the doctor draped Malcolm's body to the waist.

His blue eyes, which appeared a touch hazy, brightened. He nudged himself onto his massive shoulder to look at her. "Leona, Leona, Leona."

He skimmed her calico gown. "It's late. Why are you still dressed? Remove all of that female stuff and...*come over here.* We're alone for the night, aren't we? Sleep with me. Get naked."

She pursed her lips. It was obvious he'd had more gin over the past few hours than laudanum. The laudanum would have put him to sleep, not encouraged him to further seduce. "I have to get up in the morning to start tackling duties around the house that include far more than cleaning. Now how about we give you a cap of laudanum so you can get some good sleep?"

He stared her down through a very visible haze. "Sleep is for ninnies. Now come here." He tapped at his chest, almost missing it. "I want you naked and *here*. Where you belong. With me. You're mine now."

Her heart ached knowing that even in this condition he wanted her near. It meant their need for each other was not only genuine but mutual. "I want to, Malcolm, believe me, but after what happened between us earlier, I would rather we not."

His features sobered. He lowered his gaze to his large hand and poked a scarred finger into the bundled linen beside his thigh. "But I...*enjoyed it.*"

That much was damn obvious. "I'm certainly pleased to hear you did. But let me preface that by saying I'm confused."

He didn't meet her gaze. "Confused?" His gruff voice hinted he had no idea what she was talking about. "By what?"

"You know full well what I'm talking about. You're coherent enough to have a conversation with me right now, which means you're also coherent enough to address my confusion. What happened between us five hours ago? Would you care to explain that to me?"

He puffed out a breath. "I'm a man, Leona."

"Oh, I know *that*. There was never any doubt about *that*."

He still didn't meet her gaze. "Pardon me and the fact that I have...*needs*," he grouched.

Sensing he was getting annoyed, she sighed, knowing it was best to be honest. "That whole situation made me beyond uncomfortable. *Beyond.* I'm still..."

Remembering the way he had tongued her and stroked himself in full view and how desperate he seemed to get her to pleasure him despite the blood and the dagger made her heart pound. If it had been any other man she would have twisted the blade in his leg, grabbed up her child and ran. Instead, she had morbidly taken his cock into her mouth to appease him and what appeared to be desperation. Which meant there was as something equally wrong with her as there was with him.

She blew out a breath. "It wasn't the right time or the right place and you know it. Nor were you physically— I was torn between wanting to be scared and— What you did was— Are you out of your mind?"

He muttered something in private annoyance, and still poking a finger into the linen, confessed, "Maybe I am. But you...this...I...I don't know what I'm doing, Leona. All right? I'm merely responding to how I feel when I'm around you. So don't...*Be nice.* I've never done this with a woman before. Not even in my own head. You're the first woman I ever allowed in my life and into my bed and I...Be nice."

She blinked rapidly in complete disbelief. Upon her life. Was he serious? She had remembered him mentioning not kissing anyone since he was eighteen, but she hadn't actually thought he was also a... "You've never been with a woman before?" she echoed. "Not *ever?*"

He grudgingly flopped his hand to the pillow beside him, giving her a withering look. "Go on. Laugh about it. Tell all of London my *cock* hasn't been *christened.* Do you think I care?" His voice got progressively louder and louder to ensure she got the point. "I'll have you know, *pigeon,* I was *waiting* for the right woman. And pardon me for thinking you were the *right woman.* Was I wrong in thinking it?" He stared, lowering his mildly stubbled chin. "Did I raise the entire fucking sail for a wind that doesn't exist? You tell me. You. Tell. Me."

Her skin prickled. Aside from the language, it was overwhelming to know out of all the women in the world, he'd chosen her. *Her*. Why...her? It made her want to panic because she didn't want to disappoint him anymore than she wanted to be disappointed *by* him.

She closed the door, sensing their conversation was about to get very involved and very loud. "You could have chosen a better time to seduce me, you know. You could have made it a little more...Oh, I don't know...*enticing?* Because a blade in the thigh with blood all over the place is more like Death's idea of romance."

He still stared with his chin lowered and slurred out, "Death? *Reaaaally?* Well, now, I guess *I'm* confused what *your* idea of *romance is*. You must be as pathetically ignorant about it as I am."

She pulled in her chin. "I beg your pardon."

He squinted as if she were disappearing. "Why did you put your entire mouth on my cock if you didn't want it?"

She gasped, feeling her entire face burn. "You didn't give me much of a choice. You-you... *insisted*. You wanted me to do it!"

He snorted. "If I could get you to do *everything* I wanted you to do, we wouldn't be having this conversation. We'd be getting you pregnant right now so Jacob could have a sibling and head straight to Persia."

Of all the— She glared. "Don't make me march over to that bed and poke that wound. I'll do it. I'll hurt you. I'll treat you like a creditor."

His husky features darkened. He slowly slid the linens away from himself, tossed it to his knees and presented his left thigh buried beneath his wool robe and night-shirt. "By all means. *Do it.* Make me want you more. I dare you."

She rolled her eyes. This man was like Satan and a few hundred angels combined. "There is something seriously wrong with you."

He paused and shifted his jaw. Not meeting her gaze, he half-nodded and eventually breathed out, "I don't need this right now, Leona. I really don't. The gin is wearing off and I..." He was quiet for a moment, his features twisting. "I'm well aware there is something wrong with me.

You don't need to fling it. Now go. Leave. I'm tired and...need the rest."
He reached down for the linen with an uncooperative hand and swatted
fingers toward the linen well beyond his reach. He winced but kept trying. And trying. And...trying.

Her heart dropped to her knees then the floor. He needed her. And
not just for the linens. She trailed over to him, lowering herself to the
mattress and carefully taking the edges of the rumpled linen around his
feet, pulled it gently up and over him to the waist. She leaned in close,
the sharp lingering scent of gin penetrating the air around her as she
tucked the linen around his large frame and smoothed everything into
place.

She sighed. "I'm sorry. I'm trying to understand you, not hurt you.
I...I like you. A lot. Maybe even more than a lot. And I want to understand you. Is that wrong of me?"

He stilled and captured her gaze, his broad chest lifting and falling
unevenly.

Scooting closer to him, until she was tucked beside his good side, hip
to hip, she eventually murmured, "If you don't need any laudanum, I'll
just stay with you until you fall asleep."

His entire arm jumped around her, startling her. Tightening his
muscled hold on her shoulder to ensure she was tucked closely against
him, he sat them both against the pillows and rigidly dragged his free
hand through her hair, tugging it loose from her pins. "If you stay," he
rasped into her ear, "I won't sleep. Especially after hearing you say what
you just did. Because now I...I only want to think of all the ways I can
get you to love me. Because I want you to, Leona. I want you to love me
so fucking much, you'd be willing to accept what I am. Can't you? Won't
you?"

She breathed lightly between parted lips, unable to resist everything
he was. Her thoughts and her body felt hazy as if she had also been taken
by three bottles of gin. She actually felt like that dreamy, open-mouthed
girl she thought she abandoned so many, many years ago. The one who

wanted to naïvely believe in the beauty of the whole world until her life had been ripped from her hands and replaced with the shame of knowing she was nothing more than the last sardine in a tin no one wanted.

"Leona," he whispered. "Be mine."

In that moment, and with his unspoken promise of all the things to come, she knew she already loved him. She already loved him for being so good, so honorable, so gruff, so stupid, so determined and so everything that wasn't perfect. He didn't need to be perfect. He was perfect being *imperfect.*

The warmth of his lips dragged across her cheek as he bent his head closely to hers. His bottom teeth gently nipped their way down, down to her throat as he tightened his hold. His other hand came up and one by one, he undid the hooks on her gown. "I can be gentle," he murmured. "I can. I can do this the way any normal man can. And I will. For you, I will."

Her head heavily lulled back against his massive shoulder as he continued to unhook her to the waist, exposing her corset and chemise. A dream within a dream.

Malcolm lowered her to the mattress, staggering against the effects of the gin, and skimmed his hands down her throat. He peeled her sleeves off her shoulders and yanked them off. Pushing the gown off her hips, he shoved it past her knees.

In between heavy breaths, he skimmed his hands down her bare arms and toward her breasts hidden beneath the rigid corset. He tugged at it from the top and then the sides and paused. Then tugged again. He searched her face. "How the hell do you take this off?" he rasped. "I want it off. Why won't it come off?"

A choked laugh escaped her. "There are lacings in the back."

"Lacings?" His brows came together as he tilted her away and dug his hands beneath her, his fingers cascading down the expanse of sixteen ridges of tightened laces. He seethed out a breath. "Rot me, this is going to take forever. Why the blazes are you wearing this? It's impractical."

She bit back a smile. "Tell that to society."

He muttered something and staggered to sit up. He winced and wagged his fingers toward her. "I'm going to try to do this without using my teeth. Sit up. We're doing this."

She awkwardly sat up and peered at him from over her bare shoulder, the strip of her chemise grazing her chin. "Are you...*certain* you want to do this? You're still recovering, you know. Aren't you in pain?"

"Pain and I are good friends, Leona. Very good friends. Now let me focus." He aggressively tugged and yanked out the lacings, one by one by one. He gritted his teeth and kept tugging and pulling and tugging in an attempt to loosen them. "I damn well want to...stab whoever....invented this in the...*neck*. Why isn't this— How am I supposed to—"

"Did you untie the lace at the bottom, *pigeon*?" she offered, quirking her brow.

He yanked it loose in exasperation. "This damn thing outwitted me."

Malcolm loosened the lacing with three separate tugs, gaping it wide open. Pulling it up over her arms and head, he whipped it across the room. He bundled the chemise up past her thighs and yanked it up and over her head, as well, tossing it to the floor, as well.

He paused and let out a whistle. "Leona, I just stopped breathing."

She bit her lip knowing he was staring at her naked body.

His hot hands cupped her breasts and rounded them, sending a shiver through her.

"Come here." He captured her mouth and kissed her for a long, roaming moment, circling his tongue against hers with precise and controlled intent. Breaking their kiss, he lowered his disheveled head down to each of her nipples, letting his tongue flick across each until she was covered with goose flesh.

Her body ached for far, far more as he licked and kissed the curve of each breast until she was out of breath. She dragged her hands into his thick, soft hair and instinctively tightened her hold on it, tugging it hard to demand he push his length into her. "I'm ready," she breathed.

He groaned and choked out against her skin with the heat of his breath, "Keep it...civil. The gin is fading fast and I'm trying to—"

She tugged on his hair even harder, silently commanding him to ride her.

A savage breath escaped him. He released her, gave her a heated, long look of reprimand, then leaned over and blew out the candle, leaving them in complete darkness. "No more damn tugging of the hair," he instructed in a hard tone. "Or this ends. Do you hear me?"

She paused, her eyes blurring from the darkness. Ryder had always done the same thing. She tried not to panic. "Why did you— I wanted to see you."

"No."

"Aren't you going to let me take off your clothes?"

"No. Not tonight."

"But I wanted to—"

"Not tonight." He fell back onto the pillows, and in the darkness, dragged his nightshirt up to expose his cock. He tugged her leg up and over his hips, positioning her carefully so the wound remained untouched. "For your sake, don't rile me anymore than I already am," he finally said, his tone raw. "We're doing this your way tonight. Because I'm a gentleman like that. All right? No tugging, no biting, no pinching, and *no* touching of my wound. Keep your hands to my arms or my chest at all times. That will ensure this doesn't get out of hand."

She walked her fingers up his still robed chest. "Since when does the virgin instruct the rake?"

He grabbed her fingers and stilled them. "I may be a virgin, pigeon, but that doesn't make me any less dangerous. Keep it civil. Or I promise I'll end up spanking you."

She paused. "Spanking me—"

"*Raw.* We'll talk about the possibility of it later." He reached down between them in the darkness and rigidly holding his cock, found her opening. Setting it against her wetness, he grabbed her hips, taking full command, and yanked her fully down onto himself hard.

They both gasped and stilled.

She could feel the restraint coiled in his body as she slowly rode his length in an effort to give them both pleasure. She closed her eyes in complete disbelief as magnificent sensations gripped more than her body. It gripped her soul. He was hers and she was his. This moment marked it.

Her grabbed both her hands in the darkness and entwined his large fingers between hers, holding them tight. "In this moment, I thee wed," he said in a choked tone.

She had never felt more cherished. He might as well have confessed that he was madly in love with her. "In this moment," she choked back, "I accept being yours."

He rolled his hips into her, holding her upright with his hands. "Mine."

"Yours." She rolled her own hips against his, gripping his hands harder in an effort to keep her rhythm slow. She wanted the core tightening sensations to last. She wanted *this* to last. Because it was more than pleasure. She could feel it in his body and in his breaths. They were making love.

"Too slow, Leona," he seethed out, his chest heaving beneath her. "Move that body faster before I split open the threads holding me together, dig my teeth into your shoulder without mercy and take over. Is that what you want?"

She tsked, but entertained his request all the same. She broke her hold on their hands and caressing the strong tendons of his exposed throat, slowly set each hand against his shoulders. Capturing his lips with her own and tonguing him deeply until they were both frantic, she pumped her wetness harder and harder against his rigid length, angling herself to ensure his cock hit her nub. She gave in to ecstasy, riding him faster. She trembled from the realization that the glorious release awaiting her was just the beginning. He. This. It was just the beginning.

He groaned against her mouth, his large fingers digging viciously into her hips. He nipped her lower lip. Hard.

She winced against him and the pain, momentarily drawn out of pleasure, and tapped at his rough hands that kept digging far too deeply into her skin. "Malcolm," she managed against his mouth. She paused, realizing the acrid tinge of blood streaked her tongue. Her lip. It was bleeding. "Aside from my lip, which is damn well bleeding, can you try not to—"

He licked her lip as if to remedy it and choked out, "I'm trying. Believe me. It's not easy. It's not—" He thrust frantically up into her, his breaths puffing out. "I didn't bite your lip *that* hard. You said you gave birth standing. Now take it."

Her body gave into those deep thrusts that hit her nub so perfectly. She no longer could focus on her lower lip. There was something erotic about mixing the pleasure with a bit of pain. It made the pleasure all the more perfect. Her core tightened against the rapid sensations, and she cried out, her body trembling in response to the sweeping bloom.

He thrust up into her one last time and yelled out in the darkness of the room, stilling beneath her as his cock pulsed its seed into her. He shuddered and yanked her down onto his heaving chest, squeezing the very breath out of her as he tightened his hold beyond crushing.

"I would curse, but it wouldn't be right," he said in between pants. "Leona, that was...*everything*. And more."

She flinched against the crushing grip, no longer enjoying the bloom or the glow. "Too tight," she managed, her face mashed against his chest. "I can't— I can't breathe."

He loosened his hold but didn't let go. "I can't breathe, either. So we're even. How is that lip of yours?"

She slid her tongue over her bottom lip, which was now only a touch sore. "It's no longer bleeding, if that is what you're asking."

"Good." He sounded pleased. He nestled his chin against her head and was quiet for a long moment. "Leona?"

She sighed and nestled against his sizable chest, reveling in it and smoothed her entire hand against his wool robe. "Yes?"

He hesitated. "I'll get you that ring we earlier spoke of. We'll get married at a Christian church here in London before we go to Persia. It'll take us about two months to get there. But once we do—"

She groaned against him, wishing he wouldn't insist on dragging her onto a boat. "Malcolm. I already told you how I feel about going anywhere near water."

"You have nothing to fear. I'll be with you."

"That won't change the depth or the temperature of the water. I'm not going to Persia."

He peered down at her in the darkness that was dulled by the light of the moon outside the window. "It's where my entire life is. It's where—"

"Can't we stay here?" She softened her voice in an effort to beguile him. "Can't you find another position outside of being an admiral to a bunch of Persians?"

He stiffened beneath her. "Leona, I have to go back. Aside from the fact that those 'Persians' are my family, admiral is who I am. An entire country, and its leaders, depend on my return. Does that mean nothing to you?"

A soft breath escaped her. "I didn't say it meant nothing to me. It does. I simply...a boat..." Her throat tightened at the thought of being surrounded by water. "I've tried more than a few times, Malcolm. Even as recent as a year ago when Jacob wanted to paddle in a small boat across the Thames. The *Thames*. That isn't even a sliver of the size of the ocean and I was heaving until I almost lost consciousness. I can't do it. I can't."

His voice hardened. "Can't or won't?"

"Can't *and* won't." She almost shook him. "My fear is real, Malcolm. *Real.* Do you honestly think I would counterfeit such a thing? Do you honestly think—"

"What if I teach you how to swim?"

"That isn't the problem. Can you teach a boat how to float when it hits the rocks?"

"Leona, the danger is well worth the reward."

"Is it? My father *died* somewhere out there. His bones are *still* in that water. A water I have no intention on going near. Ever. Not ever. I'm not—"

He gripped her shoulders hard. "Leona. I'm facing my fears in your name. I expect you to do the same for me."

She glared. "I don't know what sort of *fears* you're talking about, but—"

"Don't chastise me. Don't." His chest rose and fell unevenly. "What the hell is this? Are you really mine? Or is this a ploy to be rid of me?"

She groaned again. "Malcolm, I am yours. I wouldn't have crawled into your bed if I wasn't. But I— A boat isn't safe! A boat isn't—"

"I'll tell you what isn't safe," he bit out. "Your damn association with me." He lifted her up and off himself, and unceremoniously tossed her onto the mattress. "You're getting on that damn boat or we're done. Is that what you want?"

She popped out a hand and caught herself from rolling naked off the end of the mattress. She glanced toward him in the shadows, her heart pounding. "I'm confessing my greatest fear to you and you're setting ultimatums?"

He dragged his nightshirt and robe over himself, shifting away from her. "Damn right I am." He hunkered back against the pillows, staring out into the darkness before him. "We can't be together, Leona, unless you get on that boat. And let me tell you why. I'd be willing to give up my position as admiral for you and stay here in England until we both grow old and die, but the reality is, if you can't face your worst fear by getting on that damn boat, you're not ready to face me. You're not ready to face what I really am and will always be. You're not. You're fucking not. Getting on a boat is *nothing* compared to what I am."

Her breath burned in her throat. She grew numb from the reality that he was setting ultimatums not only with her own fears but her heart. Her nostrils flared as she snatched up her chemise and yanked it over her nude body. "It appears the real Lord Brayton has finally made a bow and introduced himself."

He continued to stare out. "I can say the same about you," he replied in a low tone, taut with anger. "How is it you're willing to take on a cart full of men for a toy bear but can't get on a boat for me? Can you explain that to me, Leona? Because the woman I thought I knew is fearless. The woman I want and need in my life *should* be fearless. It's the only way you and I can be together. Be the damn leopard I need you to be. Because if I had wanted a mere kitten, I would have settled down years ago."

She narrowed her gaze and snatched up her gown that was bundled on the bed. "Oh, yes. It must be so nice being all manly and burly and not knowing anything about real fear. It must be nice flexing a muscle at even the sea and watching the whole world bow."

He was quiet.

She stalked over to the other side of the room, snatching up her mangled corset. "Setting ultimatums and belittling my fears in order to get what you want isn't love, Malcolm. It's blackmail. I hope you know the difference." She refrained from stomping over to the door that was barely outlined in the darkness.

"Where are you going?" he demanded.

Yanking open the door, she glanced back. "To bed."

He was now watching her. Not even the shadows could hide it. "I didn't ask you to leave."

She swallowed. "I didn't need permission to. In fact, I may not be around come morning. I thought I'd just say that."

"I see." He stared her down. "I received word not even an hour ago that no court in England will entertain your Mr. Blake or whatever lawyer he hires. He is being barred from every last bench in not only London but England. Which means your son will remain in your arms thanks to me. Thanks. To. *Me*. And this is how you reward me, Leona? By threatening to leave after I just gave you my body and my heart? Is this the sort of woman you are?"

Anguish seized her. He had just confessed his...love. His heart. He was giving it to her. As if she were worthy of it.

He shifted his jaw and averted his gaze again. He said nothing more.

A shaky breath escaped her. "Malcolm, I..." Another shaky breath escaped her. "Thank you. Thank you for letting me keep what I cherish most: my boy. As for your heart, I wish to assure you with all of *my* heart that I—"

"*Don't*." He adjusted the linens over himself. "Don't you dare. I would rather you not say words that can never be erased from my mind only to find I'm going to Persia without you. Because I am getting on that boat, Leona. I have to. An entire nation depends on it."

She wanted to be angry with him, but given what he did to keep her son in her hands, she owed him just enough not to be bitter. She owed him just enough to face the one fear she hadn't been able to face since she was twelve years old. Water.

Tears burned her eyes. More than a nation was depending on her getting on the boat. Their relationship depended on it. And she knew enough about herself to say she did agree with him. The danger was well worth the reward. She was tired of living on an island. She needed to swim for what she wanted. And she wanted this. She wanted him and that beautiful strength. She needed it and wanted him to teach it to her son.

She dug her nails into her palm and choked out, "I'll get on that boat. Given what you did for Jacob and me, I'll—"

"How kind of you, Miss Webster. I appreciate that." His tone indicated otherwise. "What made you change your mind? Have you decided you're in love with me? Or have you decided no one else will pay your bills?"

She attempted to throttle her confused emotions into order. "You're being cruel."

He slowly shook his head. "No. If a bleeding lip and a boat on water offends you so easily, I really don't stand a chance. You'll never love me. Not in the way I need you to."

She dragged in uneven breaths. "You aren't making any sense. You aren't—"

"Nothing about me makes sense, Leona. No one knows that more than I." He let out a harsh breath. "Go to bed. Don't...don't let our argument taint what we shared tonight. When I'm ready, we'll talk another time. Because I can't do this right now."

"But—"

"Go," he insisted. "I need the rest."

Knowing he was pushing her out, she tried to steady her voice and keep it from cracking. "Are you certain you don't need any laudanum?"

"Quite."

She felt herself inwardly breaking. Even if she did face her fears and get on that ship, whatever did he mean she wouldn't be able to face *him*? She was so confused.

Unable and no longer wanting to even think, she choked out, "I do love you. You've been close to perfect up until now. To not only me but Jacob. I only wish you'd trust me more. Despite what you think, there is really only one thing keeping us apart: *you*. Whatever you're not telling me, whatever it is you're hiding, please know I'm strong enough to take it. Trust that. But I can't hold a weight you plan on carrying all on your own. You have to trust me, Malcolm, if we are ever going to push past this. If you feel *anything* for me, and I know you do, I'm asking you to trust me."

He said nothing.

She dragged in a breath, knowing he was pushing her away. "I wish you a good night."

His voice softened by more than a touch. "Good night...pigeon."

The raw softening of that voice and endearment wasn't enough to kill all doubts or the fact that he still had told her nothing. She hesitated, waiting for him to say something. Anything. When he didn't, she turned and quietly closed the door, feeling as if she were closing it on her heart.

LESSON ELEVEN

Do you want her or not?

-The School of Gallantry

Days later, early morning
On the doorstep of James Zachery Thayer

Malcolm wanted to go in, but he couldn't bring himself to do it. He couldn't. By going in, and seeing his brother, he would be changing the one thing he had always fought to be: his own man. A normal man. A man who didn't share the same face or the same desires with...another.

After countless minutes ticked by, Malcolm finally turned away from the door. He hobbled against the tightly bundled cloth that bound his healing wound in place beneath his trousers and sat with a wince on the top stone step facing out toward the street of a quiet neighborhood in London belonging to the middle classes.

Much like him, James had learned to live in modesty. Their father had instilled it into them.

Leaning forward and fully stretching his one leg for comfort, Malcolm propped up the collar of his morning coat, pulled out his prayer book from his pocket and let out a breath, paging through Latin words that in that moment made no sense. His faith wasn't what it needed to be. He couldn't keep pushing the entire world away. It was going to kill him.

The door behind him creaked open, making him pause.

He didn't have to glance back to know who it was.

Malcolm's chest tightened as the door closed and the towering figure of his brother casually hunkered down beside him, bumping his large shoulder into his.

"Dorothea told me you were in London," James said. "I was hoping you would come by."

Malcolm closed his prayer book, tightening his hold on it to inwardly draw strength from it, and veered his gaze to his twin.

Ice blue eyes with piercing concern and gruff features that mirrored his own right down to everything but the scar, angled closer. "I'm sorry about the way we parted," James admitted.

Malcolm shrugged, trying to pretend it was nothing. Even though it was everything.

James grabbed Malcolm's face and shook it. "I know why you did what you did, damn you. Dorothea told me everything. And you're a better brother than I. And I...I appreciate it. I was far too young to be responsible with what I wanted to share with her. Dorothea and I have always been close. Almost closer than you and I, which is unacceptable. I've pushed boundaries I shouldn't have touched and I'm admitting it. I'm more responsible with what I am. You'd be proud."

Malcolm tugged him close and tightened his hold, letting out the breath he felt he'd been holding since he was eighteen. "I thought about you so damn often."

"I thought about you every single day. Your voice was the one that always pulled me away from doing things I knew you would have never approved of. You were always the better half of us. And I thank you for that. I'm not doing half of what I used to. I found my level of...normal. And I'm happy with it."

Dragging himself away, Malcolm sighed. It would seem thirteen years had finally knocked some sense into his brother. "What about the pistols you and she play with?"

James smirked. "Were you spying on us?"

"Maybe."

"Your version of maybe is always yes."

"Maybe."

James rammed his elbow into Malcolm, making Malcolm wince. "Someone over on Charlotte Street told me you're going to that school everyone is talking about. The one Madame de Maitenon is opening. Are you?"

Malcolm groaned and tapped the closed prayer book against his forehead. "I'm supposed to be starting in a few days thanks to a Persian prince who thinks he owns more than Persia. How did you— Are you telling me people know?"

"Only the ones who take a keen interest in Madame. Be careful. You're not like these other men. She won't be able to help you in the way you think."

Malcolm eyed him. "She already has. I'm here because of her."

James paused. "What do you mean?"

Malcolm smoothed a hand over his prayer book before tucking it back into his pocket. "She told me the only way I was going to be able to face what I am is by accepting what I am. And I've decided she is right. I'm done fighting it. Prior to going to the monastery, you told me I would never be anything but what I already am. And you were right. This is who I am. I have to accept it."

His brother slowly grinned. "I like being right."

"I know you do."

James smacked his hands together and let out an astounded laugh. "I don't believe it! After all the nagging you put me through for years and years and— Do you have *any* idea what this means? Jesus Christ, you and

I are going to take over the Whipping Society and burn London to the ground. We're going to—"

"No. No, no, no. Keep sweet Jesus and your society out of this. There will be *no* burning of London. I leave in a few weeks."

"*Annnnd...it's* back to boring." James puffed out a breath. "I thought you wanted to be a fellow earl of the lash? I thought—"

"I do. But..." Malcolm hesitated. "It's a touch complicated. I basically plan to get married to a woman who is *nothing* like your Dorothea or the people you associate with. Leona is...she is incredibly passionate and well-grounded and stunning and everything I could ever want her to be, but...she isn't our sort of passionate, if you know what I mean. I will have to either entirely give up what I am and hide it over the course of our marriage or altogether risk losing her. Neither of which are an option. So the question is...what happens next?"

Those dark brows went up. James gaped. "You've bloody *involved* yourself with a milk-and- water female? Are you *fucking mad?*"

Cringing, Malcolm offered, "She has more milk than water."

James smacked him hard upside the head.

Malcolm winced, accepting the reprimand. He deserved it. "Ow."

"*End it,*" James bit out. "She won't ever accept you and you'll be miserable for the rest of your life. Is that what you want?"

Malcolm glared. "I'm already in love with her, damn you. So avoiding misery really isn't an option. *I'm already miserable!*"

James muttered something with the shake of his head and shifted against the landing they sat on. "You always were a ponce." He sighed. "How far have you tried to take her tolerance of pain?"

A snort escaped Malcolm. "Not very. I bit her damn lip and her hand and got reprimanded both times. She isn't even *remotely* interested."

"Are you certain?"

"Quite."

James puffed out a breath. "You won't be able to train her. She may tolerate a few spankings here and there, but...these milk-and-water females like their pleasure in the guise of too much honey and not enough blade. Which means you'll have to focus on getting her to deliver all the pain. Is that something you'd be willing to work with? Are you fine with that?"

Malcolm rolled his tongue inside his mouth, knowing he had *always* preferred receiving pain more than giving it. It wasn't a loss. At all. "I'm more than fine with it. You damn well know that. Better to receive than to give, I say."

"Good." James patted Malcolm's knee. "You still have to train her lest you end up dead. We had one of those last week." He let out a low whistle. "It made the newspapers, which miffed Mrs. Berkley to damn pieces given he was part of the club and made us look like— This fucking moron took on a milk-and-water female prostitute and when he forced her into stabbing him in the name of pain, she panicked and darted out of his house so damn fast, she left him tied to the bed. He bled out in less than four hours before anyone could find him. You don't want that."

"Uh...no. I don't."

"Exactly. You may want to start your girl with techniques that don't involve any marks, bruises or blood. Then scale the wall from there and see where it takes you. A little at a time. I myself don't actually specialize in soft play, so you're going to have to get advice elsewhere." James smirked. "Maybe at your so-called...*school?* Madame knows soft."

"That woman knows more than soft. Have you met her?"

"No. I only know what Mrs. Berkley wags at me. What was she like?"

"Brilliant. I liked her." Throwing back his head, Malcolm stared up at the cloud-ridden, grey sky that threatened to release rain. "Madame mentioned I needed to wait for the perfect moment to reveal myself."

James wrapped an arm around him and jostled him. "There is no perfect moment. Not given what we are. Spend a lot more time with her. Get her to feel more comfortable with the idea of her giving you pain and then...*hit her.*"

Malcolm paused.

James chuckled. "Not in that way. You know...with the news."
Malcolm sighed.

****

Later that afternoon

The best cure to keep one's mind fully occupied was to scrub the very
floor she was tired of walking on. It was dirty, anyway. Leona dipped the
large rag into the tin bucket, splashing soapy water across the parlor
floor, and hitching up her skirts to allow better movement, slapped it
onto the wooden planks she earlier swept.

She then scrubbed and washed and scrubbed and washed, scooting
her way across the length of the floor, only stopping on occasion to dip
the filthy rag back into the soapy water and start again.

Jacob ran into the room, his small booted feet echoing as he rounded
her. He bustled over to the far side of the room and yanked open one of
several trunks, throwing everything out of it.

Leona paused on all fours and glanced over at him. "Jacob, that isn't
yours."

"I know," he called back.

"What are you doing?"

"Looking." He buried his head far forward into the trunk, his feet
scrambling in an effort to balance himself as he lifted something out. He
turned toward her and triumphantly held up a checkered board in one
hand and a carved wooden box in the other. "Malcolm told me to get it.
We're all going to play right now. You, me, and Malcolm. Chess re-
quires three players. *Three.* Malcolm said so. Put away the bucket, Mama. Hurry up. Before Malcolm gets here."

She sighed, sat back on the heels of her slippers and flopped the rag
into the tin bucket. She didn't even know how to play chess. Only
draughts. "I'll play later. I have to finish washing the floor."

"Wash it later. We *have* to play. Malcolm said so." Jacob scampered over and in the middle of the floor, set down the board and sat cross-legged, opening the wooden box. He dumped out all the pieces into his lap and dug through them, setting the black and ivory pieces all randomly onto the wooden board. "Mama, I'm waiting."

Despite herself, Leona allowed for a smile and swiped her hands into her apron. Pushing up onto her feet, she abandoned her bucket and walked over to the middle of the floor. She sat beside Jacob and peered at the organization he was doing.

His little fingers set the black and ivory pieces in between the painted squares, alternating the colors all on one side of the board to create a wall, which he nudged as closely together as possible. He plucked up a piece and held it up. "It looks like a horse, Mama. Look. See its head?" He wagged it in the air.

Leona took the piece and pretended to gallop it through the air. "Its legs appear to be missing," she chided. "Whatever shall we do?"

Jacob tsked. "It isn't supposed to have legs, Mama." He took the piece back and trotted it across the board. "It balances better this way. See?" His hair fell into his eyes as he continued trotting it.

Reaching out her hand to brush away the hair from his eyes, Leona's heart squeezed knowing she didn't have to worry about Ryder anymore. It was just him and her and—

Heavy booted steps crossing toward them made her look up and drop her hand away. Her breath caught.

Malcolm lowered himself to the floor beside them and stretched out long, trouser-clad legs beside them. He winced, giving away that the healing wound hidden from sight still bothered him. He let out a calming breath as if adjusting to the discomfort. Tugging his morning coat around himself, he then propped up on an elbow, to ensure he was close beside her and tilted his dark head toward her, his blue eyes brightening. "Good afternoon, pigeon."

Her heart skipped. She had grown stupidly accustomed to that endearment. Strangely, over the past few days, he acted as if nothing had happened. Absolutely nothing. As if they hadn't argued. As if they had made love and were now merrily heading straight for the altar.

Men. She adjusted her bundled hair and quirked a brow. "You appear incredibly cheerful."

His mouth quirked. "I spent the entire morning and early afternoon with my brother. I haven't seen him in thirteen years. It was nice."

Her brows went up. "You have a brother?"

He nodded, averting his gaze. "Yes. And when I'm crazy enough to do it, I'll introduce you. But first, you have to get used to me." He cleared his throat and averting his attention to Jacob, pointed to the board. "The black and white pieces have to be separated, Jacob. The black pieces go on one side of the board and the white pieces on the other side."

Jacob blinked and set the horse he was playing with onto the middle of the checkered board. "Why separate the blacks from the whites? They want to be together. Look. Look how happy they are." He nudged them all even closer, no longer keeping them in their squares. "It's a city. Everyone likes each other. And if they don't follow the rules, they go back into the box."

Malcolm smirked. "It's genius. I don't know how I didn't come up with it." He eyed the board. "I have an idea. How about today we play chess your way and tomorrow, we play chess the way everyone else plays it?"

Jacob perked. "Yes!" Jacob squinted at the pieces and gathered a few up, holding it out to Malcolm. "These are for you. Don't lose them."

With the bow of his head, Malcolm took the four pieces and splayed out his large hand. "Thank you. Now what?"

"Now you have to give them all names. They can't be real until they have names."

Leona couldn't help but inwardly melt watching them both interact. This man was a natural with children. It made her want at least three more. Which meant…Persia. With him at her side, fear wouldn't exist. Biting her lip, she leaned closer to Malcolm's shoulder, pretending to only be interested in the pieces in his large hand. "I'm very good with names."

"I bet you are," Malcolm drawled. "I remember the sort of names you came up with for the creditors on the street. Rumpot was my favorite."

She nudged him with her shoulder. "Cease." She tapped on each piece. "This here is Anna, Beatrice, Mary and…Sarah."

Malcolm's gaze flicked up to her face. "There should be at least one male in this crowd." He rattled the pieces. "Where is he?"

Leona shrugged, trying to remain serious. "I don't see him."

Jacob leaned in and scooped up the pieces. "It's time for them to sleep." Jacob shoved them all into the box, including the ones on the board. He closed the lid and then gathered the board and box and stumbled to his feet. "I'll go show Andrew."

Malcolm lifted a brow. "Andrew is still sleeping."

Jacob sighed. "Is that all he ever does? I'll go wake him up. He won't mind. I've done it before." He turned and with the checkered board hefted under one arm and the box under the other, he trudged out. "I'll be back in thirteen minutes," he called out over his shoulder.

"Should we stop him?" Leona chided.

"No. Andrew had to be somewhere in an hour anyway." Malcolm hesitated and edged in closer. "Leona?"

She paused. "Yes?"

He searched her face. "I don't want us arguing ever again. It's not who we are."

Her skin prickled in awareness. She half-nodded. "I agree."

He was quiet for a moment then murmured, "*Deltangam.*"

She leaned in. "What does that mean?"

"It's what I carved into the wall. It means…my heart is tight." He averted his gaze. "It's uh…it's how I feel when I'm around you."

A deep ache almost overtook her ability to breath. "I feel the same."

His gaze veered back to hers. "Do you?"

She nodded. "Yes."

"Good. I needed to know." He wet his lips and pushed himself up into a sitting position. He eased out a long breath and then smoothed his cravat before patting his leg. "Can you lean on this with both hands? It needs attention."

Her brows came together. Realizing his large hand patted the muscled thigh that was still recovering, she flicked her gaze to his. "You don't want me leaning on that, Malcolm."

His features tightened. He patted his thigh again. "I can take it. Start with one hand and lean into it."

Her lips parted. "Lean into it? Aren't there still threads in your leg?"

He shrugged. "Only a few. Lean into it. And then kiss me. I need you to kiss me."

Something wasn't right. She lowered her chin. "I'm not leaning into it."

He shifted his jaw. "But I'm asking you to. I want you to."

"And I'm telling you I won't. I'll hurt you."

"I know."

"You know?"

"Yes. I know. Now lean into it, pigeon. Go on. Hurt me." His eyes brightened. "It makes me feel alive."

This was...unusual. She edged back, scooting her bum away from where he sat. "Malcolm, if I didn't know any better, I'd say you enjoy being in pain."

"Exactly." He met her gaze, the amusement fading. "Are you fine with that?"

She swallowed. "I don't...I don't understand."

He sighed and reaching for her, grabbed her waist and dragged her back toward himself. Taking her hand, he set it against his thigh and pressed her hand into it. He drew in a ragged breath through his teeth, clearly struggling to breathe his way through the discomfort and then said in a low tone, "It's like sex when you do it. Every time you press, it makes me want it more."

She jerked her hand away, her heart pounding. "Malcolm, what is this? This...I...this isn't..."

He grabbed her hand back hard and bringing it to his lips savagely kissed it, holding her gaze. "This is who I am, Leona. And it would be the greatest honor I have *ever* known if you would share my life and bestow me with the sort of pain I deserve."

She gasped and yanked her hand away from his. She scrambled up onto her feet and stumbled, her chest heaving. Now she understood. He enjoyed having the dagger in him. He had enjoyed it so much he had pleasured himself before her very eyes proving it.

Malcolm lifted somber eyes to hers, remaining on the floor. "Take all the time you need to understand it, Leona. It took me my entire life to understand it. Simply know, that when we marry, our lives will be like any other. I will honor and cherish you and be the father you expect me to be. In the bedchamber, however, I will expect a little more than pleasure. I'll ease you into it when we start. I wish to assure you, I'm softer in my tastes. I won't need a dagger in my leg. That was actually a bit much, even for me, but...crops would be nice. They wouldn't be for you, of course. Only me."

Her throat tightened in panic. A crop wasn't even pleasure. Nor was it a way of giving love. It was nothing but...pain. Something she could *never* do. Not even to someone she hated.

Still staying on the floor, Malcolm grudgingly met her gaze. "Leona. Talk to me. You're too quiet and I don't like the look on your face."

Setting a trembling hand against her mouth, she choked out, "I can't do this. It isn't—"

"Normal. I know." A breath escaped him. He pushed himself up from the floor, his features twisting as he righted himself and fully stood. He reached out for her, that large scarred hand whispering of all the things he'd done to himself. "Come here."

She shook her head and kept shaking it, stepping back.

He dropped his hand heavily to his side and stared. "Don't treat me like this. Don't act like you're suddenly scared of me. I'm still the same man."

She shook her head again. "No. You aren't. The man I have come to love and know wouldn't hurt anyone. Not even himself."

He glared. "If I could rip it out of myself in your name, Leona, I would. But I can't. This is who I am."

"It can't be," she rasped. "You're too kind in nature to be this cruel to yourself. You're too kind to—"

"What is cruel is your inability to accept me for what I am." He hit his chest. "I can't change this. I've tried. And I'd only be lying to myself and to you if I didn't give into it. And I'm done lying about it, Leona. I'm done lying."

He swung away and stalked toward the door, the brass chandelier above her head trembling from his pronounced weight hitting the floorboards. Before leaving the room, he swung back. "You have five weeks to pick up a crop and be the woman I need you to be or I leave to Persia without you. Because I'd rather live without you knowing I am true to myself than live with you and betray all that I am. And if being true to *yourself* means being unable to pick up that crop...I will respect that. I will respect we simply were never meant to be."

He hesitated, looking anguished about the words he shared. "When we first kissed, you challenged me to come to you, no matter the hour, no matter the reason, asking that I show you're the only woman I would ever want in my arms and in my life. And I'm doing that. As you had once said, 'I want a life where I'm not limited to someone who refuses to give me the one thing I not only deserve but want: *everything*.' And I do want everything, Leona. I want everything including you and unlike before, I'm not settling for less." Averting his gaze, he walked out and didn't look back.

Numbly wandering over to the bucket of water that was as flat and murky as she felt in that moment, Leona sank to the floor beside it. A crop. He wanted her to wield a crop and treat him like an undisciplined animal by taking it to his body.

She wasn't even capable of spanking her own child beyond a mere tap.

And he expected her to...?

She grabbed up the rag floating in the water and frantically scrubbed the floor, wishing she could scrub out the vision of Malcolm's scarred hand reaching out to her, expecting her to further scar him.

All she wanted to do was love him in the only way she knew how. Not—

Whipping the rag against the floor, she closed her eyes in anguish and let out a sob burning within her, knowing her dream of them being together was cracking down its center. Malcolm was making her choose between hurting herself or hurting him.

And she honestly wasn't ready to do either.

****

11 Berwick Street

A man knew he was outdone when for the sixth week in a row, he was sitting in a one-room school house setting with four other grown men seated side by side awaiting instruction on women, love and seduction. All that was missing was a slate and some chalk.

He knew why he kept staggering through the cramped, underground tunnel leading into the adjoining building where 'lessons' were being held. He was doing it to hold on to a glimmer of hope that Leona would kneel to him as he knelt to her.

After the ever brilliant Madame de Maitenon suffered an unfortunate physical collapse that led to her being bedridden for at least a few weeks, her granddaughter had taken over the school with equal flare.

The petite Miss Maybelle Maitenon, who appeared to avoid men, knew far more about intimate relationships than he knew about his own left hand.

Sometimes, while in class, he silently prayed without anyone knowing. After all, God had a lot to be angry about, given he, Malcolm Gregory Thayer, the Earl of Brayton and Admiral of the Persian navy, had fornicated with an incredible, beautiful woman who wasn't his wife. An incredible woman who still had *no* idea whether she wanted to love a pain-obsessed freak or not.

Not knowing her decision was killing him.

So he...kept coming to each and every class in the hope he was preparing himself for their union. He kept waiting for there to be a topic about the art of seduction by pain (not pleasure), but annoyingly, it never came up. How was he supposed to learn anything? His time in London was running out. His time with Leona was running out.

When erotic texts were plopped into their laps one by one by Miss Maitenon, asking them to dissect what was wrong with the eroticism portrayed (other than the fact they were all written by males), Malcolm knew he had to forget about the other four men, that included Holbrook's own brother, and just ask. What did he care? They were about as pathetic as he was.

He raised his hand high above his head. As a good student would.

Miss Maitenon paused from paging through the erotic text she held. Her brows went up as her blue eyes brightened. "Yes, Lord Brayton? Did you have a question?"

He sure the hell did. "Yes." He lowered his hand.

The Duke of Rutherford, Lord Hawksford, Lord Caldwell and Lord Banfield all leaned far forward in their seats to look at him like men about to watch a horse race.

Malcolm ignored them. Unlike them, he was here to learn. "Are there any pain focused techniques a man and a woman can share in that won't involve bruising, marks, scabs, blood or any other visible signs of damage to the skin? Because I need to learn them."

There was a pulsing silence.

Miss Maitenon lowered her chin. "Pain focused techniques?"

Why was she looking at him like that? "Yes."

"Explain," she prodded.

He sighed. "I'm looking for techniques that won't leave marks on my body. Why? Because I'm in love with a woman who doesn't share my vast appreciation for pain. Which is a problem. After thinking and thinking on how to introduce her to it, I've come to realize the only way to approach this is as softly as humanly possible. That means no whips, no chains, no birch, and no blades. But I still want the pain. It's what I enjoy."

Hawksford snorted. "That explains *everything*."

Malcolm narrowed his gaze.

Caldwell kicked out a foot to Hawksford. "Are you looking to die?"

"*Lord Hawksford*," Miss Maitenon snapped, pointing the erotic book at him. "Do you need a dildo for that mouth?"

Hawskford puffed out a breath and sat back. "No. I'm capable of keeping this mouth shut."

"I thought so." Miss Maitenon brought the book back to her corseted waist, returning once again to her cheerful self. She pertly smiled. "Now what was the question again, Lord Brayton?"

What, indeed. "Your grandmother knows quite a bit about my penchant. She and I talked about it. She was incredibly helpful to me and is the only reason why I'm here. Since you've taken over the class, I've been patiently waiting for the topic of pain to come up, but it's like I'm surrounded by sugar cookies and marzipan. None of which I need. Pain, please. *That* is what I need. Because I have plans that depend on me having a technique that won't break skin or leave marks. And pinching doesn't count. It does *nothing* for me. Is there such a thing? My brother mentioned there was."

Every last male gaze veered from Malcolm to the teacher.

She let out a breath and slapped the book she was holding shut, setting it on the small desk behind her. "My grandmother never mentioned your penchant for pain."

At least his privacy was being respected. "Thank her for that. Now are there any…

techniques? Something? *Anything?* Because I've been strangling myself with this damn situation long enough."

A small smile touched her lips. "While I will admit, I'm not at all versed in the art of pain, my grandmother did bring a Chinese gentleman once to the house to teach me something that might be helpful to you. She was worried about my travelling abroad to Egypt with only a chaperone and therefore had this gentleman introduced me to a very effective measure of defense."

Oh, hell. "The Chinese idea of defense includes combing the flesh off of their enemies with metal picks that expose the bone. I've seen it. I'm looking for something more—"

"I know. Techniques for pain that won't bruise or break the skin." She swept toward him and paused before his chair. "Stand, please."

The duke sat up, clearly worried.

Malcolm rolled his eyes and stood, towering over the petite blonde like a gorilla over a banana. He widened his stance and dubiously met her gaze from above. "Now what?"

She patted his arm. "Am I allowed to demonstrate the technique?"

He spread his arms. "By all means. Have at it, Miss Maitenon."

She politely reached up and under his arm, toward his back. Setting her fingers against a group of muscles, she clamped her thumb and forefinger together through his morning coat, pinching what felt like a bundle of too many nerves.

Amplified pain seared straight up the length of his legs and up his back, causing him to suck in a breath. He staggered in disbelief, his chest tightening.

She released him and stepped back, primly folding her hands. "How was that?"

If Leona did that to him, he'd never leave the house. He hissed out a breath, trying to regain composure and a sense of calm as the tendrils of pinching already subsided. It had seized him as quickly as it had left. "That was...unexpected." He swallowed and reached under the area she had accessed.

Miss Maitenon set her chin. "According to this Chinese gentleman, there are bundled nerves all over the body. Given pain is your penchant, I suggest you play with the idea of finding them."

Damn. Now he wanted to go take Leona to China. "Thank you. I'll do exactly that. I...can you show me other areas on my body I might be able to use?"

The Duke of Rutherford stared him down lethally. "No. She can't."

Malcolm paused. Maybe he was taking this school a little too seriously.

LESSON TWELVE

Some women need time to become who they already are.

-The School of Gallantry

Four days before Persia

A flash and the sharp crack of thunder startled Leona from deep sleep.

Sitting straight up, she paused.

Rain drummed against the small, lattice window, echoing in the quiet darkness of the room. Looking around, she slowly recognized the shapes of the house and the small hearth across from the foot of the bed that barely glowed. She was still in the rickety bed she and her son had snuggled into. She blew out a slow breath and yanked up the thick coverlet around her, the one that smelled like Malcolm and made her stupidly yearn for him.

The man always tucked them both into bed at night.

Or rather...Malcolm tucked *Jacob* into bed at night, and she was merely there to see it. The man was barely around. He always left early in the morning, propping his collar up high as if to hide his face from the world, and only returned shortly before the sky turned dark.

While he did speak to her, and sometimes lingered in her presence, it was always with a removed distance that was very visible not only on his face but also in the tension of his shoulders he always set whenever she walked into the room.

She missed him. She missed being the center of his regard.

It made her want to pick up a damn crop in his name and just—

Lightning streaked the sky again, illuminating the dark room. Leona sunk into the warm coverlet and scooted closer toward Jacob's side of the bed.

She paused and patted the empty space beside her.

"Jacob?" She sat up and threw aside the comforter. He was gone.

Thunder rumbled, punctuating the realization.

"Jacob?" She scooted off the bed and noticed the door to the room was slightly open, the dim light of flickering candles from the corridor illuminating the open crevice. She groaned. Not again. The boy was now *always* playing chess with Andrew or Malcolm.

Did the male species never sleep? Damn them.

She puffed out a breath, her bare feet padding across the room as her wool nightdress tangled around her. Throwing open the door, she peered out into the dimly lit corridor, looking left, then right.

"Jacob?" she called out. "Jacob, it's late. I think it time you come back to bed."

No answer. Huh. Maybe they were downstairs.

Her bare feet tapped the wood boards as she meandered down the flickering candle-lit corridor, toward the stairs that led down into the narrow entrance of the townhouse.

Just as she came to the end of the corridor, at the top of the stairs, a large shadowy figure loomed before her, blocking her path. She yelped, skidding into the massive body.

Large hands grabbed her, keeping her in place. The crisp scent of *davana ittar* surrounded her. "Don't tell me thunder scares you more than I do," someone rumbled out.

Her heart skipped, knowing it was Malcolm. Leona gripped those muscular arms, finding enough strength in them to breathe again. She looked up. His rugged face was strained and ready for whatever it was she had to say.

"No, I...I'm actually trying to be a good mother and put my child back to sleep. Jacob needs rest and can't keep going to bed this late every night. I appreciate the time you're giving him, especially given you and I don't..." She sighed. "Are you and he done playing chess? Because it's late and—"

Thunder shook the house.

Leona jumped and instinctively gripped Malcolm's arms harder.

He paused, leaning into her. "Jacob and I weren't playing chess. I was actually sleeping but got woken by the thunder." He stared. "Are you saying Jacob isn't with you?"

Dread suddenly scraped its way through Leona. "No. I thought he was with you."

"No. He isn't."

Oh, dear God. "Is he with Andrew?" she demanded.

Malcolm released her arms, jerking toward the closed door a few feet away. "Andrew retired hours ago."

Her eyes widened. "Then where is Jacob?"

"God protect him." Malcolm swung toward the corridor leading toward the rest of the house. "I just walked through the entire house, blowing out candles I could have sworn I had already put out."

Panic gurgled within. "Something isn't right. Something isn't—" She rushed around him. "What if Ryder sent someone to take him? What if—"

Malcolm grabbed her arm, yanking her toward him. His eyes flickered over her nightdress and snapped back to her face. "Stay here. I'll find him."

"No, I'm going with you," she insisted, pushing past him and breaking into a run.

He sprinted past her and thumped down the stairs before she could even get to them.

She thumped her way after him, gasping breaths escaping her. Although she swore to never open her heart to the possibility of begging a higher being that she even doubted existed, her pride was no match against her heart, *Please, God. Malcolm claims that You are capable of mercy and goodness. Show me that goodness. Please. For the love I have for Jacob, please—*

Malcolm rushed to the entrance door and paused, his chest heaving. "The latch is broken."

"*No!*" Leona frantically shoved past and banged open the door.

A lashing gust of wind and heavy rain assaulted her. She squinted to see beyond the dull gas lights of the street and into the darkness, but too many drops of rain blurred her vision.

She rushed out into the deserted street in bare feet, frosty rain instantly drenching her. "*Jacob!*" she screamed above the whirling wind, tears and rain blinding her. The rain might as well have been the sea her father had been lost in. It was too much. Too much. "*Jacooooob!*" She sobbed, her bare feet sinking into icy mud as torrents of rain continued to whip unmercifully all around her.

"Leona, go inside!" Malcolm commanded, grabbing her arm. "I'll find him! I swear it!"

Leona jerked toward Malcolm, realizing he was as drenched as she was, his dark hair clinging to his forehead, and his white linen shirt, waistcoat and trousers adhered to every inch of him.

She sobbed, her bare feet numb from standing in the freezing puddle. "Ryder took him. He took him. I know he took him!"

"*I have him!*" a separate male voice hollered out through the wind, drawing closer. "*It's all right! The boy is all right!*"

Her head snapped toward the voice, her heart pounding.

Through the pelting rain, the dark, dim outline of a large figure in a great coat stalked toward her, guiding a tiny figure splashing through puddles. Jacob! Leona drew in a sharp breath of cold air and pushed it back out with weakened relief. *Thank you God. Thank you for...answering.*

She darted toward Jacob, trying not to sob anymore than she already was.

Jacob paused in front of her, his small chest heaving as he tried catching his breath. His bear sagged to one side of his arm, drenched in his thin arms, looking as pitiful as he did. His dark hair clung to his forehead.

"Don't cry, Mama." Jacob's small, cold hand sloppily patted her cheek to assure her.

Leona let out a choked laugh, grabbed and kissed his cold fingers. "How brave you are. How very brave. Are you all right?"

Jacob nodded in exaggeration. "Everyone was sleeping when Papa came into the house. I snuck out of the room. He told me not to wake you. He and I played downstairs for a while but then he tried to take me. It wasn't really that scary. Because James took him to the ground and tied Papa's whole body to a railing down the street so he wouldn't go anywhere. And then James and I were having a bit of fun in the rain making our way back. Only you won't believe it. *Look!*" He pointed up at the man beside him.

Her son certainly seemed to be inspired by her rescuer. "Thank you, sir, for—" Leona glanced up at the large man beside her son and froze. Imposing ice blue eyes met hers as water streamed down an all too familiar rugged face. It was Malcolm. Only...he was wearing different clothes than the ones she had just seen him in. And the jagged scar on his face was...*gone?*

She blinked against the rain, slowly drawing her arms around herself in an effort to give herself warmth as the rain seemed to slowly ebb and dull. She paused, sensing someone was behind her and swung toward the direction she thought Malcolm had earlier been. Another figure with the exact same height and the exact same ice blue eyes and rugged face met hers from behind. A jagged scar from ear to jaw traced that face.

She choked and scrambled back, slapping a trembling hand against her mouth. Oh. Dear. God. There were two. There were two Malcolms. There. Were. *Two*!

Her chest heaved, unable to believe it as she glanced from one to the other.

Leona lowered her hand from her mouth. She had heard of such oddities out in the country, but had never actually seen a set of twins in person. They really were the same in every way. Height. Breadth. Eye color. Hair color. Face. The only thing distinguishing them was one had a scar slashed across his face and the other one didn't. "You have a *twin*?"

"Yes." Malcolm's strained face and voice softened. "A twin who keeps reminding me why the hell I ever loved him in the first place. Thank you, James. Thank you for—" Malcolm swiped his face. "Leona, this is James Zachery Thayer. My younger brother by three minutes. James, this is Leona Webster." He grinned, pointed at James and chided, "You're officially soft."

The other Malcolm snorted. "Don't give me that. I've been waiting for you to call on me again. Why the hell didn't you call on me?"

"For the same reason you didn't call on me," Malcolm tossed back.

James widened his stance. "Well, I'm calling on you now. Some prick was standing outside your townhouse most of the night when I earlier rode by, so I stuck around. Glad I did. I finally get to outdo my brother. I'm the real hero now."

Malcolm rumbled out a laugh, jumped forward and grabbed James, shoving his head into an arm lock. "I'm the fucking hero. You're just a fucking lunatic who breaks glass."

Leona frantically covered her son's ears. "Uh...gentleman. I hate to interrupt this glorious little family reunion, but my son can hear everything you're both saying."

Both men froze.

Malcolm eyed Leona and cleared his throat. "Unfortunately, it's going to get worse. You may want to take the boy inside. We're a little rough with each other."

If it hadn't been for Malcolm's brother, her son would have been...taken. She edged forward. "Thank you, James."

James wrestled out of Malcolm's grasp and shoved him, making Malcolm stumble. James straightened, adjusting his wet clothes and inclined his head. "A pleasure."

The door from behind them swung open in the darkness, spilling out light. Andrew squinted out toward them, fastening his robe. "Why the hell is everyone outside? It's two in the morning and it's raining. Even I'm not that stupid."

Leona dragged Jacob closer to herself and smiled. Kissing his soaked head several times, she smoothed that small, wet face that was too chilled for her liking. "We should get you warm. Come along. It's time for bed." She pushed him past and around Malcolm's large frame, hurrying them to the stairs of the house.

"But I'm not cold or tired," Jacob whined. "I'm not."

"You're completely soaked and were almost kidnapped. And you're not cold, scared *or* tired?"

"Most certainly not!" Jacob tossed back. "One day, Mama, I plan to not only take a blade to my thigh without crying like Malcolm did, but I plan to take a villain's head, like James did, and bash it into—"

Egad. "*Nooo.* No blades in thighs and no bashing. No, no, *no.*" Whilst she was relieved that Jacob didn't seem in the least bit rattled by his experience of being taken it was obvious Malcolm's company over these past few weeks had *overly* inspired him.

"But, Mama, can't I stay outside a few minutes longer and—"

"No." Leona turned her son toward the house, marching him forward and up the stairs to Andrew. She pushed her son through the door past Andrew and into the warmth of the house. "Go in. I'll be right there."

Jacob trailed water across the tile floor of the house, and hugged his dripping bear against his chest. He turned toward her. "Can Andrew read me a story?"

Leona pointed toward the staircase. "Go upstairs and start stripping those wet clothes. I'll be right up and read you that story myself. Andrew needs to sleep."

Her son scowled. "But I want Andrew to read me a story. He does all the voices. And you...you don't." He sighed as if the thought of it depressed him. He then hitched up the wet bear he held and turned on his wet heel, tracking more water up the stairs.

Andrew eyed Leona and then veered his gaze back to Malcolm and James. "One was bad enough. Two is like inviting Satan over for tea." He puffed out a breath. "Don't worry. I'll take care of Jacob and put him in some dry clothes. I'll even read him the newspaper. That always puts him to sleep."

Leona smiled, leaned in and kissed Andrew on the cheek in gratitude. "Thank you. You know how he adores you."

"What isn't there to adore?" Andrew wrapped his arm around her, growing overly cocky. "Seeing you and Brayton are no longer...you know...maybe you and I could—"

Malcolm rigidly pointed at them and boomed, "*Ey!* What the hell is going on over there? Get your hands off my woman before I tie your damn cock around your throat."

Andrew snorted and called back, "I appreciate you thinking it's *that* long."

Malcolm swung fully toward Andrew and hardened his tone. "Get inside, you damn rake. *I mean it.*"

Andrew cringed, ducked and darted out of sight.

Leona sighed and swiped a hand over her wet face, edging back toward the warmth of the house and out of the rain. She wished she could say she was flattered by Malcolm's territorial behavior, but neither of them had really *tried* to progress their relationship beyond their last conversation regarding his penchant for...crops.

She was still debating.

James jogged backward, putting up a large gloved hand. "I still have that bastard tied to the railing. After a few more punches, I'll be delivering him to Scotland Yard with a few orders. You two have a good night. I'll be in touch. Oh and...*Malcolm?*"

Malcolm paused.

James smirked. "If you ever get bored of that dinky little School of Gallantry you attend every day in the name of impressing a woman you still haven't impressed, head on over to where you really belong: Charlotte Street." He swung away and strode out into the night that was beginning to slowly clear from all the rain.

Leona blinked. And then blinked again. "What on earth is he talking about?"

Malcolm lingered in the street for a moment, looking after his brother. He then heaved out a breath and swiveled toward her. Shifting his jaw, he jogged up the stairs and past her.

For some reason, he didn't answer her question.

"Malcolm?" She turned toward him.

He said nothing.

"I'm the one who should be agitated," she pointed out.

"I thought you were." He nudged her into the house and slammed the door. Stalking into the adjoining parlor, he hefted up a trunk, came back and set it against the door with a thud. "We'll get the latch fixed in the morning. It's late."

A cold stream of water trickled down the length of her and pooled around her bare feet, sending a shiver through her. Feeling rather sorry for herself, she muttered, "We can't keep ignoring each other. You leave in four days."

Malcolm stepped toward her, blocking her view of the staircase with his body. "Are you saying you have an answer for me?"

Veering her gaze up to his, she cringed at the possibility that maybe, just maybe, because he clearly, clearly wanted it, she could...?

She watched a large drop of water drip from a strand of his dark hair. It slowly traced his temple, then slid down his cheek and disappeared off the end of his chin. She envied the very water that clung to him so naturally, so provocatively. "I do miss you," she gushed, not knowing what else to say. "I miss everything about us. It isn't fair. It isn't fair that I have to take a crop to you to be able to show my love. *Who does that?* I'm not...you're ridiculously large in size. Ridiculously. My arm would grow tired if I tried to—" She puffed out a breath and eyed him.

He said nothing.

"I don't want you to leave without me or Jacob," she grouched. "I don't."

He searched her face. "What are you saying?"

It was pointless. She couldn't do it. Leona moved around him, the cold settling in on her body like a winter storm. Every inch of her shook.

He grabbed her arm and yanked her back toward himself. "Leona."

She swallowed but didn't meet his gaze. "What?"

He brought her hands to his cool lips and kissed them. Twice. He lowered himself to his knee, not breaking their gaze. "I love you. No matter what you decide."

Her hands stilled against his. He was on one knee and begging. Begging. "I..."

Obnoxious, lip-smacking kissing sounds echoed around them, making them both pause.

Malcolm released her hand, jumping up to both feet and glanced up the stairwell, calling out, "That will come later, I assure you. Now take your little noises elsewhere. Leona and I need some privacy, if you please."

Leona swung toward the stairwell.

Jacob giggled.

Andrew smirked, snatched up Jacob with one arm and yelled back, "I'll keep him upstairs for the rest of the night if you both promise to keep the noise down!" Andrew pointed at them, then jogged out of sight, flipping Jacob over and up on his shoulder, making Jacob giggle even more.

Everything grew quiet again.

Malcolm grabbed Leona by the waist hard, startling her, and tossing her up into his muscled arms, he proceeded to stalk them down the corridor into the kitchen, trailing water from their drenched clothes across the floor. "Do you trust me?"

She eyed him awkwardly as he continued stalking them into the kitchen. "Yeeees."

He gave her a hard pointed look. "Sound a little more confident about it, Leona. Or I'll damn well walk you back." He tightened his hold, shaking her to emphasize it. "Do you trust me?"

She eyed him again, their wet clinging clothes practically pasted against each other. "Yes, of course. You know I do."

"Good." He angled them into the narrow doorway of the kitchen, slamming the door behind them with his leather boot and crossed them over to the table in two long-legged steps. He sat her down on it, letting her bare and muddy feet dangle as her heavy skirts dripped water onto the floor.

He stepped back and holding her gaze in the candlelight of the kitchen, unbuttoned his waistcoat. "I leave in four days." He shrugged off the wet waistcoat and let it drop to the floor. "It's important you see my body. It might help you make a decision."

She snorted and gripped the edge of the table she sat on, her pulse roaring. "A touch of an ego, have we?"

"I'm being damn serious." He unraveled his sagging cravat, unwound it from around his neck and tossed it, his features gruff but calm. He undid the top two buttons at his throat with the lift of his shaven chin and opened the wide slit of the linen shirt. He turned away from her, purposefully giving her his broad back, and yanked the wet linen off, exposing the shifting muscle beneath.

Her eyes widened as her heart almost stopped in disbelief. He had so many thick scars fingering the expanse of his back that the patches of his skin didn't even look like skin. "Malcolm," she rasped. "Oh God. Did you do all of this to yourself?"

"No." He dropped his wet trousers around his muscled legs, which were also heavily scarred. He shoved his soaked undergarments down and stepped out of them, leaving himself completely and gloriously naked. He turned back toward her, not even bothering to cover his cock, and revealed a massive, almost overly muscled body that was covered from abdomen to arms to chest with similar thick, slash-like gashes.

It didn't even include the still healing wound on his sculpted thigh.

He met her gaze. "I was punished quite a bit at the monastery when I was younger. Unlike most of the boys there, however, I was a creature they really weren't familiar with. I wasn't scared of getting whipped as much as I was scared of...enjoying it. Had God not made me like this, I honestly don't think I would have survived at the hands of the monastery. Every scar you see, I didn't mind getting. I stand here before you, Leona, with nothing to hide. This and my heart is yours if you will take it."

Only the support of the table beneath her kept her from staggering. Although she wanted to bury her face into her hands so she wouldn't have to look at the extent of the pain his body had been through, she couldn't move nor allow herself to blink.

There was, however, something utterly magnificent in the way he humbly stood before her, asking her to accept every last scar. Some laid out their hearts with words. This man laid out his heart with scars.

Every inch of that marred, massive body was actually beautiful, rigid, muscular and tight. She felt tense looking at him.

As he slowly drew closer, his leg muscles moved like rippling satin. His chest and those broad shoulders and long arms had more bulk than she had originally imagined through his clothes.

She swallowed again, her skin burning as if it were on fire.

Silence filled the room, deafening her.

"You're not saying anything." His voice was thick with concern. "Why? Do you detest what you see? Be honest."

She tensed, her fingers digging into the wet material of her wool gown. There was no sense in lying to him or herself. "No. You're annoyingly beautiful."

He stopped and his features brightened. His mouth quirked. "I knew you'd like it."

And the ego was back.

Moving toward her again, his eyes flickered over her wet gown as a cocky smile cracked the surface of his harsh features. He paused before her and widened his stance as if fully clothed. He held her gaze. "So why do you think I picked the kitchen to do this? Do you know?"

She swallowed hard, lifted her chin and boldly met his blue eyes. She knew.

He leaned in, blocking all view. "Start with a wooden spoon if you have to. Whatever makes you comfortable."

A warning whispered in her head, telling her it was wrong, but her heart chanted it would be all right because it was what he wanted. Trying to focus, she blurted, "Do you want me to get it out of the cupboard now?"

He grazed his lips across hers.

Her eyes fluttered closed as she let the heat of his mouth penetrate her own.

His tongue slid between her lips as he angled his head to penetrate deeper, dragging his tongue across the inside of her teeth. He broke away.

She swayed against the empty space and opened her eyes.

Malcolm hovered menacingly over her, stepping in between her legs, which he yanked apart against the table, his rough fingers pinching the skin beneath her wet clothing. He watched his own hands skim up her thighs and waist and further up past her breasts.

Her lips parted, unable to believe he was touching her again. Like she wanted.

He slowly hooked his large hands into the opening of her nightdress that was held together by hooks and gripped and twisted the material hard enough to cause the water to stream down his bare hands. The muscles in his arms and chest visibly tensed, bunched and corded as he rigidly held the material bound around his fists.

Every inch of her skin seemed to sizzle from his heat as she unevenly breathed in and out, trying to steady the frantic beat of her heart. Lips still parted, she waited for him to unleash the savage power he dominantly displayed.

Holding her gaze, his jaw shifted. "When I rip this, it's up to you to punish me. The more force you use, the more I'll reward you. Do you understand?"

Leona half-nodded and tried to breathe without gasping. "Yes."

With the violent jerk of both hands, she winced as he ripped open her nightgown with enough force to split it straight down to her thighs, exposing the clinging, thin chemise beneath. He shoved the wet gown down her arms and yanked it out from under her, causing the table to jump as she almost stumbled off the table with a yelp.

He whipped the torn nightgown to the floor, his cock growing visibly hard. His broad chest heaved upward and down as he stared her down, silently waiting for what they agreed on.

Her body trembled as she scrambled off the table. Pulse roaring, she yanked down her clinging chemise to cover her exposed thighs, but realized it was rather pointless given the material was sheer. She gestured toward the nearest cupboard. "I'll...go get a spoon."

He lowered his chin. "You do that," he said softly, mockingly.

She was rather surprised to find this felt more like a game. It made it a touch...palatable. Even fun. "Shall I get the largest one there is?" she offered.

Amusement flashed in those eyes. "You do that."

She turned and knowing he was intently watching her, and that her chemise was sheer and clinging, she did her best to provocatively sashay across the kitchen for him. Her bare, wet feet squeak-squeak-squeaked on the wooden floorboards, making her cringe with each sashaying step. So much for provocative.

Arriving before the cupboard she organized with all the utensils weeks earlier, she daintily opened it and peered in. Her fingers grazed an array of fourteen wooden spoons she had arranged by size. She tapped her way through them, wondering which one would cause the most harm. Which was ridiculous, really, because she knew she had never even been able to kill a roach with a good swat of any of them.

"Any spoon," he chided. "Wood is wood."

Right. She snatched the largest one, turned and as calmly and as regally as she knew how she squeak-squeak-squeaked her way back. Although she exuded poise, inside, her heart continued to thump out of control knowing what she was about to do.

She edged in as close to him as possible trying not to get distracted by his well-erected, large cock pointing straight at her. She pinched her lips, held up the wooden spoon and wagged it toward his chest in an effort to aim, determined to prove she was a very capable lover intent on delivering him what he wanted. She tightened her hold on the spoon and rigidly tapped the flat end against his bare chest. "There."

He gave her a pointed stare. "Did you even try?" he drawled. "A fish could swing harder."

She returned his pointed look. "Fish don't have arms."

"Exactly."

She huffed out a breath and positioned the spoon again. Swiping away frigid water from her face and neck that continued to trickle from her wet hair, she flung it off to the side. "I'm too wet. I can't focus."

He quirked a brow, brought both hands down to the root of his cock and aimed it at her. "Can you focus now, pigeon?"

He was making fun of her. Even though she was trying.

Exasperated by everything he had put her through, and for even making her sob over him weeks earlier, she gritted her teeth and wacked him hard in the one place he didn't expect. The cock he was holding out.

He choked, jerking far forward to protect it with both hands and hissed out a long breath. His chest rose and fell as if stunned. He eventually glanced up at her, his features playfully darkening. "Well done. She *can* be trained."

She triumphantly tapped the spoon against the palm of her hand, rather liking the power a mere spoon bestowed. "Don't *ever* rip my nightgown again," she played along. "Or I'll render that cock useless."

Letting out a low growl, he grabbed her, yanked her chemise up to her waist, startling her, and shoved her against the nearest wall, causing them both to stumble. The spoon clattered out of her hand as he stripped off her chemise and whipped it aside.

Panting against each other, they scrambled to make their naked bodies align.

He jerked her up onto his hips by hoisting her up with open thighs and slammed the length of his cock into her wetness, making her gasp as her back hit the wall. Covering her mouth with his own, to quiet her, he pumped her relentlessly, guiding one of her hands to a place beneath his arm and toward his back.

Against her mouth, which he kept jerking into with his tongue between each full measured thrust, he said tersely, "Dig your fingers together like a pinch and we're done. We'll keep our first try at this simple. I promise."

Everything began to blur from the pleasure that overwhelmed her core. Sensation coiled as his hips and his cock pounded into her harder and harder.

Sensing he was waiting for her to obey his earlier command, she dug her fingers into the spot he guided her hand to and mindlessly dug her fingers together in the hope it delivered him the same ecstasy he was delivering to her.

He stiffened in visible pain and choked out, "More."

She tightened the pinch, determined to give him exactly that.

He slid them down the wall and to the floor, his features twisting. "No more," he rasped. "Too. Much."

She released her hold.

A breath escaped him as he lowered them in a weakened state to the floor.

Between ragged breaths, Malcolm smoothed her hair with large hands and kissed her lips, her cheeks and her throat. "Leona," he whispered, slowly stroking his cock into her, clearly no longer interested in giving either of them pain. "Leona, you make me suffer in unending bliss, and I thank you for that."

To see him reveling in such ecstasy was well-worth taking the role of his pain mistress.

He rolled his hips and licked her mouth again and again, his movements becoming more precise and edging slower still but deep. So deep.

Feeling lightheaded against the pleasure rippling through her core, she gasped and gave into the strokes that hit her nub so perfectly. She cried out, her fingers digging into his scarred skin.

He gripped her hair hard and tugged, stilling his massive body against her as he groaned out against her. His seed filled her.

The pounding of their hearts eventually lulled.

Leona blissfully lay on the kitchen floor beneath him and drawled, "It was a good thing I washed the floors this week."

A gruff laugh escaped him. "There won't be any more of that. You're going to be an admiral's wife and live in a palace with your own servants."

Her brows went up in astonishment. "A palace? You lie."

Malcolm captured her gaze, repositioning himself over her and smoothed her hair. "I forgot to mention that I'm incredibly good friends with the Persian prince. It will be the greatest adventure you'll ever know. You'll want for nothing."

She pinched her lips. "Except for the ring you still owe me."

He eyed her. "It's not my damn fault you didn't see the box."

She paused. "Box?"

He rolled off and propped himself up onto an elbow naked. "Why do you think I wanted you to use a wooden spoon? It's been sitting in that cupboard for three weeks. Which isn't too much of a surprise, I guess, given you don't cook."

Her lips parted. He— "Malcolm," she breathed. "You are such a romantic."

He smacked his lips and glanced around. "Don't you forget it."

She laughed. Rolling toward him, she grabbed his face and kissed it twice. "We can't have it sitting in there any longer." She scrambled onto her bare feet and snatched up her wet chemise to cover herself. She cringed, given how cold it was to the touch and tossed it, knowing she was better off without it.

Padding over to the cupboard that was still open, she peered in. In the shadows off to the side, just beyond the wooden spoons, was a small velvet box. Biting her lip, she reached in and plucked it up. Cradling it in her hand, she hurried back to Malcolm. Sitting next to him, so they were thigh to naked thigh, her eyes widened at the gold inlay of initials on the lid of the box: RBR. *"Rundell, Bridge and Rundell,"* she gushed in disbelief. "They are jewelers to the king!"

Malcolm half-nodded. "So I'm told. Over on Ludgate Hill."

She frantically lifted the lid and gasped. It wasn't a simple gold band. It was a gold band with a glinting ruby the size of a roasted chestnut. She still gaped. "We can afford this?"

"Maybe."

She paused. "Can we or can't we?"

He nudged her. "Maybe is my version of yes."

A breath escaped her. "Thank the heavens, because I'm already too in love with it to let it go." She took it out of the box and held it out to him. "Here."

He lowered his gaze to the ring and paused. "What?"

She kept holding it out. "You're supposed to put it on my finger. It's rather anticlimactic for me to do it."

He cleared his throat. "Right." He took it and lifting her hand, he turned her palm up, kissed it and then nipped it before turning it back over and gently sliding it onto her ring finger.

She smiled and held it up, admiring the way it glinted against the candlelight around them. "It's so beautiful." She lowered her hand and eyed him. "Malcolm?"

"Yes?"

"Can we afford to send some money to Mrs. Henderson? She wasn't particularly the kindest person I ever knew, but she always ensured I never starved and I would like to return the favor given my aunt never will."

"I'll ensure she receives a generous amount. Enough to make her pray harder than she already does."

She smiled. "Thank you."

"You are most welcome." He nuzzled his stubbled chin against her. "Are you ready to go to Persia and live like a princess half the time and a

British lady here half the time? We can alternate. That way, you enjoy both worlds and I get to see my brother."

She paused. "Do I have to go to anywhere? Can't we stay here?"

He paused, his smile fading.

She snorted and poked him twice. "I expect you to blindfold me and carry me on that boat. Or it won't happen."

He smirked. "I'll do more than blindfold you, I'll tie you up."

EPILOGUE

Take a breath and revel in what will always be yours.

-The School of Gallantry

Months later, Persia

The As-Din Qajar Palace

The heat of the late September sun penetrated Malcolm's bare shoulders as he dipped and re-dipped the cloth of his turban into the water of the pool he waded in. Squeezing out just enough of the water from the bundled linen to retain a fair amount of moisture, he wrapped the long strip of material around his head, streaming it down around his neck and shoulders. A well-pleasured breath escaped him as he reveled in its coolness.

He was celebrating the fact that Russia and Persia had negotiated another treaty.

Which meant...more time to play.

"Look, Papa, look!" Jacob called out, his bare feet slapping the smooth stone leading to the oversized pool of water in the courtyard whose walls were covered with vines. "I'll do it without stopping!" He skid to the edge, stopped, adjusted his bathing clothes from out of his rear and

then pinched his nose and jumped into the water. He paddled his arms across the vast pool. "It's so hot. Can't we sleep in the water tonight?"

Malcolm bit back a laugh, spraying water toward the rascal with his arm and called out, "When you grow gills and learn how to breathe like a fish, we'll talk. Right now, just enjoy..." He paused as a petite figure breezed past the pool. He let out a low, long whistle.

Flowing red and gold silk flapped against the incoming hot wind, outlining the curvy figure of a pregnant woman draped from head to toe in a chādar clasped into place by gold buttons. Draped on her shoulder was a leather satchel filled with arrows. In her hand was a bow.

The woman had found a sport worthy of her.

Swimming his way toward Leona, he came to the edge of the pool and propped an arm against the stone ledge. "Do you need a target, Lady Brayton?" he playfully drawled.

She paused, only her bright green eyes visible through the flowing silk. Lowering the veil to reveal her entire face, her mouth quirked. "I do. But I love you too much to let you die."

He coughed out a laugh and pushed himself up and out of the water in one sweep, letting water spray and spill across the stone as he made his way toward her. "I appreciate the fact that you love me." He glanced back at Jacob who was already paddling his way toward them and quickly leaned in and captured her lips. "Enjoy your afternoon. Jacob and I are going to swim for another hour and then head into the village with Nasser. We'll see you at the banquet tonight. I'm thrilled the shah took the news so well. According to Nasser, the man knew all along but was waiting to hear it."

She smiled. "I'm so happy all is as it should be."

"So am I." He cleared his throat theatrically and tapped at the leather satchel with arrows. "Are you getting any better or are you still accidentally shooting camels three miles away?"

She gave him a withering look and stepped back. "I've been practicing every day." Yanking out an arrow, she propped it against the side of the bow and said, "Pick a target. Anywhere in the courtyard. I'll decimate it."

He smirked and playfully hit his chest twice. "Right here."

She swung toward him and aimed, fully pulling back the string until her arms quivered.

His eyes widened as he popped up a hand. "Ey, ey! Woman, you had better stop taking things out of the bedchamber. You're getting out of hand."

She grinned and swung away toward a palm tree several feet away. Squinting, she released it and let the arrow effortlessly punch into the trunk of the tree.

Malcolm's brows went up. He lowered his hand in disbelief. "If I wasn't in love with you before I am now," he drawled. "Damn."

She waggled her brows and then called out to Jacob, "Keep your father out of trouble in the village! You know how the women flock to him when he wears a turban."

Jacob grappled up and out of the water. "I'll write down every woman's name, Mama!"

Malcolm snorted and pointed at the boy. "You do that. She severely punishes me for things like that."

Leona tsked. "Mind your tongue. He doesn't need to hear it." She paused and rubbed her belly, softening her tone. "And neither does this one." Blowing him and Jacob each a kiss, she smiled and breezed onward to retrieve the arrow from the tree.

Lowering himself to the warmth of the stone, Malcolm let out a breath he didn't realize he was holding and wondered how he ever got so damn lucky to be able to say he had found a woman capable of giving him...*everything.*

CPSIA information can be obtained at www.ICGtesting.com
Printed in the USA
LVOW10s1619080816

499499LV00005B/1206/P

9 781505 206364